Because his three published novels have their locale in the state of Nevada, WALTER VAN TILBURG CLARK has come to be considered a Westerner. Actually he was born in East Orland, Maine on August 3, 1909. When he was eight years old, his father became president of the University of Nevada. Clark attended high school in Reno and received a B. A. and M. A. from the University of Nevada. After two years devoted to philosophy and literature at the University of Vermont, he accepted a post at Cazenovia, New York as a teacher and basketball coach. With the appearance of *The Ox-Bow Incident* in 1940, Walter Van Tilburg Clark came into immediate prominence as a writer. His novel was acclaimed by the critics and later was made into what has been acknowledged to be one af the finest motion pictures ever produced in Hollywood. *The City of Trembling Leaves,* published in 1945, further established Clark's literary reputation as spokesman for the new generation in the West. This novel was followed in 1949 by a Western legend, *The Track of the Cat* (which also became a movie), and in 1950 by a volume of short stories entitled *The Watchful Gods.*

The Ox-Bow

With an Afterword by Walter Prescott Webb

WALTER VAN TILBURG CLARK

Incident

A SIGNET CLASSIC from
NEW AMERICAN LIBRARY
TIMES MIRROR
New York and Scarborough, Ontario
The New English Library Limited, London

SIGNET, SIGNET CLASSICS, MENTOR, PLUME, MERIDIAN AND NAL
BOOKS are published *in the United States* by
The New American Library, Inc.
1633 Broadway, New York, New York 10019,
in Canada by The New American Library of Canada Limited,
81 Mack Avenue, Scarborough, Ontario M1L 1M8,
in the United Kingdom by The New English Library Limited,
Barnard's Inn, Holborn, London, EC1N 2JR, England.

29 30 31 32 33 34 35 36 37

PRINTED IN THE UNITED STATES OF AMERICA

Gil and I crossed the eastern divide about two by the sun.
We pulled up for a look at the little town in the big valley
and the mountains on the other side, with the crest of the
Sierra showing faintly beyond like the rim of a day moon.
We didn't look as long as we do sometimes; after winter
range, we were excited about getting back to town. When
the horses had stopped trembling from the last climb,
Gil took off his sombrero, pushed his sweaty hair back
with the same hand, and returned the sombrero, the way
he did when something was going to happen. We reined to
the right and went slowly down the steep stage road. It
was a switch-back road, gutted by the run-off of the winter
storms, and with brush beginning to grow up in it again
since the stage had stopped running. In the pockets under
the red earth banks, where the wind was cut off, the spring
sun was hot as summer, and the air was full of a hot, melt-
ing pine smell. Rivulets of water trickled down shining
on the sides of the cuts. The jays screeched in the trees

and flashed through the sunlight in the clearings in swift, long dips. Squirrels and chipmunks chittered in the brush and along the tops of snow-sodden logs. On the outside turns, though, the wind got to us and dried the sweat under our shirts and brought up, instead of the hot resin, the smell of the marshy green valley. In the west the heads of a few clouds showed, the kind that come up with the early heat, but they were lying still, and over us the sky was clear and deep.

It was good to be on the loose on that kind of a day, but winter range stores up a lot of things in a man, and spring roundup hadn't worked them all out. Gil and I had been riding together for five years, and had the habit, but just the two of us in that shack in the snow had made us cautious. We didn't dare talk much, and we wanted to feel easy together again. When we came onto the last gentle slope into the valley, we let the horses out and loped across the flat between the marshes where the red-wing black-birds were bobbing the reeds and twanging. Out in the big meadows on both sides the long grass was bending in rows under the wind and shining, and then being let upright again and darkening, almost as if a cloud shadow had crossed it. With the wind we could hear the cows lowing in the north, a mellow sound at that distance, like little horns.

It was about three when we rode into Bridger's Wells, past the boarded-up church on the right, with its white paint half cracked off, and the houses back under the cottonwoods, or between rows of flickering poplars, every third or fourth one dead and leafless. Most of the yards were just let run to long grass, and the buildings were log or unpainted board, but there were a few brick houses, and a few of painted clapboards with gimcracks around the veranda rails. Around them the grass was cut, and lilac bushes were planted in the shade. There were big purple cones of blossom on them. Already Bridger's Wells was losing its stage-stop look and beginning to settle into a half-empty village of the kind that hangs on sometimes where all the real work is spread out on the land around it, and most of the places take care of themselves.

Besides the houses on the main street and the cross street that ran out into a lane to the ranches at the north and south ends, there wasn't much to Bridger's Wells:

Arthur Davies' general store, the land and mining claims office, Canby's saloon, the long, sagging Bridger Inn, with its double-decker porch, and the Union Church, square and bare as a New England meeting house, and set out on the west edge of town, as if it wanted to get as far from the other church as it could without being left alone.

The street was nearly dried, though with wagon ruts hardened in it, so you could see how the teams had slithered and plowed in it. It drummed hard when we touched up to come in right. After all the thinking we'd done about it, the place looked dead as a Piute graveyard. There were a few horses switching at the tie rails in front of the inn and Canby's, but only one man in sight. That was Monty Smith, a big, soft-bellied, dirty fellow, with matted, gray streaked hair down to his shoulders and a gray, half-shaved beard with strawberry patches showing through, sore and itchy. Monty had been a kind of half-hearted rider once, but now he was the town bum, and kept balanced between begging and a conceited, nagging humor that made people afraid of him. Nobody liked him, but he was a tradition they'd have missed. Monty was leaning against a post of the arcade in front of Canby's, picking his teeth with a splinter and spitting. He looked us over out of his small, reddened eyes, nodded as if he was thinking of something else, and looked away again. We didn't see him. We knew that soon enough he'd be in to sponge on us. The notion made Gil sore, I guess, because he pulled in so sudden I had to rein Blue Boy around sharp to keep from climbing him.

"Take it easy," I told him.

He didn't say anything. We swung down, tied up, crossed the boardwalk, our boots knocking loudly, and went up the three steps to the high, narrow double door with the frosted glass panels that had Canby's name on them, inside two wreaths. Smith was watching us, and we went in without looking around.

It was dark and cool inside, and smelled of stale beer and tobacco. There was sawdust on the floor, the bar along one side and four green-covered tables down the other. There were the same old pictures on the wall too. Up back of the bar a big, grimy oil painting in a ponderous gilded frame of fruits and musical instruments showing

7

a woman who was no girl any longer, but had a heavy belly and thighs and breasts, stretched out on a couch pretending to play with an ugly bird on her wrist, but really encouraging a man who was sneaking up on her from a background so dark you could see only his little, white face. The woman had a fold of blue cloth between her legs and up over one hip. I'd been around back once, and knew the picture had a little brass plate which said, dryly, *Woman with Parrot,* but Canby called it "The Bitching Hour." On the other wall was a huge, yellowish print, like a map, of a reception at the Crystal in Virginia City. On it President Grant and a lot of senators, generals, editors and other celebrities were posed around so you could get a good, full-length view of each. The figures were numbered, and underneath was a list, telling you who they all were. Then there was a bright-colored print of a bleached Indian princess in front of a waterfall, a big painting of a stagecoach coming in, the horses all very smooth, round bellied and with little thin legs all in step and all off the ground, and an oval, black and white picture of the heads of three white horses, all wild eyed and their manes flying.

Four men were playing poker at a back table with a lamp over them. I didn't know any of the men. They looked as if they'd been playing a long time, hunched down to their work, with no life showing except in the slits of their eyes or a hand which one of them moved once in a while to pick up his glass or a silver dollar from his pile, or to throw out a card. They were quiet.

Canby was behind his bar, a tall, thin, take-your-time kind of man with seedy gray hair combed to cover a bald spot. All Canby's bones were big and heavy, and those in his wrists were knobby and red. His arms were so long that he could sit on the back counter, where his glasses and bottles were arranged, and mop the bar. It was clean and dry now, but he mopped it while he waited for us. He looked at us, first one and then the other of us, but didn't say anything. He had watery, pale blue eyes, such as alcoholic old men sometimes have, but not weak, but hard and uninterested. They suited the veined, pitted, but tight-to-the-bone look of his face, which always seemed too large, the nose too large, the mouth too large, the cheekbones and black eyebrows too prominent. I wondered

8

again where he'd come from. He looked like a man who knew he'd been somebody. Nobody ever found out, that I know of. He drank a lot, but he didn't talk except to pass the time of day, and he always kept that quiet, who-the-hell-are-you look.

"Well?" he said, when we just stood looking from the Bitch to the bottles.

Gil pushed his hat back so his red, curly hair showed, and folded his arms on the bar, and kept looking up at the Bitch. Gil has a big, pale, freckled face that won't darken and never shows any expression except in the eyes, and then only temper. His nose has been broken three times, and his mouth is thick and straight. He's a quick, but not a grudgy kind of fighter, and always talks as if he had a little edge, which is his kind of humor. It was Canby's kind too.

"That guy," said Gil, still looking at the picture, "is awful slow getting there."

Canby didn't look at the picture, but at Gil. "I feel sorry for him," he said. "Always in reach and never able to make it."

They said something like this every time we came in. It was a ritual, Gil always taking the side of the woman with the parrot, and Canby always defending the man. Canby could deliver quite a lecture on the mean nature of the woman with the parrot.

"I got a feeling she could do better," Gil said.

"You're boasting," Canby told him, and then said again, "Well?"

"Don't rush me," Gil said.

"Take your time," Canby said.

"It don't look to me," Gil said, "like you was so rushed you couldn't wait!"

"It's not that. I hate to see a man who can't make up his mind."

"What do you care?"

"I either have to put them to bed or listen to their troubles, depending on what they drink," Canby said. His mouth only opened a slit when he talked, and the words came out as if he enjoyed them, but had to lift a weight to get them started.

"I ain't lookin' for either sleep or comfortin'," Gil said. "And if I was, I wouldn't come here for it."

"I feel better," said Canby. "What'll you have? Whisky?"

"What have you got?"

"Whisky."

"Did you ever know such a guy?" Gil said to me. "All this time I'm thinkin', and all he's got's whisky."

"And that's rotten, ain't it?" he asked Canby.

"Rotten," Canby agreed.

"Two glasses and a bottle," Gil said.

Canby set them out in front of us and uncorked the bottle.

"I wouldn't have the heart to open any of this other stuff," Canby said, taking a bottle of wine down and polishing it with his cloth. "I've had it ever since I was a boy; same bottles."

We put our fingers around the tops of the glasses, and Gil poured us one apiece, and we took them down. It was raw, and made the eyes water after being dry so long. We hadn't had a drop since Christmas.

"First time in?" Canby asked.

"Yessir," Gil said with pleasure. Canby shook his head.

"What's the matter?" Gil asked him.

Canby looked at me. "Do you always have this much trouble with him?" You always felt Canby was grinning at you, though his face stayed as set as an old deacon's.

"More, mostly," I said, and told him about the fight we'd had, which Gil had finished by knocking me across the red-hot stove. We drank slowly while we talked, and Gil listened politely, as if I were telling a dull story about somebody else. "It was just being cooped up together so long," I finished, remembering the one-room shack with the snow piled up to the window ledge and more of it coming, blowing against the glass like sand; the lonely sound of the wind, and Gil and I at opposite ends of the room, with two lamps burning, except for a truce at meal times. "It got so he wouldn't even ride with me. We took turns tailing up and feeding."

"He's naturally mean," Canby said. "You can tell that."

"A man needs exercise," Gil said. "He's not much of a fighter, but there wasn't anything else handy." He poured us another. "Besides, he started them all."

"Like hell I did," I said. "Do we look like I'd start them?" I asked Canby. I'm as tall as Gil is, but flat and

10

thin, while Gil is built like a bull; his hands are twice as big as mine. Gil looks like a fighter too, with a long heavy chin and those angular eyes with a challenging stare in them. I could see myself in the mirror under the *Woman with a Parrot*. My face was burned dark as old leather already, but it's thin, with big eyes.

"You should have heard the things he said," Gil told Canby.

"By January," I put in, "he'd only talk about one thing, women. And even then he wouldn't be general. He kept telling the same stories about himself and the same women."

"Well, he wouldn't talk," Gil said, "and somebody had to. He'd sit there reading his old books like he had a lesson to learn, or writing all the time, scratch, scratch, scratch. It got on my nerves. Then I'd try to sing, and he'd get nasty. Once he went to the door, in the middle of a good song too, and stood there like he was listening for something, and all the time the wind blowing in, and thirty below outside. When I asked him what the matter was, he said nothing, he was just listening to the steers bawling; they sounded so good."

"Gil has a fine voice," I said, "but he only knows three songs, all with the same tune."

We kept on talking off our edge, Canby putting in a word now and then to keep us going, until Monty Smith came in. He started to say something to Gil, but Gil just looked at him, and Monty came over on my side and edged up to be friendly, with his back to the bar, as though it didn't mean a thing to him. I can't look a man down the way Gil can, so I just didn't look at him and didn't answer. I put a half dollar out on the bar, Canby poured out a couple of drinks, and Smith took them. He tried to be polite about it, saying, "Here's mud in your eye," and I felt mean to make him feel so much like a beggar. But Gil gave me the elbow, and I didn't say anything. Smith hung around for a minute or two, and then went out, hitching his belt in the doorway to get his conceit back.

When the door was closed Canby said, "Now that you two are peaceable again, what's on your mind?" He was talking to Gil.

"Does something have to be on my mind?" Gil asked.

11

"When you talk that long just being unsociable," said Canby, filling the glasses again, "yes." Gil turned his glass around and didn't say anything.

"What's he so bashful about?" Canby asked me.

"He wants to know if his girl is still in town," I told him.

"*His* girl?" said Canby, mopping a wet place and stooping to put the empty bottle under the bar.

"Take it easy," Gil said. He stopped turning his glass.

"If you mean Rose Mapen," Canby said, straightening up, "no. She went to Frisco the first stage out this spring."

Gil stood looking at him.

"It's a fact," Canby said.

"Hell," Gil said. He finished his drink in a toss. "Christ, what a town," he said furiously. His eyes were watering, he felt so bad about missing it.

"Have a drink," Canby said, opening another bottle, "but don't get drunk while you're feeling like that. The only unmarried woman I know of in town is eighty-two, blind and a Piute. She's got everything."

He poured another for each of us, and took one himself. You could see it tickled him that Gil had given himself away like that. But Gil was really feeling bad. All winter he'd talked about Rose Mapen, until I'd been sick of her. I thought she was a tart anyway. But Gil had dreamed out loud about buying a ranch and settling.

"It's my guess the married women ran her out," Canby said.

"Yeh?" Gil said.

"Oh, no tar and feathers; no rails. They just righteously made her uncomfortable. Not that she ever did anything; but they couldn't get over being afraid she would. Most of the men were afraid to be seen talking to her, even the unmarried ones. The place is too small."

Gil kept looking at him, but didn't say anything, and didn't look so personal. It's queer how deeply a careless guy like Gil can be cut when he does take anything seriously.

"Anything come of this gold they were talking about last fall?" I asked Canby.

"Do I look it?" he asked.

"No," he went on. "A couple of young fellows from Sacramento found loose gold in Belcher's Creek, up at

12

the north end, and traced it down to a pocket. They got several thousand, I guess, but there was no lode. A lot of claims were staked, but nobody found anything, and it was too near winter for a real boom to get started." He looked at me with that malicious grin in his eyes. "Not even enough to get more than two or three women in, and they left before the pass was closed."

"It's nothing to me," I lied.

"What is there to do in this town, anyway?" Gil demanded.

"Unless you aim to get in line and woo Drew's daughter," Canby began.

"We don't," I informed him.

"No," he agreed. "Well, then, you have five choices: eat, sleep, drink, play poker or fight. Or you can shoot some pool. There's a new table in the back room."

"That's just great," Gil said.

The door opened, and Moore, Drew's foreman, came in. Moore was past forty and getting fat so his belt hung under his belly. He looked even older than he was, his face being heavily lined and sallow and his hair streaked with gray, with one white patch, like ash, on the back of his head. Moore was really a sick man, though he wouldn't stand for having anybody ask how he felt. He was past any fancy riding now, and even an ordinary day's work in the saddle would tire him out so his face got pasty. He had a lot of pain, I guess; his insides were all shot from staying at broncho busting too long. But he'd been a great rider once, one of the best, and he was still worth his salt. He knew horses and cattle and country as he knew his own mind, which was thoroughly. His eyes were still quiet and sure, and he never blew off or got absent-minded, no matter how bad he felt. Only I suspected he hadn't saved any money, any more than the rest of us did, and was really scared he wouldn't be fit to work much longer. He was a way more than average short on those questions about how he felt.

He came over to the bar, said hello to us, and threw a silver dollar onto the bar, nodding at Canby. Canby poured him a glass, finger around, and he downed it. Canby filled him another, which he let sit while he rolled a cigarette and licked it into shape.

"I see Risley's still around," Canby said. Moore nodded.

13

Risley was the sheriff for this territory, but he wasn't often closer than Reno, except on special call. I could see Moore didn't want to talk about it, hadn't liked Canby's mentioning Risley in front of us. But I was curious.

"There was talk about rustling last fall, wasn't there?" I asked Moore.

"Some," he said. He sucked two little streams of smoke up his nostrils and drank half his whisky before he let the smoke out. When it came out there wasn't much of it, and that thin. He didn't look at me, but at the three rows of dark bottles behind Canby. Canby wiped the dry bar again. He was ashamed. It was all right for Moore, but I didn't like Canby acting at if we were outsiders. Neither did Gil.

"Do they know anything about it?" he asked Moore. "Is that why Risley's out here?"

Moore finished his whisky, and nodded at the glass, which Canby filled up a third time. "No, we don't know anything, and that's why he's here," he said. He put his change in his pocket, and took his whisky over to the table by the front window. He sat down with his back to us, so Canby could talk.

"It's getting touchy, huh?" Gil said.

"They don't like to talk about it," Canby said, "except with fellows they sleep with."

"It's a long way from any border," he said after a minute, "and everybody in the valley would know if there was a stranger around."

"And there isn't?" I asked.

"There hasn't been, that knew cattle," said Canby, sitting back up on the counter, "except you two."

"That's not funny," Gil told him, and set his glass down very quietly.

"Now who's touchy?" Canby asked him. He was really grinning.

"You're talking about my business," Gil said. "Stick to my pleasures."

"Sure," Canby said. "I just thought I'd let you know how you stand."

"Listen," Gil said, taking his hands down from the bar.

"Take a drink of water, Gil," I said. And to Canby, "He's had five whiskies, and he's sore about Rose." I didn't really believe Gil would fight Canby, but I wasn't sure after his disappointment. Whenever Gil gets low in spirit, or confused in his mind, he doesn't feel right again until he's had a fight. It doesn't matter whether he wins or not, if it's a good fight he feels fine again afterward. But he usually wins.

"And you keep your mouth shut about Rose, see?" Gil told me. He had turned around so he was facing right at me, and I could tell by his eyes he was a little drunk already.

"All right, Gil," I reassured him. "All right. But you don't want to go pitching into your best friends on account of a little joke, do you? You can take a joke, can't you, Gil?"

"Sure I can take a joke," he argued. "Who says I can't take a joke?" He stared at us. We kept quiet. "Sure I can take a joke," he said again, but then turned back to his drink. "Some jokes though," he said, after a swallow, but then took another swallow, and let it go at that. I looked at Canby and bent my head a little toward Gil. Canby nodded.

"No offense meant, Carter," he said, and filled Gil's glass again, pouring slowly, as if he were doing it very carefully for somebody he thought a lot of.

"It's all right, it's all right," Gil said; "forget it."

Canby put two plates on the bar, and then got some hard bread and dried beef from under the counter and put them on the plates. Gil looked at them.

"And I don't need any of your leftovers to sober me up, either," he said.

"Just as you like," Canby said. "It's a long time since lunch. I just thought you might be hungry." He put some strong cheese on the plates too, and then took some cheese and a bottle over to Moore at the table. He stood by Moore, talking to him for a while. I was glad neither of them laughed.

I ate some of the dry food and cheese. It tasted good, now that I was wet down. We'd had a long ride, and nothing to eat since before daybreak. Finally Gil began to eat too, at first as though he weren't thinking about it, but just picking at it absent-mindedly, then without pretense.

15

"Are they sure about this rustling?" I asked Canby when he came back.

"Sure enough," he said. "They thought they'd lost some last fall, but with this range shut in the way it is by the mountains, they'd been kind of careless in the tally, and couldn't be too sure. Only Bartlett was sure. He doesn't run so many anyway, and his count was over a hundred short. He started some talk that might have made trouble at home, but Drew got that straightened out, and had them take another tally, a close one. During the winter they even checked by the head on the cows that were expected to calve this spring. Then, it was about three weeks ago now, more than that, a month, I guess, Kinkaid, who was doing the snow riding for Drew, got suspicious. He thought one of the bunches that had wintered mostly at the south end was thinning out more than the thaw explained. He and Farnley kept an eye out. They even rode nights some. Just before roundup they found a small herd trail, and signs of shod horses, in the south draw. They lost them over in the Antelope, where there'd been a new fall of snow. But in the Antelope, in a ravine west of the draw, they found a kind of lean-to shelter, and the ashes of several fires that had been built under a ledge to keep the smoke down. They figured about thirty head, and four riders."

"And the count came short this spring?"

"Way short," Canby said. "Nearly six hundred head, counting calves."

"Six hundred?" I said, only half believing it.

"That's right," Canby said. "They tallied twice, and with everybody there."

"God," Gil said.

"So they're touchy," said Canby.

"Did everybody lose?" I asked after a minute.

"Drew was heaviest, but everybody lost."

"But they would, wouldn't they, with that kind of a job," Gil said angrily.

"The way you say," Canby agreed.

We could see how it was, now, and we didn't feel too good being off our range. Not when they'd been thinking about it all year.

"What's Risley doing here? Have they got a lead?" Gil asked.

16

"You want to know a lot," said Canby. "He's down just in case of trouble. It's Judge Tyler's idea, not the cattlemen."

I was going to ask more questions. I didn't want to, and yet I did. But Moore got up and came back to the bar with the partly emptied bottle. He pushed it across to Canby, with another dollar beside it.

"Three out of that," he said.

"Lost any over your way?" he asked us.

"No," I admitted. "No more than winter and the coyotes could account for."

"Got any ideas?" Gil asked him. Canby paused, holding Moore's change in his hand.

"No ideas, except not to have any ideas," Moore said. He reached for his change and put it in his pocket. "Game?" he asked, to show we were all right.

Canby fished a deck out of a back drawer for us, and the three of us sat down at the front table. Moore played his cards close to his vest, and looked up at the ceiling with narrowed eyes every time before he'd discard. We played a twenty-five-cent limit, which was steep enough. Canby sat in with us until others began coming. Then he went back and stood wiping the bar and looking at them; he never liked to speak first. Most of the men who came in were riders and men we knew. I thought they looked at Gil and me curiously and longer than usual, but probably that wasn't so. Each of them nodded, or raised a hand, or said "hi," in the usual manner. They all went to the bar first, and had a drink or two. Then some of them got up a game at the table next to ours, and the rest settled into a row at the bar, elbows up and hats back. The place was full of the gentle vibration of deep voices talking mostly in short sentences with a lot of give and take. Now and then some man would throw his head back and laugh, and then toss off his drink before he leaned over again. Things didn't seem any different than usual, and yet there was a difference underneath. For one thing, nobody, no matter how genially, was calling his neighbor an old horse thief, or a greaser, or a card sharp, or a liar, or anything that had moral implications.

Some of the village men came in too: old Bartlett, who was a rancher, but had his house in the village, Davies, the store owner, and his clerk, Joyce, a tall thin sallow

17

boy with pimples, a loose lower lip which made him look like an idiot, and big hands, which embarrassed him. Even the minister from the one working church, Osgood, came in, though he ostentatiously didn't take a drink. He was a Baptist, bald-headed, with a small nose and close-set eyes, but built like a wrestler. His voice was too enthusiastic and his manner too intimate to be true, and while he kept strolling pompously among the men, with one arm flexed behind him, the fist clenched, like the statue of a great man in meditation, the other hand was constantly and nervously toying with a seal on the heavy gold watch chain across his vest. I noticed that none of the men would be caught alone with him, and that they all became stiff or too much at ease when he approached, though they kept on drinking and playing, and spoke with him readily, but called him Mr. Osgood.

Bartlett came over to the table and watched. He was a tall man, looking very old and tired and cross. The flesh of his face was pasty and hung in loose folds, even his lower lids sagging and showing pools of red, like those of a bloodhound. He breathed audibly through his mouth, and kept blowing his mustache. He had on boots, but a flat Spanish sombrero and a long black frock coat, such as only the old men were wearing then. When Jeff Farnley came over too, Moore invited them to sit in. Farnley had a thin face, burned brick red, stiff yellow hair and pale hostile eyes, but a quick grin on a stiff mouth. He wiped his hands on his red and white cowhide vest and sat. Bartlett sat down slowly, letting himself go the last few inches, and fumbled for a cigar in his vest. When he got to playing he would chew the cigar and forget to draw on it, so that after every hand he had to relight it.

Osgood stood behind Moore and watched Gil and me playing. We were new to him, and I had an uneasy feeling, from the way he was sizing us up, that we were due to get our souls worked over a little. There was that about Osgood; he wouldn't know the right time from the wrong. Not that he'd try it here, but we'd have to move sharp when we left.

Then I forgot Osgood because I had something else to worry about. Gil was tight enough so I could see him squinting, sometimes two or three times, to make out what he had in his hand, but he was having a big run of luck.

I knew he wasn't cheating; Gil didn't. Even if he'd wanted to he couldn't, with hands like his, not even sober. But with his gripe on he wasn't taking his winning right. He wasn't showing any signs of being pleased, not boasting, or bulling the others along about how thin they'd have to live, the way you would in an ordinary game with a bunch of friends. He was just sitting there with a sullen dead-pan and raking in the pots slow and contemptuous, like he expected it. The only variation he'd make would be to signal Canby to fill his glass again when he'd made a good haul. Then he'd toss the drink off in one gulp without looking at anybody or saying a "mud," and set the glass down and flick it halfway to the middle of the table with his finger. If there hadn't been anything else in the air you couldn't play long with a man acting like that without getting your chin out, especially when he was winning three hands out of four. I was getting riled myself.

It didn't seem to be bothering Moore. Once when Gil took in the chips three times running on straight poker, Moore looked at him and then at me, and shook his head a little, but that was all. A couple of other riders who'd sat in after Bartlett and Farnley, started prodding Gil about it, but they stayed good natured and Gil just looked at them and went on playing cold. But that made their jokes sound pretty hollow, and after a little they didn't joke any more, though they didn't seem sore either. Old Bartlett, though, was beginning to mutter at his cards; nothing you could hear, just a constant talking to himself. And he was throwing his hands in early and exasperated, and not bothering to relight his cigar any more. But it was Farnley I was really worried about. He had a flaring kind of face, and he wasn't letting off steam in any way, not by a look or a word or a move, but staring a long time at his bad hands and then laying the cards down quietly, sliding them onto the table and keeping his fingers on them for a moment, as if he had half a mind to do something else with them.

I hoped Gil's luck would change enough to look reasonable, but it didn't, so I dropped out of the game, saying he'd had enough off me. I thought maybe he'd follow suit, but even if he didn't, it would look better without his buddy in there. He didn't, and he kept winning. I didn't want to get too far from him, so I did the best I could and stood right behind him, where I could see his hand, but nobody else's.

After two more rounds Farnley said, "How about draw?" He said it quietly and watching Gil, as if changing the game would make a real difference. Gil was dealing and Farnley had no business asking for the change; it was picking the worst time he could. I knew by the set of his head that Gil was staring back at him like he'd just noticed he was there and wanted to get a clear impression. He held the cards in his fist for a moment and ruffled the edge of them with his other thumb. Moore was going to say something, and I had my fist all doubled to persuade Gil, but then Gil said,

"Sure. Why not?" So I saw the muscles bunch on Farnley's jaws; and Gil began to deal them out.

"Double draw, for a real change," Farnley said.

That's no poker player's game; draw's bad enough, but double draw's for old ladies playing with matches.

"Wait, Jeff," Moore started. Farnley looked at him quick, like he'd paste him if he said another word.

"Double draw it is," Gil said, without breaking his deal.

"Look 'em over careful, boys," he said, when they were all out. "Maybe somebody has two aces of spades."

Farnley let it go. He picked up his cards, and his face didn't change from its set look, but I could tell from the way he looked them all over again, and then bunched them together with his other hand before fanning them to stay, that he thought he had something this time. He drew two cards out and slid them onto the table face down, and this time didn't keep his fingers on them.

I looked at Gil's hand. He had the queen, jack and ten of spades, the ten of clubs and the four of hearts. He looked at it for a moment, but this was double draw. He threw off the club and the heart.

"How many?" he asked.

They drew around, Gil dropping Farnley's cards where he had to reach for them. Farnley looked at them longer this time. Then he put one down very slowly, like he wasn't sure. Four of a kind played cute, or keeping one for luck, I thought.

"Come again," he said.

"Don't hurry me," Gil said, putting down the deck to look at his own draw. He had the nine of spades and the queen of hearts. He thought again, but threw off the queen.

"Place your bets," he said sharp.

Moore, on his left, tossed his hand in. So did the next man. Farnley bet the limit. Bartlett and the other puncher, a fellow with curly black sideburns like wire-hair, stayed, though Bartlett muttered.

Gil threw a half dollar out on top of his quarter so it clinked.

"Double," he said.

"There's a limit," Moore said.

"How about it?" Gil asked Farnley, as if the other two weren't in the game.

Farnley put in the quarter, then threw a silver dollar after it.

"Again," he said.

Bartlett balked, but I guess he had something too. When they didn't pay any attention to him he stayed. So did the other man, but sheepishly.

Gil matched the dollar.

"How many?" he asked again.

Moore pushed his chair back from the table to get his legs clear. The change in the game had got to the men at the bar. Five or six of them came over to watch, and the others turned around, leaning on the bar with their elbows, and were quiet too. Canby stood in the ring with his towel over his shoulder and that dry look of malicious pleasure on his face, but watching Gil and Farnley just the same.

"One," Farnley said. It was quiet enough so his voice sounded loud, and we could hear Gil slide the card off, and its tap on the table.

"You?" he asked Bartlett.

The old man had changed his mind. He'd taken just one the first time, but now he took two.

Farnley picked up his card slowly and looked at it. Then he put it slowly into the hand, closed the hand up, fanned it again, and sat there waiting for Gil to finish. The man standing behind Farnley couldn't help lifting his eyebrows and looking at Canby, who could see the hand too. Canby didn't appear to notice, but glanced at Gil. Gil was tending to business. He didn't even look up when

Bartlett snorted violently and slapped his hand down, face up.

"Cover them cards," Moore said. Bartlett glared at him, but then turned the hand over.

The sheepish man took two.

"I'm taking one," Gil said, and put the deck down away from his hand, and slid one off the top and rubbed it back and forth on the felt for Farnley to see it was only one. Even at that Farnley didn't give any sign. Gil drew the card into his hand and picked them all up. He'd drawn the king of spades.

The sheepish man plucked at his mustache a couple of times and threw in.

"Your bet," Gil told Farnley.

Farnley tossed out another silver dollar. Gil threw out two. Farnley raised it another. Men stirred uneasily, but were careful to be quiet. Only when Farnley made it five Canby said, "Enough's enough. See him, Carter, or I'll close up the game."

Gil put out the dollar to see, and we started to relax, when he counted five more off the top of his pile and shoved them out.

"And five," he said.

That still didn't make it any sky-limit game, but it was mean for the kind of a game this had started out to be. There was plenty left in Gil's stack, but when Farnley had counted out the five there was only one dollar left on the green by his hand.

"Make it six," Gil said, and put in the extra one.

"Pick it up, Gil," I said. "You were seen at five."

There was some muttering from others too. Gil didn't pay any attention. He sat looking at Farnley. Farnley was breathing hard, and his eyes were narrowed, but he looked at his hand, not Gil.

"That's enough," Canby said, and started to pick up. It was Farnley, not Gil, who looked at him.

"Your funeral," Canby said.

"Maybe," Farnley said, and threw in the sixth dollar.

"I'm seeing you," he said, and laid out his hand carefully in a nice fan in front of him but opening toward Gil. We craned to see it. It was a full house, kings and jacks.

Gil tossed his cards into the center so they fell part covered and reached for the pot.

"Hold it," Moore said. Gil leaned back and watched Moore as if he was being patient with a fool. Moore spread the cards out so everybody could see them. One of the watchers whistled.

"Suit you?" Gil asked Moore.

Moore nodded and Gil reached the money in and began to put it in neat stacks, slowly and with pleasure.

Farnley sat staring at Gil's cards for a moment.

"Jesus," he said, "that's damned long luck," and suddenly let off by banging the table with his fist so hard that Gil's stacks slid down again into a loose pile. Gil had the canvas sack out of his jeans and was just ready to scoop the silver into it. He stopped and held the sack in the air. But Farnley wasn't going to start anything. He got up and turned toward the bar. He was doing well, I thought; you could tell by his face he was near crazy mad. Gil was the fool.

"Wouldn't suggest it was anything but luck, would you?" he asked, still holding the sack out in the air.

At first Farnley stood there with his back turned. Then he came back to the table, but slow enough so Moore had time to get to his feet before he spoke.

"I wasn't going to," he said; "but now you mention it."

Gil stood up too, letting the sack drop onto the coins on the table.

"Make it clear," he said, his voice thick and happy.

Gil was taller and a lot more solid than Farnley, and Farnley was so far gone I was scared. He had the look of a kill-fighter, not a man who was happy to rough it up. I saw his hand start for his belt, and I reached too. Gil doesn't think of a gun when he gets like that; he wants to slug. And he was drunk. But Farnley didn't have a gun; no belt on. He remembered it too, before he'd reached all the way, and wiped both hands on his seat to cover.

"There's a lot of things around here aren't clear," he said.

And then Gil had to say, "You're talking about cows now, maybe?"

I got set to hit him. There wasn't any use grabbing.

"You're saying it this time too," Farnley told him.

"Come on, boys, the game's over," Canby put in. "The drinks are on you, Carter. You're heavy winner."

He took my mind off what I was doing. I swung, but

23

Gil was already part way round the table. In spite of his weight and all he'd had to drink, he was quick, clumsy quick, like a bear. Canby reached but missed. Gil shoved Moore nearly off his feet and was on Farnley in three jumps, letting go a right that would have broken Farnley's neck. Farnley got under that one, but ducked right into a wild left that caught him on the corner of the mouth. He spun part way around, crashed across two chairs, and folded up under the front window, banging his head against the sill. Gil stood swaying and laughing as if he loved it. Then his face straightened and got that deadly pleased look again.

"Called me a rustler, did he?" he said thickly, as if somebody had just reminded him of it again. I knew the look; he was going to pile Farnley and hammer him. Nobody seemed to move. They were standing back leaving Gil alone by the table. I yelled something and started around, bumping into Moore, who was just getting set on his feet again. But I was too far behind. Canby turned the trick. Without even looking excited, he reached back to the bar, got hold of a bottle, and rapped Gil, not too hard either, right under the base of skull. He must have done it a thousand times to be that careful about it. For a moment Gil's tension held him up. Then his knees bellied like cloth and he came down in a heap and rolled over onto his back, where he lay with a silly, surprised grin on his face and his eyes rolled up so only the whites showed. He slid against the table when he fell, and jarred it, so some of the coins and one glass of whisky slipped off, while another glass tipped over and the whisky streamed briefly, and then dribbled into a little pool by Gil's head. One of the coins lit on its edge and started rolling away by itself, and a man jumped out of the way of it like it was a snake. There was a little laughing.

"Looks happy, don't he?" Canby said, standing over Gil with the bottle in his hand.

"He'll be all right," he told me. "I just gave him a touch of it."

"It was neat," I said, and laughed. Others laughed too, and the talk began.

I helped Canby with Gil, who was heavy and limp and hard to prop in a chair. When we had him there I turned to the table to get some whisky to throw in his face, and

24

had to laugh again. Bartlett was still sitting there, with a look on his face as if he didn't know yet what had happened, and the edge of the table shoved into him so it creased his big middle.

Canby had already thrown water in Gil's face, and was taking his gun out of the holster.

"He'll be all right," I said. "He always comes out of it nice."

Canby studied me for a moment, then nodded and let the gun slip back.

"How about him, though?" I asked, meaning Farnley.

Canby had hold of Gil's head between his two long hands and was working it around loosely and massaging the back of his neck. Still working, he looked over his shoulder at Farnley, where Moore had him in another chair by the window. Farnley was still out, but he was coming. His face was already beginning to swell, and his mouth was bleeding some from the corner. I didn't like the way he was coming back, slow, and without any chatter or struggle. Canby watched him too, until Farnley got back of his eyes again, and then, as if everything was all at once clear, sat up and shook off the hands working on him, and leaned forward, propping himself with his arms on his knees.

Gil was beginning to come up too. Canby turned back.

"Yeh," he said to me. "That's a different matter. Better pick up his dough," he added.

I got the sack and scooped the winnings from the table into it. Osgood, who had been standing around trying to think of something useful, picked up the coins that had fallen onto the floor, even tracking down the one that had rolled off.

Gil started to talk before he was out of it, muttering and sort of joking and protesting. He rolled around some on the chair. When he really woke up he pushed us off, but gently, not wanting to jar himself. Then he took hold of his head with both hands and leaned way over.

"Holy cow," he said, and worked his hands in and out from his head to show how it was feeling.

Everybody laughed but Farnley, who looked across slow, and didn't seem to think anything was funny.

Gil got up, testing his legs, and turned his head carefully.

"I must have hit myself," he said. They laughed again.

Farnley got up, and the laughing stopped. But he only walked to the bar and got himself a drink. He didn't talk to anyone or look at anyone.

Gil closed his eyes, then his mouth, and got a queer, strangled look on his face. He put a hand up to his mouth and turned and hurried out through the back room. I followed him with his Indian sack in my hand. He was staggering some, and bumped against the outside kitchen door, but he got out quickly. I could hear the men laughing again behind us. They liked the way Gil took it; he made it all right for them to laugh, and he did look funny, that big, red-headed bear trotting out like a little kid holding his pants.

When I got to him he was standing in a little cleared, black space where Canby burned his rubbish, with his hands on his knees, leaning over some green tumbleweed that was still rooted in. He was pretty well emptied out already, and just getting hold of himself again.

He stood up with his eyes watering and his face red.

"Holy cow," he gulped.

"It must have been Canby," he said. "Now I've got to start all over again."

"Take your time," I advised. "You've got head enough."

Gil stood there breathing in and looking around like he was really starting life again, though doubtfully. The clouds had risen higher in the west, and now and then one blew free across the valley, making a deeper, passing shadow on the shadow of the bending grass.

From somewhere down the side street we caught the sound of a running horse on the hard-pan. By the clatter, he was being pushed.

"Somebody's in a hell of a hurry," Gil said.

We got a glimpse of the rider as he rounded onto the main street. The horse banked around at a considerable angle, and was running hard and heavily. There was white dropping away from his bit. The rider had been bent over with his hat pulled down hard, but even in the little space we could see him, he straightened back and began to rein in strong. Then they were out of sight behind Canby's. There'd be trouble stopping that horse. He looked to me like he'd been run till he couldn't quit.

"I'm not, though," Gil said.

I liked it out there too. It was good after the stale darkness inside. A long roundup makes you restless inside houses for a while. Now and then in the freshening wind we could hear a meadow lark "chink-chink-a-link," and then another, way off and higher, "tink-tink-a-link." I could see how they'd be leaping up out of the grass, fluttering while they just let off for all the spring was worth to them, and then dropping back into the grass again.

Gil, though, was thinking about something.

"He didn't use his fist, did he?"

"What?"

"Canby. He didn't knock me out with his fist, did he?"

"No, a bottle."

"That's all right, then. I thought it must have been that." And after breathing in a couple of times more, "He shouldn't have stopped me though. I don't feel any better."

"It takes a lot to please you," I told him. "Anyway, lay off Farnley. You were pretty low on that."

"Listen who's giving the orders," he said, but grinning.

"Yeh, I guess I was at that," he said seriously. "Maybe I ought to give him back his money. Say, the money," he said quickly.

"I've got it," I told him, and gave him the sack. He weighed it in his hand and ran his tongue over his lower lip.

"You think I ought to give it back?" he asked unhappily.

"Not all of it," I said. "Most of it was won fair. But not the last pot; that was no poker."

That cheered him up. "Yeh, the last pot," he agreed, "that was the one."

He stared at the sack. "Maybe you'd better give it to him," he said. "How much was it?"

"No, you give it to him," I said. "That will fix it better."

He looked at me, thinking about it.

"You don't need to say anything, just that you were pretty drunk," I advised.

That seemed to satisfy him.

"How much was it?" he asked again.

"Ten dollars is near enough," I said.

"Is that all?" he said, feeling better.

He poured coins out into his hand, counted out ten dollars, dropped the rest back in, drew the sack tight, tied

27

it around the neck and slipped it into his pocket. It still made a big bulge. With the ten dollars in his hand he started for the back door.

"Better kind of sidle up," I said.

He stopped short and looked at me. "The hell I will," he said. He was coming back all right. He had a wonderful strong head when his belly was clean. "Why should I?" he asked, as if he was willing to be reasonable if I didn't expect too much.

"You hit him plenty hard," I said, "and you made him look foolish."

"Did I?" he asked. Then, "Did I get him?"

"You got him. I thought you'd busted his neck."

Gil grinned. "Well, I'll try and go easy," he said.

We went in through the kitchen and the back room where Canby served meals and had a pool table now. But when we got to the bar door I could see right away something was wrong. Farnley was standing at the other end, by the front door, looking like he hadn't come out of his daze yet, and Moore had hold of him by the arm and was talking to him. Davies was trying to say something too. Just when we stopped, Farnley shook Moore off, though still standing there.

"The lousy sons-of-bitches," he said, and then repeated it slowly, each word by itself.

At first I was going to try to get Gil out the back way again. It wouldn't be easy. When he heard Farnley he pulled the sack out of his jeans again and dropped the ten dollars back into it. And it wasn't his drunk fighting face that was coming on now, either.

Then I saw how the men were, all gathered together along the bar there, looking quiet and angry, and not paying any attention to us. When they heard our boots a few glanced at us, but didn't even seem to see us. They'd been watching Farnley at first, and now they were looking at a new rider who was talking excitedly, so I couldn't get what he said. He was a young fellow, still in his teens, I thought, and he was out of breath. He was feeling important, but wild too, talking fast and waving his right hand, and then slapping the gun on his thigh, which was tied down like a draw-fighter's. His black sombrero was pushed onto the back of his head, and his open vest was flapping. There was a movement and mutter beginning among the men, but at the end the kid's voice came up so we could hear what he was saying.

"Shot right through the head, I tell you," he cried, like somebody was arguing with him, though nobody was.

Farnley reached out and grabbed the kid by the two sides of his vest in one hand, yanked him close and spoke right in his face. The kid looked scared and said something low. Farnley still held him for a moment, staring at him, then let him go, turned and pushed through to the front door and out onto the walk.

Some of the men followed him, but most of them milled around the kid, trying to get something more out of him, but not being noisy now either.

"Come on," I told Gil, "it's not us."

"It better not be," Gil said, starting slow to come with me.

"It's the kid that was riding so fast," I explained.

They were all beginning to crowd outside now. Only Smith was trying to push in past them, with his eye out for drinks they'd left on the bar. And they'd left a lot, seven or eight that weren't empty. And Canby saw Smith and didn't say anything either, but went and stood in the door behind the others, looking out. Something was up.

"What's up?" I asked Canby, trying to see past him. He didn't turn his head.

"Lynching, I'd judge," he said, like it didn't interest him.

"Those rustlers?" I asked.

"Maybe," he said, looking at me kind of funny. "They don't know yet who. But somebody's been in down on Drew's range and killed Kinkaid, and they think there's cattle gone too."

"Killed Kinkaid?" I echoed, and thought that over quick. Kinkaid had been Farnley's buddy. They'd been riding together from the Panhandle to Jackson Hole ever since they were kids. Kinkaid was a little, dark Irishman who liked to be by himself, and never offered to say anything, but only made short answers when he had to, and then you had to be close to hear him. He always seemed halfway sad, and though he had a fine, deep singing voice, he wouldn't often sing when he knew anybody could hear. He was only an ordinary rider, with no flair to give him a reputation, but still there was something about him which made men cotton to him; nothing he did or said, but a gentle, permanent reality that was in him like his bones or his heart, that made him seem like an everlasting part of things. You didn't notice when he was there, but you noticed it a lot when he wasn't. You could no more believe that Kinkaid was dead than you could that a mountain had moved and left a gap in the sky. The men would go a long way, and all together, to get the guy that had killed Kinkaid. And I was remembering Canby's joke about Gil and me.

"When?" Gil asked.

Then Canby looked at him too. "They don't know," he said; "about noon, maybe. They didn't find him till a lot later." And he looked at me again.

I wanted to feel the way the others did about this, but you can feel awful guilty about nothing when the men you're with don't trust you. I knew Gil was feeling the same way when he started to say something, and Canby looked back at him, and he didn't say it. But we couldn't afford to stand in there behind Canby either. I pushed past him and went down onto the walk, Gil right behind me.

Farnley was climbing onto his horse. He moved slowly and deliberately, like a man with his mind made up. A rider yelled, as if Farnley was half a mile off, "Hey, Jeff. Wait up; we'll form a posse."

"I can get the sons-of-bitches," Farnley said, and reined around.

Moore said, "He's crazy," and started out into the street. But Davies was ahead of him. He came alongside Farnley in a little, shuffling run, and took hold of his bridle. The horse, checked, wheeled his stern away from Davies and switched his tail. The way Farnley looked down, I thought he was going to let Davies have it in the face with his quirt. But he didn't. Davies was an old man, short and narrow and so round-shouldered he was nearly a hunchback, and with very white, silky hair. His hollow, high-cheeked face, looking up at Farnley, was white from indoor work, and had deep forehead lines and two deep, clear lines each side of a wide, thin mouth. The veins made his hollow temples appear blue. He would have been a good figure for a miser except for his eyes, which were a queerly young, bright and shining blue, and usually, though not now, humorous. Farnley looked at those eyes and held himself.

"There's no rush, Jeff," Davies said, coaxing him. "They have a long start of us, anyway."

Farnley said something we couldn't hear.

Davies said, "You don't know how many of them there are, Jeff. There might be twenty. It won't help Larry to get yourself killed too."

Farnley didn't say anything, but he didn't pull his horse away. The horse yanked its head up twice, and Davies let go of the bridle, and put a hand on Farnley's knee.

"We aren't even certain which way they went, Jeff, or how long they've had. You just wait till we know what we're doing. We're all with you about Kinkaid. You know that, son."

He kept his hand on Farnley's knee, and stood there with his hat off and the sun shining in his white hair. The hair was long, down over his collar. Farnley must have begun to think a little. He waited. Moore went out to them.

Osgood was standing beside me on the walk. "They musn't do this; they musn't," he said, waving his hands and looking as if he were going to cry. Then he thrust his hands back into his pockets again.

Gil was behind us. He said to Osgood, "Shut up, gran'ma. Nobody expects you to go."

Osgood turned around quickly and nervously. "I'm not afraid," he asserted. "Not in the least afraid. It is quite another consideration which prevents . . . "

"You can preach later," Gil cut him off without looking at him, but watching Moore talk to Farnley. "There'll be more of us needing it, maybe."

"You ain't even got a gun yet, Jeff," Moore was repeating.

Osgood suddenly went out to the two men by the horse. He went busily, as if he didn't want to, but was making himself. His bald head was pale in the sun. The wind fluttered his coat and the legs of his trousers. He looked helpless and timid. I knew he was trying to do what he thought was right, but he had no heart in his effort. He made me feel ashamed, as disgusted as Gil.

"Farnley," he said, in a voice which was too high from being forced, "Farnley, if such an awful thing has actually occurred, it is the more reason that we should retain our self-possession. In such a position, Farnley, we are likely to lose our reason and our sense of justice.

"Men," he orated to us, "let us not act hastily; let us not do that which we will regret. We must act, certainly, but we must act in a reasoned and legitimate manner, not as a lawless mob. It is not mere blood that we want; we are not Indians, savages to be content with a miserable, sneaking revenge. We desire justice, and justice has never been obtained in haste and strong feeling." I thought he intended to say more, but he stopped there and looked at us pathetically. He talked with no more conviction than he walked.

The men at the edge of the walk stirred and spit and felt of their faces. It was not Osgood, really, who was delaying them, but uncertainty, and perhaps the fear that they were going to hunt somebody they knew. They had been careful a long time.

Davies saw that Osgood had failed. His mouth tightened downward.

Farnley paid no attention, but having admitted he would wait, just sat his saddle rigidly. His horse knew something was wrong, and kept swinging his stern, his heels chopping. Farnley let him pivot. He reared a little and swung his tail back toward the Reverend. Osgood backed away hurriedly. One of the punchers laughed. Osgood did look queer, feinting and wavering out there. Moore looked back at us angrily. Farnley's back had gone stiff under the cowhide vest. The man who had laughed pulled his hat down and muttered.

"We'll organize a posse right here, Jeff," Moore promised. "If we go right, we'll get what we're after." For Moore, that was begging. He waited, looking up at Farnley.

Then Farnley pulled his horse around slowly, so he sat facing us.

"Well, make your posse," he said. He sat watching us as if he hated us all. His cheeks were twitching.

Canby was still leaning in the door behind us, his towel

33

in his hand. "Somebody had better get the sheriff, first thing," he advised. He didn't sound as if it mattered to him whether we got the sheriff or not.

"And Judge Tyler," Osgood said. He was impressed by the suggestion, and came over to stand in front of us, closer. "Judge Tyler must be notified," he said.

"To hell with that," somebody told him. That start~d others. "We know what that'll mean," yelled another. A third shouted, "We know what that'll mean is right. We don't need no trail for this business. We've heard enough of Tyler and his trails." The disturbance spread. Men began to get on their horses.

The kid, Greene, had been forgotten too long. He pushed through toward Osgood with his fist doubled. But Osgood faced him well enough. Greene stopped at the edge of the walk. "This ain't just rustling," he yelled.

"Rustling is enough," Bartlett told him; then he pulled off his hat and waved it above his head. His head looked big when it was uncovered. There was a pasted-down line around it from the sweat under his hatband. He curled his upper lip when he talked angrily, showing his yellow, gappy teeth and making his mustache jerk.

"I don't know about the rest of you," he cried. He had a big, hollow voice when he was angry enough to lift it. "I don't know about the rest of you, but I've had enough rustling. Do we have rights as men and cattlemen, or don't we? We know what Tyler is. If we wait for Tyler, or any man like Tyler," he added, glaring at Osgood, "if we wait, I tell you, there won't be one head of anybody's cattle left in the meadows by the time we get justice." He ridiculed the word justice by his tone. "For that matter," he called, raising his voice still higher, "what is justice? Is it justice that we sweat ourselves sick and old every damned day in the year to make a handful of honest dollars, and then lose it all in one night to some miserable greaser because Judge Tyler, whatever God made him, says we have to fold our hands and wait for his eternal justice? Waiting for Tyler's kind of justice, we'd all be beggars in a year.

"What led rustlers into this valley in the first place?" he bellowed. "This is no kind of a place for rustlers. I'll tell you what did it. Judge Tyler's kind of justice, that's what did it. They don't wait for that kind of justice in

34

Texas any more, do they? No, they don't. They know they can pick a rustler as quick as any fee-gorging lawyer that ever took his time in any courtroom. They go and get the man, and they string him up. They don't wait for that kind of justice in San Francisco any more, do they? No, they don't. They know they can pick a swindler as well as any overfed judge that ever lined his pockets with bribes. The Vigilance Committee does something—and it doesn't take them six months to get started either, the way it does justice in some places.

"By the Lord God, men, I ask you," he exhorted, "are we going to slink on our own range like a pack of sniveling boys, and wait till we can't buy the boots for our own feet, before we do anything?

"Well, I'm not, for one," he informed us, with hoarse determination. "Maybe if we do one job with our own hands, the law will get a move on. Maybe. And maybe it never will. But one thing is sure. If we do this job ourselves, and now, it will be one that won't have to be done again. Yes, and what's more, I tell you we won't ever have to do any such job again, not here.

"But, by God," he begged, "if we stand here yapping and whining and wagging our tails till Judge Tyler pats us on the head, we'll have every thieving Mex and Indian and runaway Reb in the whole territory eating off our own plates. I say, stretch the bastards," he yelped, "stretch them."

He was sweating, and he stared around at us, rolling his bloodshot eyes.

He had us excited. Gil and I were quiet, because men had moved away from us, but I was excited too. I wanted to say something that would square me, but I couldn't think what. But Bartlett wasn't done. He wiped his face on his sleeve, and when he spoke again his voice went up so high it cracked, but we could understand him. Faces around me were hard and angry, with narrow, shining eyes.

"And that's not all," Bartlett was crying, piping. "Like the boy here says, it's not just a rustler we're after, it's a murderer. Kinkaid's lying out there now, with a hole in his head, a Goddamned rustler's bullet hole. Let that go, and I'm telling you, men, there won't be anything safe, not our cattle, not our homes, not our lives, not even our women. I say we've got to get them. I have two sons, and we all know how to shoot; yes, and how to tie a knot in a rope, if that's worrying you, a knot that won't slip.

"I'm for you, Jeff," he shouted at Farnley, waving his hat in a big arc in front of him. "I'm going to get a gun and a rope, and I'll be back. If nobody else will do it, you and I and the boys will do it. We'll do it alone."

Farnley raised one hand, carelessly, in a kind of salute, but his face was still tight, expressionless and twitching. At his salute the men all shouted. They told him loudly that they were with him too. Bartlett stirred us, but Farnley, sitting there in the sun, saying nothing, now stirred us even more. If we couldn't do anything for Kinkaid now, we could for Farnley. We could help Farnley get rid of his lump. He became a hero, just sitting there, the figure which concentrated our purpose.

Thinking about it afterward I was surprised that Bartlett succeeded so easily. None of the men he was talking to owned any cattle or any land. None of them had any property but their horses and their outfits. None of them were even married, and the kind of women they got a chance to know weren't likely to be changed by what a rustler would do to them. Some out of that many were bound to have done a little rustling on their own, and maybe one or two had even killed a man. But they weren't thinking of those things then, any more than I was. Old Bartlett was amazing. It seemed incredible that so much ferocity hadn't killed him, weak and shaky as he appeared. Instead, it had made him appear straighter and stronger.

He turned around and pushed through us in a hurry, not even putting his hat on. I could hear him wheezing when he shoved past me, and his lower lip stuck out, reaching for his mustache.

Osgood called to the men. "Listen, men," he called. Most of them were already on their horses. "Listen, men," he called again. Old Bartlett stopped out in the sun on the walk beyond us. He was going to come back and collar the preacher. "Listen to me, men. This insane violence . . ."

Gil walked over close to Osgood. "You listen to me, preacher," he said. "I thought I told you once to shut up." Osgood couldn't help backing away from him. He backed off the walk, and stumbled in the street. This mortified him so he grasped his forehead with both hands for a moment, as if trying vainly to get himself back together again; or else to protect his skull. When we all laughed, businesslike, contemptuous laughter, in a short chorus, old Bartlett grinned and turned around and went off up the walk again.

Suddenly Osgood uncovered his head and ran to Davies, holding both hands out in front of him, first like a child running to beg for something, then weaving them back and forth while he talked.

"They won't listen to me, Mr. Davies," he babbled. "They won't listen. They never would. Perhaps I'm weak. Any man is weak when nobody cares for the things that mean something to him. But they'll listen to you. You know how to talk to them, Davies. You tell them.

"Oh, men," he cried out, coming back at us, "think, won't you; think. If you were mistaken, if . . ."

He gave up, and stared at us, still moving his hands like birds with their legs caught.

Davies, without moving away from Farnley, said clearly, "Mr. Osgood is right, men. We should wait until . . ."

"What do you know about it?" Gil asked him.

A voice from the door called, "The trouble with Davies is that he can't see no profit in this. It's hard to move Davies when he can't see no profit. Now, if you'd offer to buy the rope from him . . ." It was Smith. He still had a whisky glass in his hand, and he'd pushed past Canby and was standing on the top step with his legs apart and his other hand in his belt, where it hung under his belly.

Davies did look sharp at that, but Moore acted for him. He reached up and grabbed Smith by the belt, and pulled him down among us.

"If we go, you're going, porky."

"You don't have to tell me," Smith laughed. He pushed Moore off. "I wouldn't miss it," he said. "The only thing would get me out faster, would be your necktie party, Moore." A few men watching them laughed, and this encouraged Smith. "Who knows," he added, "maybe this *is* yours."

They'd all been afraid for months that they'd know the man. This was a hit. Moore, though, just looked Smith in the eye until the big drunk couldn't face him. Then he said, "I'll remember that. I'll see that you get to handle a rope!"

Gil had been pleased, his words to Osgood having made things better for us. Now suddenly he was quieter, and sober.

Canby said, "You're wasting a lot of time. Whoever you're after has made five miles while you argued."

"You gotta get guns," Greene piped. "They shot Kinkaid. They got guns."

Only two or three of the men had guns. Gil and I had ours, because we were on the loose and felt better with them. They called to Farnley they'd be back and went off after guns, some of them riding, some running on the walks.

To the rest of us Davies said, "There are only a few of you now. Will you listen to me?" Moore and Osgood were looking at us too.

"We listened once," Smith said, "listened, and heard nothing. As for me," he grinned, "I think I'll have a couple of drinks on the house. I want to be primed."

Canby blocked the door. "Not here, you don't," he said. "Two more and you'd have to be tied on. If you went."

"It's past talk, Davies," a puncher told him. "You can see that." He didn't sound angry.

"Yes," Davies said. "Yes, I guess you're right."

"I'm going to have a drink," Gil said; "I want a hell of a long drink."

I told him that suited me. There were only a few men left now, talking quietly in the blue shadow of the arcade. Up and down the street you could hear the others, their boots on the boardwalk or their horses trotting. A few called to each other, reminding that it might be a long ride, or to bring a rope, or advising where a gun might be borrowed, since most of them were from ranches outside the village. The sun was still bright in the street, but it was a late-in-the-afternoon light. And the wind had changed. The spring feeling, warm when it was still, chilly when the air stirred, was gone. Even right out in the sun it was pretty cold now. I went out in the street to take a look west. The clouds over the mountains had pushed up still more, and were dark under their bellies.

Davies stood on the walk while I was looking at the sky. I thought he was waiting for me, and took longer than I had to, hoping he would go in. But there's only about so much to look at in one sky; I'm no painter. I gave it up and he came in with me, though not saying anything. He stood up to drink with us too. There were half a dozen of us drinking. Canby had left the door open, and through it I could see Farnley still sitting in his saddle in the sun. Nobody was going to change his mind with Farnley sitting there. Gil kept looking out at him too. Gil felt partly to blame for how hard Farnley was taking this; or maybe it was the ten dollars.

"What made you so hot for a drink?" I asked Gil, to keep ahead of Davies.

"Nothing; I'm thirsty," he said, drinking one and pouring another.

"Yes, there is too," he admitted. "I'd forgot all about it until Moore told Smith he could hold a rope that way. I was layin' up in Montana that winter, stayin' with an old woman who put out good grub. Sittin' right on her front porch I saw them hang three men on one limb."

He took his other drink down. That didn't worry me now. Feeling this way he could drink twenty and not know it. He poured another. He talked low and quick, as if he didn't mind my hearing it, but didn't want anyone else to.

"They kicked a barrel out from under each one of them, and the poor bastards kept trying to reach them with their toes." He looked down at his drink. "They didn't tie their legs," he said, "just their arms."

After a minute he said, "That was an official posse though, sheriff and all. All the same . . ." He started his third drink, but slowly, like he didn't want it much.

"Rustlers?" I asked him.

"Held up a stagecoach," he told me. "The driver was shot."

"Well, they had it coming," I said.

"One of them was a boy," he said, "just a kid. He was scared to death and kept crying, and telling them he hadn't done it. When they put the rope around his neck his knees gave out. He fell off the barrel and nearly choked."

I could see how Gil felt. It wasn't a nice thing to remember with a job of this kind in front of you. But I could tell Davies was listening to Gil. He wasn't looking at us, but he was just sipping his drink, and being too quiet.

39

"We got to watch ourselves, Gil," I told him, very low, and looking up at the woman with the parrot.

"To hell with them," he said. But he didn't say it loudly.

"Greene was all mixed up," I said, still muttering over my chin. "He wasn't sure of anything except Kinkaid was shot in the head. But he thought it was about noon."

"I know," Gil said.

Then he said, "They're gettin' back already. Hot for it, ain't they?" It sounded like remembering that Montana job had changed his whole way of looking at things.

I could tell without turning who was coming. There wasn't a big, flat-footed clop-clop like horses make on hard-pack, but a kind of edgy clip-clip-clip. There was only one man around here would ride a mule, at least on this kind of business. That was Bill Winder, who drove the stage between Reno and Bridger's Wells. A mule is tough all right; a good mule can work two horses into the ground and not know it. But there's something about a mule a man can't get fond of. Maybe it's just the way a mule is, just as you feel it's the end with a man who's that way. But you can't make a mule part of the way you live, like your horse is; it's like he had no insides, no soul. Instead of a partner you've just got something else to work on along with steers. Winder didn't like mules either, but that's why he rode them. It was against his religion to get on a horse; horses were for driving.

"It's Winder," Gil said, and looked at Davies and grinned. "The news gets around, don't it?"

I looked at Davies too, in the glass, but he wasn't showing anything, just staring at his drink and minding his own thoughts.

Winder wouldn't help Davies any; we knew that. He was edgy the same way Gil was, but angry, not funning, and you couldn't get at him with an idea.

We saw him stop beside Farnley and say something and, when he got his answer, shake his head angrily and spit, and pull his mule into the tie rail with a jerk. Waiting wasn't part of Winder's plan of life either. He believed in action first and make your explanation to fit.

Gabe Hart was with him, on another mule. Gabe was his hostler, a big, ape-built man, stronger than was natural, but weak-minded; not crazy, but childish, like

40

his mind had never grown up. He was dirty too; he slept in the stables with his horses, and his knees and elbows were always out of his clothes, and his long hair and beard always had bits of hay and a powder of grain chaff in them. Gabe was gentle, though; not a mean streak in him, like there generally is in stupid, very strong men. Gabe was the only man I ever knew could really love a mule, and with horses he was one of them. That's why Winder kept him. Gabe was no use for anything else, but he could do everything with horses, making clucking, senseless talk in his little, high voice and just letting them feel his hands, which were huge even for a man his size. And Winder liked his horses hard to handle. Outside of horses there were only two things in Gabe's life, Winder and sitting. Winder was his god, and sitting was his way of worshipping. Gabe could sit for hours if there wasn't something to do to a horse. Sometimes I've thought Gabe just lived for the times Winder took him on the coach because he had a really ugly team or had some heavy loading to do. Riding on the coach got everything into Gabe's life that mattered, Winder, sitting and horses, and he'd sit up there on the high seat, holding on like a scared kid, with his hair and tatters blowing and solemn joy in his huge face with the little, empty eyes.

Winder had a Winchester with him, but he left it against the tie rail and came in, Gabe behind him, and looked at Davies like a stranger, and ordered a whisky.

Canby offered Gabe a drink too, just to see him refuse it. He looked at Canby and grinned to show he meant to be pleasant and shook his head. Then he stood looking slowly around as if he'd never been in the place before, though he'd followed Winder in, almost every day for years.

Winder winked at Canby. "Gabe don't care nothin' for drinkin' or smokin' or women, do you, Gabe?"

Gabe grinned and shook his head again, and then looked down at the floor like he was going to blush. Winder cackled.

"He's a good boy, Gabe is," he said.

This joke was as old as Canby's and Gil's about the woman in the picture.

Winder drank one down, put his glass out to be filled

again, and looked at Davies. He was a short, stringy, blond man, with a freckled face with no beard or mustache but always a short, reddish stubble. He had pale blue eyes with a constant hostile stare, as if he was trying to pick a fight even when he laughed.

"They're takin' their time, ain't they?" he said.

"They might as well," Davies said.

"Yeh?" Winder demanded.

"They haven't much to go on yet," Davies told him.

"They got enough, from what I heard."

"Maybe, but not enough to know what to do."

"How do you mean?"

"Well, for one thing they don't know who did it."

"That's what we aim to find out, ain't it?"

"You can't tell who it might be."

"What the hell does that matter? I'd string any son-of-a-bitchin' rustler like that." He slapped the bar. "If he was my own brother, I would," he said furiously.

Gabe made a little noise like he was clearing his throat.

"You're getting Gabe stirred up," Canby said.

"Yes, suh, if he was mah own brothah," Gabe said in his high voice. He was watching Davies, and swinging his hands back and forth on the ends of the long arms, close to his legs. We all knew there were two things made Gabe angry, seeing Winder angry, and being teased about niggers. Winder could handle him about getting mad himself, which was a good thing, he was mad so much; but Gabe was from Mississippi, and the worst about niggers I ever knew. He wouldn't eat where they'd eaten, sleep where they'd slept, or be seen talking to one. That seemed to be the one idea he'd kept from his earlier days, and it had grown on him.

"Well, there's another thing," Davies said.

"What's that?" Winder wanted to know.

"What's that?" Gabe asked too.

"Shut up, Gabe," Winder told him. "This ain't none of your affair. Go sit down."

Gabe looked at him like he didn't understand.

"Go on, sit down." Winder waved at the chairs along the back wall.

Gabe shuffled back to them and sat down, leaning on his knees and looking at the floor between his feet, so all you could see was the swell of his big shoulders, like the shoulders of a walrus, and the top of his head with the hair matted and straw in it, and those tremendous, thick paws hanging limp between his knees. He made a strong smell of horses and manure in the room, even through the stale beer odor.

"This sorta thing's gotta stop," Winder said, "no matter who's doin' it."

"It has," Davies agreed. "But we don't know how many of them there are; or which way they went, either. There's no use going off half-cocked."

"What the hell way would they go?" Winder asked him. "Out the south end by the draw, wouldn't they? There ain't no other way. They wouldn't head right back up this way, would they, with the whole place layin' for them? You're damn shootin' they wouldn't."

"No," Davies said. He hadn't finished his drink; was just sipping it, but he filled the glass again and asked Winder, "Have one with me?"

"I don't mind," Winder said.

Canby filled Winder's glass again, and then Gil's. He held the bottle at me, but I shook my head.

"We might as well sit down," Davies said. "They're waiting on Bartlett anyway." He included Gil and me in the invitation. I didn't like it, but I didn't see how to get out of it. We sat down at the table where we'd been playing cards. Canby had that want-to-grin look in his eyes.

Winder pushed his hat back. "All the more reason to get going," he said.

"No particular hurry, though. If they're from around here, they aren't going far. If they aren't, they're going a long ways, too long for a few hours to matter when they've already got a big start."

"The sooner we get started, the sooner we get them."

"It looks that way to me, too," Gil said.

I tried to kick him under the table. I had a feeling Davies was working most on us anyway. He knew better than to think he could reach Winder.

"And how do you know they've got a start?" Winder asked.

"That's what young Greene said."

"Oh, him."

"He was tangled, but if he had anything straight it was the time. He figured Kinkaid must have been killed about noon."

"Well?"

"It's four-thirty now. Say they have a four-hour start. You aren't going to ride your head off to pick that up, are you?"

"Maybe not," Winder admitted.

"No," Davies said. "It's a long job at best, and stern chase. And it's more than five hundred miles to the first border that will do them any good. Part of that will be a tracking job too. The same way if they're heading for a hide-out to let things cool. It'll be dark in a couple of hours; three anyway. We won't even get down to the draw in that time."

"It's that much of a start if we get there tonight," Winder said.

"Yes, but there's no hurry. We can take our time, and form this posse right."

"Who the hell said anything about a posse?" Winder flared.

"He did," Gil put in; "but it didn't seem to go down so good."

"Why the hell would it?"

"Risley's here," Davies said.

"Risley's been here all summer," Winder said. "It didn't stop Kinkaid gettin' killed, did it?"

"One man can't be every place," I had to chip in. "This is a big valley."

Gil grinned at me to say now who needed a kick.

"He could be a hell of a lot more places than Risley is," Winder told me, staring across at me so I wanted to get up and let him have one.

"Risley's a good man," Davies said, "and a good sheriff."

"You 'mind me of Tyler and the preacher. What have they got us, your good men? A thousand head of cattle gone and a man killed, that's what they got us. We gotta do this ourselves. One good fast job, without no fiddlin' with legal papers, and that's all there'll be to it."

Davies had his hands out on the table in front of him, knobby fingers extended and fingertips together, and was looking at them. He didn't answer.

44

"It's like those damn, thievin' railroads," Winder said, staring around at all three of us to dare us to disagree. "They got the law with them; they're a legal business, they are. They killed off men, didn't they? You damn shootin' they did; one for every tie their son-of-a-bitchin' rails is laid on. And they robbed men of honest to God men's jobs from Saint Looey to Frisco, didn't they? And for what? For a lot of plush-bottomed, soft-handed bastards, who couldn't even drive their own wagons, to ride across the country and steal everything they could lay their hands on in Californy the same way they been doin' in the East for a hundred years. That's what for. And they got the law with them, ain't they? Well, it's men like us shoulda taken the law in their own hands right then. By God, I hate the stink of an Injun, but an Injun smells sweet comparin' to a railroad man. If we'd wanted to keep this country for decent people, we'da helped the Injuns bust up the railroad, yes, by God, we woulda. And that's the same law you're tryin' to hold us up for, ain't it—the kind of law that'll give a murderer plenty of time to get away and cover up, and then help him find his excuses by the book. You and your posses and waitin'. I say get goin' before we're cooled off, and the lily liver that's in half these new dudes gets time to pisen 'em again, so we gotta just set back and listen to Judge Tyler spout his law and order crap. Jesus, it makes me sick."

He spit aside on the floor, and then glared at Davies.

That hatred of the railroad was Winder's only original notion, and when he got mad that always came in some way. Everything else was what he'd heard somebody, or most everybody, say, only he always got angry enough to make it sound like a conviction. His trouble was that he was a one-love man, and stagecoaching was his one love. Guard and driver, he'd been in it from the start with Wells Fargo on the Santa Fe, but it had such a short life he'd outlasted it, and by now, 1885, Lincoln dead and Grant out, the railroads had everything but these little sidelines, like Winder's. The driving was still tough enough, but the pay was poor as a puncher's and the driver was no hero any more. Winder took it personally.

Davies knew how he was, and let him cool. Then he

said, without looking up, "Legal action's not always just, that's true."

"You're damn shootin' it ain't."

"What would you say real justice was, Bill?"

Winder got cautious. "Whadya mean?" he asked.

"I mean, if you had to say what justice was, how would you put it?"

That wouldn't have been easy for anyone. It made Winder wild. He couldn't stand getting reined down logical.

"It sure as hell ain't lettin' things go till any sneakin' cattle thief can shoot a man down and only get a laugh out of it. It ain't that, anyway," he defended.

"No, it certainly isn't that," Davies agreed.

"It's seein' that everybody gets what's comin' to him, that's what it is," Winder said.

Davies thought that over. "Yes," he said, "that's about it."

"You're damn shootin' it is."

"But according to whom?" Davies asked him.

"Whadya mean, 'according to whom'?" Winder wanted to know, saying "whom" like it tasted bad.

"I mean, who decides what everybody's got coming to him?"

Winder looked at us, daring us to grin. "We do," he said belligerently.

"Who are we?"

"Who the hell would we be? The rest of us. The straight ones."

Gabe was standing up and looking at us again, with his hands working. Winder saw him.

"Sit down, you big ape," he yelled at him. "I told you once this is none of your business." Gabe sat down, but kept watching us, looking worried. Winder felt better. It pleased him to see Gabe mind.

Davies said, "Yes, I guess you're right. It's the rest of us who decide."

"It couldn't be any other way," Winder boasted.

"No; no, it couldn't. Though men have tried."

"They couldn't get away with it."

"Not in the long run," Davies agreed. "Not if you make the 'we' big enough, so it takes in everybody."

"Sure it does."

46

"But how do we decide?" Davies asked, as if it were troubling him.

"Decide what?"

"Who's got what coming to him?"

"How does anybody? You just know, don't you? You know murder's not right and you know rustlin's not right, don't you?"

"Yes, but what makes us feel so sure they aren't?"

"God, what a fool question," Winder said. "They're against the law. Anybody . . ." Then he saw where he was, and his neck began to get red. But Davies wasn't being just smart. He let his clincher go and made his point, mostly for Gil and me, that it took a bigger "we" than the valley to justify a hanging, and that the only way to get it was to let the law decide.

"If we go out and hang two or three men," he finished, "without doing what the law says, forming a posse and bringing the men in for trial, then by the same law, we're not officers of justice, but due to be hanged ourselves."

"And who'll hang us?" Winder wanted to know.

"Maybe nobody," Davies admitted. "Then our crime's worse than a murderer's. His act puts him outside the law, but keeps the law intact. Ours would weaken the law."

"That's cuttin' it pretty thin," Gil said.

He'd let himself in. Davies turned to him. "It sounds like it at first," he said earnestly, "but think it over and it isn't." And he went on to prove how the greater "we," as he called it, could absorb a few unpunished criminals, but not unpunished extra-legal justice. He took examples out of history. He proved that it was equally true if the disregard was by a ruler or by a people. "It spreads like a disease," he said. "And it's infinitely more deadly when the law is disregarded by men pretending to act for justice than when it's simply inefficient, or even than when its elected administrators are crooked."

"But what if it don't work at all," Gil said; and Winder grinned.

"Then we have to make it work."

"God," Winder said patiently, "that's what we're tryin' to do." And when Davies repeated they would be if they formed a posse and brought the men in for trial, he said, "Yeah; and then if your law lets them go?"

"They probably ought to be let go. At least there'll be a bigger chance that they ought to be let go than that a lynch gang can decide whether they ought to hang." Then he said a lynch gang always acts in a panic, and has to get angry enough to overcome its panic before it can kill, so it doesn't ever really judge, but just acts on what it's already decided to do, each man afraid to disagree with the rest. He tried to prove to us that lynchers knew they were wrong; that their secrecy proved it, and their sense of guilt afterward.

"Did you ever know a lyncher who wasn't afraid to talk about it afterward?" he asked us.

"How would we know?" Winder asked him. "We never knew a lyncher. We'll tell you later," he added, grinning.

I said that with the law it was still men who had to decide, and sometimes no better men than the rest of us.

"That's true," Davies said, "but the poorest of them is better fitted to judge than we are. He has three big things in his favor: time, precedent, and the consent of the majority that he shall act for them."

I thought about it. "I can see how the time would count," I said.

He explained that precedent and the consent of the majority lessened personal responsibility and gave a man more than his own opinion to go on, so he wasn't so likely to panic or be swung by a mob feeling. He got warmed up like a preacher with real faith on his favorite sermon, and at the end was pleading with us again, not to go as a lynching party, not to weaken the conscience of the nation, not to commit this sin against society.

"Sin against society," Winder said, imitating a woman with a lisp.

"Just that," Davies said passionately, and suddenly pointed his finger at Winder so Winder's wry, angry grin faded into a watchful look. Davies' white, indoor face was hard with his intensity, his young-looking eyes shining, his big mouth drawn down to be firm, but trembling a little, as if he were going to cry. You can think what you want later, but you have to listen to a man like that.

48

"Yes," he repeated, "a sin against society. Law is more than the words that put it on the books; law is more than any decisions that may be made from it; law is more than the particular code of it stated at any one time or in any one place or nation; more than any man, lawyer or judge, sheriff or jailer, who may represent it. True law, the code of justice, the essence of our sensations of right and wrong, is the conscience of society. It has taken thousands of years to develop, and it is the greatest, the most distinguishing quality which has evolved with mankind. None of man's temples, none of his religions, none of his weapons, his tools, his arts, his sciences, nothing else he has grown to, is so great a thing as his justice, his sense of justice. The true law is something in itself; it is the spirit of the moral nature of man; it is an existence apart, like God, and as worthy of worship as God. If we can touch God at all, where do we touch him save in the conscience? And what is the conscience of any man save his little fragment of the conscience of all men in all time?"

He stopped, not as if he had finished, but as if he suddenly saw he was wasting something precious.

"Sin against society," Winder repeated the same way, and got up.

Gil got up too. "That may be all true," he said, "but it don't make any difference now."

"No," Winder said, "we're in it now."

Gil asked, "Why didn't you tell them all this out there?"

"Yeah," Winder said.

"I tried to," Davies said, "and Osgood tried. They wouldn't listen. You know that."

"No," Gil said. "Then why tell us?" He included me. "We're just a couple of the boys. We don't count."

Davies said, "Sometimes two or three men will listen."

"Well," Gil said, "we've listened. What can we do?"

Winder grinned like he'd won the argument by a neat point, and he and Gil went back to the bar.

Davies sat staring at the table, with his two hands lying quiet on top of it. Outside we could hear the men beginning to come back, the hoofs and harness and low talk. Finally he turned his head slowly and looked at me. His mouth had a crooked smile that made me sorry for him.

"Why take it so hard?" I asked him. "You did all you could."

He shook his head. "I failed," he said. "I got talking my ideas. It's my greatest failing."

"They had sense," I said.

But I wasn't sure of this myself. I'm slow with a new idea, and want to think it over alone, where I'm sure it's the idea and not the man that's getting me. And there's another thing I've always noticed, that arguments sound a lot different indoors and outdoors. There's a kind of insanity that comes from being between walls and under a roof. You're too cooped up, and don't get a chance to test ideas against the real size of things. That's true about day and night too; night's like a room; it makes the little things in your head too important. A man's not clear-headed at night. Some of what Davies had said I'd thought about before, but the idea I thought was the main one with him, about law expressing the conscience of society, and the individual conscience springing from that mass sense of right and wrong, was a new one to me, and needed work. It went so far and took in so much. Only I could see how, believing that, he could feel strongly about law, like some men do about religion.

When he didn't say anything, I said, "Only it seems to me sometimes you have to change the laws, and sometimes the men who represent them."

Davies looked at me, as if to calculate how much I'd thought about it. I guess he didn't think that was much, because finally he just nodded and said, as though it didn't interest him, "The soul of a nation or a race grows the same way the soul of a man does. And there have always been impure priests."

There was a lot in that, but he didn't give me time to get hold of it.

"Will you do me a favor?" he asked all of a sudden.

"That depends," I said.

"I have to stay here," he said. "I have to stop them if I can, till they know what they're doing. If I can make this regular, that's all I ask."

"Yes?"

"I'm going to send Joyce for Risley and Judge Tyler. I want you to go with him. Will you?"

"You know how Gil and I stand here. We came in at

50

a bad time," I said. I didn't like being put over the fence into the open.

"I know," he said, and waited.

"All right," I said. "But why two?"

"Do you know Mapes?" he asked.

"The one they call Butch?"

"That's the one."

"I've seen him."

"Risley's made him deputy for times he's out of town, and we don't want Mapes."

"No," I said. I could see why, and I could see why he didn't want Joyce to have to go alone if there was a question of keeping Mapes out of it, though I still thought that was chiefly sucking me in. Mapes was a powerful man, and a crack shot with a six-gun, but he was a bully, and like most bullies he was a play-the-crowd man. He wouldn't be any leader.

"Tyler may not help much," Davies said, as if to himself, "but he ought to be here. Risley's the man we want," he told me.

We got up. Gil was looking at me, and so was Winder.

Before we could get out the door, Smith came in. He had on a reefer jacket and a gun belt with two guns, and he had a coil of rope in his hand. When he saw Davies he grinned.

"Well, if it ain't big-business," he said. "It looks like we'd be going after all, big-business."

He held up the rope. "Look," he said. "Moore says I'm head executioner, so I come all primed." He held the end of the rope up next to his ear, and nudged it a couple of times, as if he was tightening the knot, and then suddenly jerked it up and let his head loll over to the other side. He stuck his tongue out and crossed his eyes. Then he laughed.

"Don't tell me I don't know the trade," he said.

He pretended to be looking at Davies closely, with a worried look. He shook his head and clucked his tongue against his teeth.

"You don't look well, Mr. Davies," he said. "You don't look at all well. Maybe you'd better stay to home and get rested up for the funeral." He laughed again. "Maybe you could get the flowers," he piled it on. "The boys wouldn't begrudge showin' a few flowers, even for a

51

rustler," he said seriously. "A good dead one." And he laughed again.

Osgood had come in in time to see Smith making the hanging motions. He stood in the door watching the act, white and big-eyed, like it was a real stretch he was seeing.

Smith saw me looking at the preacher, I guess, and turned around, and when he saw him laughed again, as if he couldn't stop.

"Oh, Jee-zus," he roared, "look at that. They're all sick. The flower pickers," he bellowed, and then, in a little thin voice, "Girls, shall we lay out the poor dear rustler wustler?" and roared again.

The place was pretty quiet, most of the men not looking at Smith.

"Never see a dead man, preacher?" Smith asked him. "Should, in your trade. But not the ones that was hung, is that it? Well, better not, better not. They get black in the face, and sometimes . . ."

Gil banged his glass down and hitched up his gun belt. Smith turned at the sound, and when he saw Gil walking right at him, he half put up one arm, and wasn't laughing at all. He backed to the side as Gil came closer. But Gil didn't even turn his head to look at him, but went on out and down the steps. Smith stayed quiet, though. Davies and I went out too, Osgood pattering behind us, making a funny, half-crying noise.

"But to go like that," he cried at Davies, waving an arm back at the door. "To go like that," he kept repeating.

"I know," Davies said.

When he saw Joyce he went over and talked to him for a minute. The boy looked scared, and kept nodding his head in little jerks, as if he had the palsy.

"Where you off to?" Gil was asking me, standing beside me.

I rolled a cigarette and took my time to answer. When I'd had a drag I told him. He didn't take it the way I'd thought he would, but looked at me with a lot of questions in his eyes that he didn't ask, the way Canby had looked at both of us in the door. I was getting too many of those looks.

"Davies is right," I said. "Want to come along?"

"Thanks," he said, "but somebody's got to keep this

52

company in good ree-pute." He said it quiet. I guess Smith's act had made him wonder again, in spite of Winder.

The sky was really changing now, fast; it was coming on to storm, or I didn't know signs. Before it had been mostly sunlight, with only a few cloud shadows moving across fast in a wind that didn't get to the ground, and looking like burnt patches on the eastern hills where there was little snow. Now it was mostly shadow, with just gleams of sunlight breaking through and shining for a moment on all the men and horses in the street, making the guns and metal parts of the harness wink and lighting up the big sign on Davies' store and the sagging white veranda of the inn. And the wind was down to earth and continual, flapping the men's garments and blowing out the horses' tails like plumes. The smoke from houses where supper had been started was lining straight out to the east and flowing down, not up. It was a heavy wind with a damp, chill feel to it, like comes before snow, and strong enough so it wuthered under the arcade and sometimes whistled, the kind of wind that even now makes me think of Nevada quicker than anything else I know. Out at the end of the street, where it merged into the road to the pass, the look of the mountains had changed too. Before they had been big and shining, so you didn't notice the clouds much. Now they were dark and crouched down, looking heavier but not nearly so high, and it was the clouds that did matter, coming up so thick and high you had to look at them instead of the mountains. And they weren't firm, spring clouds, with shapes, or the deep, blue-black kind that mean a quick, hard rain, but thick, shapeless and gray-white like dense steam, shifting so rapidly and with so little outline that you more felt than saw them changing.

Probably partly because of this sky-change and partly because a lot of them were newcomers who hadn't heard that there were any doubts about this lynching, the temper of the men in the street had changed too. They weren't fired up the way some of them had been after Bartlett's harangue, but they weren't talking much, or joking, and they were all staying on their horses except those that had been in Canby's. Most of them had on reefers or stiff cowhide coats, and some even had

53

scarves tied down around their heads under their hats, like you wear on winter range. They all had gun belts, and had ropes tied to their saddles, and a good many had carbines, generally carried across the saddle, but a few in long holsters by their legs, the shoulder curved, metal heeled, slender stocks showing out at the top. Their roughened faces, strong-fleshy or fine with the hard shape of the bones, good to look at, like the faces of all outdoor, hard-working men, were set, and their eyes were narrowed, partly against the wind, but partly not. I couldn't help thinking about what Davies had said on getting angry enough not to be scared when you knew you were wrong. That's what they were doing, all right. Every new rider that came in, they'd just glance at him out of those narrow eyes, like they hated his guts and figured things were getting too public. And there were new men coming in all the time; about twenty there already. Every minute it was getting harder for Davies to crack. They were going to find it easy to forget any doubts that had been mentioned. It just seemed funny now to think I'd been listening to an argument about what the soul of the law was. Right here and now was all that was going to count. I felt less than ever like going on my missions for Davies.

When Joyce came over for me, I took a look at Davies, and he was feeling it too. When he looked at the men in the street he had a little of the Osgood expression. It was hard for him to shift from the precious idea in which he had just been submerged, to what he really had to handle. Osgood was standing near him, at the edge of the walk, his baggy suit fluttering and his hands making arguing motions in front of him. They made a pair.

But Davies was still going to try. When he saw me looking at him, and Joyce just standing there waiting for me, the muscles came out at the back jaw again, and he made a fierce little motion at us to get going. I started.

"Take it easy, law-and-order," Gil said to me. "This ain't our picnic."

I was getting touchy, and for a second I thought he was still trying to talk me out of lining up with the party that wasn't going to be any too popular, win or lose. I looked around at him a bit hot, I guess, but he just grinned at me, a soft, one-sided grin not like his usual one, and shook his head once, not to say no, but to say it was a tough spot. Then I knew he wasn't think-ing of sides right then, but just of me and him, the way it was when we were best. I shook my head at him the same way, and had to grin the same way too. I felt a lot better.

Joyce and I crossed the street, picking our way among the riders, which made us step a bit because the horses were restless, not only the way they always are in wind bringing a storm, but because the excitement had got into them too. Any horse but an outlaw will feel with his rider. They were wheeling and backing under the bridles, and tossing their heads so you could hear the clinking of the bits along with the muffled, uneasy thud-ding. Now and then a rider would turn his horse down the street and let him go a bit away from the gathering, and then turn him back in, like racers waiting for a start. Joyce was horse-shy, and dodged more than he had to, and then went into a little weak-kneed run, like an old man's, to catch up with me again. I knew the men were watching us, and I felt queer myself, walk-ing instead of riding, but Joyce had said it wasn't far, and he didn't have a horse, and I'd have felt still queerer doubling up with him. I didn't look at anybody. I could feel myself tighten up when I passed in front of Farnley's horse, but he held him, and didn't say anything.

Just when we got to the other side of the street I heard Winder calling me by my last name. That can make you mad when it's done right, and I checked, but then had sense enough to keep going.

"Croft," he yelled again, and when I still kept going yelled louder and angrily, "Croft, tell the Judge he'll have to step pronto if he wants to see us start."

Joyce was breathing in little short whistles, and not from dodging either. I knew how he felt. That yell had marked us all right. I thought quickly, in the middle of what I was really thinking, that now I didn't know any of those men; they were strangers and enemies, except Gil. And yet I did know most of them, at least by their faces and outfits, and to talk to, and liked them: quiet, gentle men, and the most independent in the world too, you'd have said, not likely, man for man, to be talked into anything. But now, stirred up or feeling they ought to be, one little yelp about Judge Tyler and I might as well have raped all their sisters, or even their mothers. And the queerest part of it was that there weren't more than two or three, those from Drew's outfit, who really knew Kinkaid; he wasn't easy to know. And the chances were ten to one that a lot more than that among them had, one time or another, done a little quiet brand changing themselves. It wasn't near as uncommon as you'd think; the range was all still pretty well open then, and those riders came from all ends of cow country from the Rio to the Tetons. It wouldn't have been held too much against them either, as long as it wasn't done on a big scale so somebody took a real loss. More than one going outfit had started that way, with a little easy picking up here and there.

"Don't mind that big-mouth," I told Joyce.

I'd underrated the kid. He was scared in the flesh, all right, but that wasn't what he was going to think about.

"Do you think he can hold them?" he asked.

He meant Davies. When Joyce spoke about Davies he said "he" as if it had a capital H.

"Sure he can," I said.

"Risley hang out at the Judge's too?" I asked him.

"When he's here," Joyce said, not looking at me. "We've got to get him, though. We've got to get him, anyway."

"Sure," I pacified, "we'll get him."

He led me onto the cross street and we walked faster. There was no boardwalk here, and the street wasn't used so much, so my bootheels sank into the mud a little. There were only a few people standing in front of their houses or on the edge of the street, looking toward the crossing, men in their shirtsleeves, hunched against the wind, but more women, wearing aprons and holding shawls over their hair. They looked at us, not knowing whether to be frightened or to ask us their questions. One man, standing on his doorstep, with a pipe in his hand, joked to try us.

"What's going on, a roundup?"

"That's it," I gave him back. "Yessir, a roundup."

Joyce got red, but didn't say anything, or look at me yet. I woke up, and saw the kid was scared of me too. I was just one of those riders to him, and a strange one at that.

"They'll wait," I picked up. "They don't know what they're going to do."

Joyce thought he ought to say something. "Mr. Davies didn't think they'd go. Not if somebody stood up against them."

I wasn't so sure of that. Most men are more afraid of being thought cowards than of anything else, and a lot more afraid of being thought physical cowards than moral ones. There are a lot of loud arguments to cover moral cowardice, but even an animal will know if you're scared. If rarity is worth, then moral courage is a lot higher quality than physical courage; but, excepting diamonds and hard cash, there aren't many who take to anything because of its rarity. Just the other way. Davies was resisting something that had immediacy and a strong animal grip, with something remote and mistrusted. He'd have to make his argument look common sense and hardy, or else humorous, and I wasn't sure he could do either. If he couldn't he was going to find that it was the small but present "we," not the big, misty "we," that shaped men's deeds, no matter what shaped their explanations.

"Maybe," I said.

"He says they have to get a leader; somebody they can blame."

"Scapegoat," I said.

"That's what he calls it too," Joyce said. "He says that's what anything has to have, good or bad, before it can get started, somebody they can blame."

"Sometimes it's just that they can't get anywhere without a boss."

"It's the same thing," he argued. "Only one's when it's dangerous."

We kept moving. Joyce had to trot a little to catch up with me. Finally I said, "Mr. Davies doesn't think we've got a leader, then?"

"No," Joyce said. "That's why he thought they'd wait."

I gave that a turn, and knew he was right. That was half what ailed us; we were waiting for somebody, but didn't know who. Bartlett had done the talking, but talk won't hold. Moore was the only man who could take us, and Moore wouldn't.

"He's not far wrong," I said.

"If we can get Risley," he said, "before they pick some-body . . ."

We passed a house with a white picket fence, and then another with four purple lilac trees in the yard. Their sweetness was kind of strange, as if we should have been thinking about something else.

"You know," I said, teasing, "I'm not so sure Davies wants those rustlers brought in at all. You sure he doesn't think even the law's a mite rough and tumble?"

He really looked at me then, and I saw why Davies might talk to him. He was pimply and narrow and gawky, but his eyes weren't boy's eyes.

"Maybe he does," he said, "and maybe he's right. Maybe it would be better if they got away."

"Just because he's gentle," he flared.

"Sure," I said, "it's a good thing to be gentle."

"But he wouldn't let them get away," Joyce said sharply. "Even if he wanted to, he wouldn't let them get away, if he thought they'd get any kind of a show."

"Sure," I said. And then asked him, "How about you? Going, if we form the posse?"

He looked where he was walking again, and swallowed hard.

"If he wants me to go, I'll go," he said. "I don't want to," he told me suddenly, "but it might be my duty."

"Sure," I said again, just to say something.

"That's the place," Joyce said, pointing across the street. I flicked my cigarette away.

Judge Tyler's house was one of the brick ones, with a Mansard roof and patterns in the shingles. There were dormer windows. It was three stories high, with a double-decker veranda, and with white painted stonework around all the windows, which were high and narrow. The whole house looked too high and narrow, and there were a lot of steps up to the front door. There was a lawn, and lilac bushes, and out back a long, white carriage house and stable. It was a new place, and the brick looked very pink and the veranda and stonework very white. It looked more than ever high and narrow because there weren't any big trees around it yet, but only some sapling Lombardies, about twice as high as a man, along the drive. The place looked as if it was meant to be crammed in be-tween two others on a city street, going up because it didn't have room to spread. That made it appear even sillier than that kind of a house naturally does, being in a village where hardly anything was more than one story high, and they all had plenty of room around them. The Judge, having settled on the edge of the village, had the whole valley for a yard, if he'd wanted it. You could see the southwest spread of it, and the snow mountains between his little poplars.

I couldn't help wondering where the Judge got the money for that house. Brick doesn't come for nothing, that far out. But then, of course, the Judge had business in other parts too, and now and then a big stake did come out of some of the mining or water litigation.

On the inside wall of the veranda, where you could see it plain from the road, was the Judge's shingle, a big black one with gold letters. There was a fancy, metal-knobbed pull bell beside the front door.

"Scrape your boots, put your hat on your arm, and straighten your wig," I told Joyce as we went up onto the porch. He grinned like it hurt.

I gave the knob a yank, and it was attached to something all right. Way inside the house there was a little, jingly tinkle that kept on after I let go of the knob. A door opened and closed somewhere inside, and there were slow, heavy steps coming. Then the door opened in front of us. It was a tall big-boned woman with a long, yellow, mistrustful face and gold-rimmed glasses, wearing a frilly house-cap and a purple dress that was all sleeves and skirt. Probably we'd just taken her out of something she was doing, but she acted like we were there to mob the Judge. She stood in the opening with her hands on her hips, so nobody could have squeezed by, and took a hard look at my gun-belt and chaps.

"Well?" she wanted to know.

I figured a soft beginning wasn't going to hurt, and took off my hat.

"The Judge in, ma'am?"

"Yes, he is."

I waited for the rest, but it didn't come.

"Could we see him?" I asked.

"You got business?"

I was getting a little sore. "No," I said, "we just dropped over for tea."

"Humph," she said, and didn't crack a bit.

"Mr. Davies sent us, ma'am," Joyce explained. "It's important, ma'am. The Judge would want to know."

"Mr. Davies, eh?" she said. "That's different. But it's not regular office hours," she added.

I started to follow her in, and she stopped.

"You wait here," she told us. "I'll ask the Judge if he'll see you. What's your name?" she asked me without warning.

I told her, and she grunted again, and went about five steps in the dark, red-carpeted hall, and gave a couple of sharp raps on a door, half turning around at the same time to keep an eye on us.

A big voice boomed out, "Come in, come in," like it had been looking forward for hours and with a lot of pleasure to that knock. She gave us another look, and went in and closed the door firmly behind her. We weren't going to get in on any secrets, anyway.

"That the Judge's wife?" I asked.

Joyce shook his head. "She died before I came here. That's his housekeeper, Mrs. Larch."

"How long she been with him?"

"I don't know. Ever since his wife died, I guess."

"Well," I said, "you can see why the Judge has times when he don't seem able to make up his mind."

Joyce grinned again as if he didn't want to. I was making up a little.

The office door opened again, and Mrs. Larch came out. She closed the door and advanced on us, but this time, when she halted, left us room to squeeze by.

"Go on in," she ordered.

"Is the sheriff here too?" I asked her.

She closed the outside door behind us, so we were trapped in the dark with her, except for a little oil flame burning in a red globe overhead.

"No, he isn't," she said, and started her slow parade toward the back of the house.

Joyce gave me a rabbity look and ran after her a few steps.

"Mrs. Larch . . ."

She stopped and wheeled into a company-front facing him.

"Do you know where he is, Mrs. Larch? The sheriff, I mean?"

"No, I don't," she said, and went on back.

After that I couldn't help knocking at the office door too, and I kept my hat off.

Joyce was whispering at me that we had to find the sheriff, we had to.

The same big voice called, "Come in, come in," again.

When we got inside the big voice kept booming, "Well, well, Croft; how are things out in your neck of the woods?"

"All right, I guess," I said.

But they weren't all right here. The Judge looked the same as I'd always seen him outside, wide and round, in a black frock coat, a white, big-collared shirt and a black string tie, his large face pasty, with folds of fat over the collar, bulging brown eyes, and a mouth with a shape like a woman's mouth, but with a big, pendulous lower lip, like men get who talk a lot without thinking much first. He got up from in front of his roller-top desk in the corner which was full of shelves of thick, pale-brown books with red labels, all pretty new-looking, and came to meet me with his hand out as if he was conferring a special favor. The Judge never missed a chance on that sort of thing. But not only Risley wasn't there, but Mapes was. He was sitting with his chair tilted back right next to the door. His gun belt and sombrero and coat were hanging on the hooks above him.

When he was done shaking hands with me, the Judge smoothed back his thick, black mane, cut off square at the collar, like a senator's, put one hand in his pocket, played with the half-dozen emblems and charms on his watch chain with the other, teetered from his heels to his toes two or three times, lifted his head, smiled at me like I was the biggest pleasure he'd had in years, and drew a great, deep breath, like he was about to start an oration. I'd seen him go through all that when all he finally said was, "How-do-you-do?" to some lady he wasn't sure he hadn't met before. The Judge had a lot of public manner.

"Well, well," he said, "you don't appear to have been pining away, exactly, since I last saw you." He took Joyce in kind of on the side.

"And what can I do for you gentlemen?"

I knew he probably hadn't the faintest notion where he'd

seen me before, but I let that go, and nodded at Joyce to show he was doing the talking. But the kid was tangled. He didn't know what to say with Mapes there. I had to risk it.

"We're here for Mr. Davies," I said.

"Yes, yes, so Mrs. Larch said. And how is my good friend Davies these days? Well, I trust?"

"He's all right, I guess," I said. "Could we see you alone for a minute, Judge?"

Mapes let his chair down, but it wasn't to go. He sat looking at us.

The Judge didn't know what to do about that. He cleared his throat and inflated again, grinning more than ever.

"So, so," he said, "matters of a rather private nature, eh?"

"Yes, sir."

Mapes stayed there, though.

Joyce got his breath. "Mr. Davies said particularly, just you and Mr. Risley, sir."

"So, so," said the Judge again, and looked at Mapes.

"Risley ain't here," Mapes said. "I'm actin' sheriff."

"That's right, quite right," the Judge assured us, before I could speak. I tried to pick up the ground we'd lost.

"Where'd he go?" I asked Mapes.

"Down to Drew's, early this mornin'."

"When'll he be back?"

"He didn't say. Maybe not for a couple of days." He grinned like he wanted to see me try to get out of that one.

"I'm acting sheriff," he said, thumbing out the badge on his vest. "Anything you can tell Risley, you can tell me."

Joyce started to speak, and decided not to. I looked at the Judge.

"That's right, quite right," he said, with that damn-fool cheerfulness. "The sheriff deputized Mr. Mapes before me, last night. It's official; entirely official." He cleared his throat and teetered again. He'd argued himself around to suit the way it had to go anyhow.

"If you have business which requires Mr. Risley's services, you may speak quite freely before Mr. Mapes."

"I saw that kid Greene, from down to Drew's, come by here hell-for-leather half an hour ago," Mapes said, standing up. "I thought it didn't look like no pleasure jaunt. What's up?"

I couldn't see any way out of it. It was more than ten miles down to Drew's. Like Davies, I didn't think the Judge would be any help, and I knew Mapes wouldn't. He'd do just what the men wanted him to do. But we couldn't get Risley, and they couldn't make things any worse than they were anyway, from Davies' point of view. If the Judge couldn't change the direction of things, at least with him there Davies wouldn't have to feel that the whole blame was his. And besides, maybe the fact that Risley was down at Drew's meant something itself.

Joyce, though, was sticking to orders.

"Mr. Davies said you and Mr. Risley, sir."

"Quit the stalling," Mapes said, his neck swelling out and his heavy, red face getting redder. "What the hell does Mr. Davies want, anyway?"

"Now, Mapes," the Judge said, "the boy has a mission. He's merely acting on instructions, I presume."

"If it's sheriff's business, I'm sheriff," Mapes said.

"Sure," I said, thinking I'd make one more try. "We know that, Butch. But it's not us. We're here for Mr. Davies. Now if you'd let us have a minute alone, we'll give the Judge our story, and then if he thinks it's your job, he'll tell you."

"Certainly, certainly," the Judge said. "If the matter touches your official capacity, I shall let you know at once, Mapes."

Mapes stood with his feet apart and stared at us, one after the other. He had a huge chest and shoulders, and a small head with a red, fleshy face, small black eyes, thick black eyebrows, and short-cropped, bristly hair and beard. Like Winder, he always looked angry, even when he laughed, but in a more irritated way, as if his blood was up but he wasn't clear what was wrong.

"All right," he said finally, as if he'd decided that whatever we had to say couldn't matter much, anyway.

At the door he turned, his face redder than ever, and told the Judge, "If it's a sheriff's job, you call me. See?"

"Of course, of course," the Judge said, flushing.

When I had closed the door behind Mapes the Judge

63

said, "And now," rubbing his hands together as if he had settled everything without a hitch, "now what seems to be the trouble?"

With Mapes out of the way, Joyce told him rapidly. I went over to the front window, but listened while Joyce told him, and the Judge, all business, asked him questions about who was there, and just what Greene had said, and other things, most of which Joyce couldn't answer very well. But I figured my job, which was bodyguard, was done, and didn't horn in. From the window, which was in a bow, I could see Mapes standing at the top of the porch steps with his thumb in his belt. The Judge didn't show any signs of doing anything but put more questions. Joyce was getting excited.

"It's not that Mr. Davies doesn't want them to go," he explained for the third or fourth time.

"No, no, of course not," the Judge agreed.

"He just doesn't want it to be a lynching."

"No. Can't let that sort of thing start, of course."

Joyce explained again how he wanted a posse sworn in.

"Assuredly," the Judge said. "Only proper procedure. Anything else inevitably leads to worse lawlessness, violence. I've been telling them that for years," he said angrily, as if he suddenly recognized a personal insult. "For years," he repeated. And then I could hear him striding back and forth and snorting.

"Mr. Davies asks will you come at once, sir. The men are already gathering, and they wouldn't listen to him or Mr. Osgood."

The Judge stopped walking.

I saw a rider coming down the street at a lope. He was one of the men who had been at Canby's when Greene came. He saw Mapes and yelled something to him. Mapes called out to him, and the rider pulled around, yelling something more.

"Mr. Davies wanted you and Mr. Risley to come, sir," Joyce was pleading.

"Eh? Oh, yes, yes. But Risley isn't here."

He started walking again. "Today of all days," he said angrily.

"If you would come, sir. You could talk to them."

"It's not in my position—" the Judge began. Then he said, even more angrily, "No, no. It's not the place of either a judge or a lawyer. It lies in the sheriff's office. I have no police authority."

The rider had wheeled his horse toward the main street and pushed him up to a lope again. Mapes was coming in. I turned around.

"Risley's at Drew's?" I asked.

"Yes, yes. Thought there might be something . . ." the Judge began.

I cut in. "If you could get the men to promise they'd take orders from Risley. They'll have to go that way, anyhow."

Mapes came in, leaving the door open again. He didn't look at us, or say anything, but took his gun down, and buckled it on, and then took down another little gun in an arm-pit holster and slung it on so it would be between his vest and coat. He had big, thick, stubby-fingered hands, and had trouble with the waist thong on the arm-holster.

"And where are you going, Mapes?" the Judge fumed.

"Rustlers got Kinkaid this morning," Mapes said, still working at the knot. He got it, and looked around at us with that angry grin.

"There's a posse forming, just in case you hadn't heard," he said.

"That's sheriff's work, ain't it, Judge?" he asked, reaching his coat down.

"That's no posse, Mapes," the Judge roared. "It's not a posse," he repeated, "it's a lawless mob, a lynching mob, Mapes."

That seemed to me to be stretching it a little. Those men may have been bent on hanging somebody without the delay of a trial, but there was a lot of difference between the way they were going at it and what I thought of as a mob. I didn't say anything, though.

"It'll be a posse when I get there, won't it, Judge?" Mapes asked.

"It will not," bellowed the Judge, a lot angrier than there was any call for, even with the way Mapes spoke.

Joyce looked from one to the other of them for a moment. His face was white, so the pimples showed in red blotches on it, or rather kind of blue. Then he slipped out the door silently.

"I'll deppitize 'em all proper, Judge," Mapes said. His

coat was on, and he put his sombrero on the back of his head.

"You can't do it," the Judge told him. "Risley's the only one empowered to deputize."

Mapes started to answer back. He put one foot upon his chair, and spit over on the corner stove first. He liked it when he had the Judge this way, and didn't want to hurry it too much. There was going to be a wrangle, but I could only see one end of it. I started out after Joyce. We'd give Davies warning, anyhow, though I didn't see what he could do with it.

I stopped in the door and said, loud enough so the Judge could hear over what Mapes was saying, "I'll tell Davies you're coming then, Judge."

"Yes, yes, of course," he said, just glancing away from Mapes for an instant, and giving me a big, fixed smile. I figured that had him hooked the best I could manage, and ducked out quick, not stopping when I heard him call out in a different voice, showing he knew now what I'd said, "Wait, wait a moment . . ." I passed Mrs. Larch in the middle of the hall, her hands folded over her belly and looking at me like she figured I was to blame for the whole disorder. I gave her a wink and went on out without bothering to close the front door. I figured she'd take care of that, and I was right. Before I could get to the road, I heard it slam, and by the time the Judge got my name from her, and opened the door again to call to me, I was far enough toward the main street so I could pretend not to hear him.

Joyce was nearly at the crossing already, running with his coat flapping around him. He could tell Davies all there was to tell. I eased off when I'd got beyond fair cry of the Judge's house. There's better things to run in than high-heeled boots, and it looked like the word had really got around now. I didn't want to make a fool of myself. There were people out in front of every house, craning down toward the corner, and I passed women in the street who were trying to call back their children. One of them looked at me with a scared face. She looked at my gun belt and twisted her apron in her hands. But it wasn't me that scared her.

"The horses," she said, like I knew everything she was thinking.

"Send Tommy home if you see him, please," she begged. She didn't even know she didn't know me.

At the next house a man in chaps was getting on his horse. There was a Winchester on his saddle. A woman, his wife I suppose, was standing right beside the horse and holding onto the man's leg with both hands. She was looking up at him and trying to say something and trying not to cry. The man wasn't answering, but just shaking his head short. His face was set and angry, like so many faces I'd been seeing, and he was trying to get her to let go of him before the horse, which was nervy, stepped on her. He was trying to do it without being rough, but she kept hanging on. A little kid, maybe two or three years old, was standing out in the brush in front of the house and crying hard, with her hands right down at her sides.

More people than before were out in the middle of the street watching the crossing, where now and then they could see one of the riders who had let his horse go that far. The excitement had got through the whole village.

One skinny old man in a blue work shirt, with his galluses out over it, and with a narrow, big-nosed head and his gray hair rumpled up so he looked like a rooster, was peering hard through his spectacles, and exclaiming furiously when a rider showed. A little old woman, as skinny and stooped and chickenlike as he was, was trying to keep him from going any farther. When he saw me he stared at me wildly. He had big eyes, anyway, and they were twice as big through those glasses.

"You goin'?" he rasped at me, shaking his stick at the corner.

"John, John," the old lady clucked, "it don't do for you to go gettin' excited."

"I ain't excited," the old man twittered, pounding his stick on the road, "I ain't excited; I'm jest plumb disgusted."

I'd stopped because he'd caught hold of my shirtsleeve.

"You're goin', ain't you?" he threatened me again.

"It looks like it, dad," I said.

He didn't like my answer.

"Looks like it?" he crowed. "Looks like it? Well, I guess

it better look like it. What kinda stuff you boys made of these days?

"You know how long they been dandlin' around down there?" He jabbed his stick at the corner again.

"They got to get information yet," I told him.

"More'n half an hour, that's what, more'n half an hour already. Half an hour since I seen how they was lally-gaggin' around and started timin' them," he said triumphantly, hauling a big, thick turnip out of his pocket and rapping it with the forefinger of the hand that had the cane in it. He glared up at me with those big eyes.

"An' God knows how long before that; God only knows. Looks like," he cackled scornfully.

"John," the old woman protested, "the young man don't even know us."

"An' a good job fer him he don't," the old man told her.

He was still hanging onto me.

"You know those men that was killed?" he asked me.

"There was only one."

"Only one. There was three. Three of Drew's men was killed. Another one of 'em just told me so. And they gotta get information." He spit off to the side.

My face was getting hot. I didn't like to just yank my arm away from an old man like that, but people along the street were beginning to look at us instead of the show down at the corner. They weren't having any trouble hearing the old man either.

"There's no great rush," I told him, sharp. "They got four or five hours' start already."

"No hurry," he said, but not so loud, and let go of my shirt. "Chee-rist," he boiled again, "five hours' start and no hurry. That's sense now, ain't it? I s'pose if they had ten hours' start you'd jest set to home and wait fer 'em.

"You get on down there," he ordered, when I'd started on anyway. He trotted after me two or three steps, cackling, "Get a move on," and gave me a rap across the seat with his stick.

I didn't look around, but could still hear him, "No hurry, Chee-rist, no hurry," and his wife trying to gentle him down.

I was pretty hot, the way you get when old people or sick people or smart kids talk up to you and make you look foolish because they know you won't do anything, or even say much. I rolled myself a cigarette as I went along, and at the corner stopped and lit it and sucked in a couple to get hold of myself. But one thing I did see. If that old cackler who didn't even have the facts straight could heat me up when I knew he was wrong, then a lot of these men must be fixed so that nothing could turn them off unless it could save their faces. The women were as stirred up as the men, and though a lot of them would have been glad if they could keep their own men out of it, that didn't make any difference. When a man's put on his grim business face, and hauled out a gun he maybe hasn't used for years, except for jack rabbits, he doesn't want to go back without a good excuse. And there were people along the walks now, too, a few old men, and a good many women and excited small boys, some of the women holding smaller children by the hands to keep them from getting out where the horses were. That meant an audience that had to be played up to from the start.

In the edge of the street opposite Canby's, where things were thickest, I saw a little fellow no bigger than the one that had been crying because her mother and father were arguing. He was barefooted, and had on patched overalls, and had a big head of curls bleached nearly white. He was all eyes for what was going on, and stood there squirming his toes on the hard mud without a notion where he was. I didn't see any other kid as small who wasn't attached, so I figured he must be Tommy.

"Young fellow, your mother's looking for you," I told him.

He said for me to look at the horsies, and explained something pretty lengthy, which I couldn't rightly follow, about the guns. It was too bad to spoil his big time, but he was in a bad place. I put on a hard face, and put it right down close to him, and said, "Tommy, you git for home," and switched him around and patted him on the pants, saying, "Git now," again. I guess I overdid it, because he backed as far as the boardwalk, looking at me all the time, and stopped there, and then his face gathered in a pucker toward his nose and he burst out bawling. I started toward him to ease it off a little, but when he saw me coming he let out a still louder wail and lit out for the corner. He slowed down there, and looked back a couple of times, digging at his eyes, but then went on out of sight up the cross street at a little half-jog that I figured was going to take him all the way. Well, I probably wouldn't ever have to see that woman again, anyway.

When I got across the street to Davies, he was done talking to Joyce, and was standing there staring blankly at the men, his face tired as it had been after the talk in the bar, but the jaw muscles still bulging.

"Bartlett not back yet?" I asked him.

He shook his head.

"Wonder what's holding him?" I said.

He shook his head again.

"I'm sorry about Risley," I said, "but I think the Judge will come."

He nodded. Then he brought his eyes back to see me, and smiled a little.

"There wasn't anything else you could do," he said. "Maybe there isn't anything any of us can do. They've made a show out of it now."

I saw I didn't have to tell him anything about that.

"Yeh," I said, looking at the riders in the street too. And there was a change in them. Farnley was still sitting there with no change but a tighter bridle hand, and three or four others, one of them Gil, were still standing at Canby's tie rail. But the rest of them, what with the wait, and the women standing on the walk watching them, looked as grim as ever, but not quite honest. There was a lot of play-acting in it now, passing pretty hard jokes without much point to them, and having more trouble with the horses than they had to.

"They'd be willing to quit if it was dark," I said.

He smiled a little, but shook his head again.

"Well, they'd go orderly pretty easy," I suggested.

"They might do that," he admitted.

I told him what I'd told the Judge about their having to go by Drew's anyway.

"You could get them to promise to pick Risley up, and he'd take care of it."

He considered that and nodded more vigorously. He thought it was a clincher too.

"It's queer what simple things you don't think of when

70

you're excited," he said. "There's a simple little thing, and it's the whole answer."

Then he added, "We'll have to let the Judge tell them, though. They wouldn't dare listen to me."

I looked at him. He shook his head. "Don't worry," he said, "I don't care who does it."

He went on as if he was thinking it farther to himself. "Yes, that will do it."

Then, "Thank you. I know it was a hard place for you."

I didn't see why he felt as sure as all that about it, but I was glad he thought it cleared me.

"That's all right," I said. "Glad to do it. But the way things are, that'll have to be my stake to you."

He looked at me with those eyes full of questions too. I thought maybe he'd get rid of them, that being more his way than Canby's. But he didn't get the chance if he was going to. Smith, being tight and bored, and having a crowd, picked this time to play the clown again. He got everybody's attention, which wasn't on much, by picking on Gabe Hart's one meanness. He called out from the steps to the bar.

"Coming along, Sparks?" he called, so the men grinned, finding that old joke funny about a nigger always being easy to scare. I hadn't noticed Sparks, but I saw him now, standing on the other side of the street with that constant look of his of pleasant but not very happy astonishment.

Sparks was a queer, slow, careful nigger, who got his living as a sort of general handy man to the village, splitting wood, shoveling snow, raking leaves, things like that; even baby tending, and slept around wherever was handiest to the jobs, in sheds or attics, though he had a sort of little shack he called his own out in the tall weeds behind the boarded-up church. He was a tall, stooped, thin, chocolate-colored man, with kinky hair, gray as if powdered, and big, limp hands and feet. When he talked his deep, easy voice always sounded anxious to please, slow but cheerful, but when he sang, which he did about most any work which had a regular rhythm, like sweeping or raking, he sang only slow, unhappy hymn tunes. He was anything but a fast worker, but he did things up thorough and neat, and he was honest to the bone, and the cleanest nigger I ever knew. He wore dungarees and a blue shirt, always like they'd just been washed, and his palms were clean tan, and clean steelblue where they met the skin from the backs of his hands. He had a dry, clean, powdered look all over all the time. It was said that he'd been a minister back in Ohio before he came west, but he didn't talk about himself, outside of what he was doing right at the time, so nobody really knew anything about him, but they all liked him all right, and there wasn't anything they wouldn't trust him with. They made jokes about him and to him, but friendly ones, the sort they might make to any town character who was gentle and could take joking right.

When the men grinned they all looked across at Sparks. He was embarrassed.

"No, suh, Mistah Smith, ah don't guess so," he said, shaking his head but smiling to show he wasn't offended.

"You better come, Sparks," Smith yelled again. "It ain't every day we get a hanging in a town as dead as this one."

The men stopped grinning. They didn't mind Smith joking Sparks, but that offended their present sense of indecision and secrecy. It seemed wrong to yell about a lynching. I felt it too, that someone might be listening who shouldn't hear; and that in spite of the fact that everybody in town knew.

Smith saw he'd made a mistake. When Sparks continued to look down and smile and shake his head, he yelled, "You ain't afraid, is yoh, Spahks," badly imitating Spark's drawl. "Not of a little thing like this," he cried in his own voice again. "You don't have to do anything, you know. The real work is all signed up. But I thought maybe we ought to have a reverend along. There'll be some praying to do, and maybe we ought to have a hymn or two afterward, to kind of cheer us up. You do know the cheerfullest hymns, Sparks."

The men laughed again, and Smith was emboldened.

"That is," he said loudly, "unless Mr. Osgood here is going along. He has first call, of course, being in practice."

"I'm not going, if it interests you," Osgood said, with surprising sharpness for him. "If you men choose to act in violence, and with no more recognition of what you're doing than this levity implies, I wash my hands. Willful murderers are not company for a Christian."

That stung, but not usefully. A bawling out from a man

72

like Osgood doesn't sit well. Some of the men still grinned a little, but the sour way.

"I was afraid the shepherd would feel his flock was a bit too far astray for him to risk herding them this time," Smith lamented. Osgood was hit, and looked it. He knew the men tolerated him at best, and the knowledge, even when he could delude himself into believing it private, made it doubly difficult for him to keep trying to win them. Sometimes, as now, he was even pitiable. But he had an incurable gift of robbing himself even of pity. After a moment he answered, "I am sorry for you, all of you."

"Don't cry, parson," Smith warned him. "We'll do the best we can without you.

"I guess it's up to you, Sparks," he yelled.

Sparks surprised us. "Maybe it is, Mistah Smith," he said seriously. "Somebody ought to go along that feels the way Mistah Osgood and ah do; beggin' yoh pahdon, Mistah Osgood. If he don' feel it's raght foh him to go, it looks lahk ah'm the onlay one laift."

This unassuming conviction of duty, and its implication of distinct right and wrong, was not funny.

Quickly Smith struggled. "Maybe Mr. Osgood will lend you his Bible, Sparks, so's we can have the right kind of reading at the burial."

This was partially successful. Osgood was obviously offended to be so freely talked of by Smith, and perhaps even to have his name coupled with Sparks'. And everyone knew Sparks couldn't read.

"You will lend him your Book, won't you, Reverend," Smith asked Osgood. He had no sense for the end of a joke. Osgood had the thick, pale kind of skin that can't get red, so he got whiter, and was trembling a little.

Sparks came across the street in his slow, dragging gait. He didn't swing his arms when he walked, but let them hang down as if he had a pail of water in each hand.

When he was close enough to talk more quietly, he said, "No, thank you, Mistah Osgood," and turning to Smith told him, "Ah knows mah text to pray without the Book, Mistah Smith.

"But ah'm a slow walkah," he said, smiling especially at Winder, "you wouldn't have anothah mule ah could borrow, would you, Mistah Winder?"

73

Winder didn't know what to say, knowing it was still a joke except to Sparks.

Smith said, "Sure he would, Sparks. Gabe, you just trot back and get the Reverend a good saddle mule, will you? An easy one, mind; he ain't much padded."

The men were quiet.

Finally, Winder said, "Your mouth's too damn loose, Smith."

"I'm talking to Gabe," Smith said, but avoided Winder's stare.

Gabe stared back at Smith, but sat solid and appeared unmoved. He muttered something that nobody could hear.

"What's that you said, Gabe?" Smith prodded him.

Gabe got it out. "I said I ain't waitin' on no nigger," he said.

"Shut up, Smith," Winder said, before Smith could make anything of this.

Smith got red, which was remarkable for him, since he could swallow almost any insult, but with Winder staring at him he couldn't think of a retort.

"It's all right, Mistah Windah," Sparks said, "but if they is a mule at yoh place ah could borrow, ah'd be obliged. Ah can get him mahself, if thayas tahm."

"They're kidding you, Sparks," Canby said from the door. He liked the nigger.

"Ah know that, Mistah Canby," Sparks said, grinning again. "But ah think maybe Mistah Smith was accidentally right when he said ah should go."

"You really want to go?" Winder asked him.

"Yessuh, Mistah Windah, ah do."

Winder studied him, then shrugged and said, "There's a horse in the shed you can use. There's no saddle, but he's got a head-stall on, and there's a rope in the back stall you can use for a bridle.

"You'll have to get him yourself, though. You know how Gabe is," he apologized.

Gabe continued to stare heavily at Smith, but he didn't seem to hold anything against Sparks.

"Yassuh, ah undahstand," Sparks said, and turned to go. Winder felt he'd been too soft.

"Move along, or you'll get left," he said. "We're only waiting for Mr. Bartlett and his boys."

Sparks turned his head back, and grinned and nodded,

and then went on down the street toward the stage depot, walking quickly for him. You could tell by his carriage that he was pleased in the way of a man doing what he ought to do.

Smith had missed being funny, and Sparks had given a kind of body, which the men could recognize, to an ideal which Davies' argument hadn't made clear and Osgood's self-doubt had even clouded. I thought it would be a good time for Davies to tackle them again, and looked at him. He saw the chance too, but found it hard to get started in the open, with all those men, and waited too long. A rider called out, "Here comes Ma," and there was as much of a cheering sound as they felt presently fitting, to greet her. Here was a person could head them up.

Ma was up the street quite a ways when they hailed her, but she waved at them, a big, cheerful, unworried gesture. It made me feel good, too, just to see Ma and the way she waved. She was riding, and was dressed like a man, in jeans and a shirt and vest, with a blue bandanna around her neck and an old sombrero on her head. She had a Winchester across her saddle, and after she waved she held it up, and then held part way up, as far as the tie would let it, a coil of rope she had hitched to the flap of the saddle. There was another cheer, stronger than the first, and jokes about Ma and her power that showed how much better the men were feeling. She changed the whole attitude in two moves, and from a quarter mile off.

Jenny Grier was the name of the woman we called Ma. She was middle-aged and massive, with huge, cushiony breasts and rump, great thighs and shoulders, and long, always unkempt, gray hair. Her wide face had fine big gray eyes in it, but was fat and folded, and she always appeared soiled and greasy. She was strong as a wrestler, probably stronger than any man in the valley except Gabe, and with that and her appearance, if it hadn't been for the loud good nature she showed most of the time, people would have been afraid of her. All the women were, anyway, and hated her too, which was all right with her. There were lively, and some pretty terrible, stories about her past, but now she kept a kind of boarding house on the cross street, and it was always in surprisingly good order, considering how dirty she was about herself. She was a peculiar mixture of hard-set ideas too. Though mostly by jokes, she'd been dead set against Osgood from the first day he came. She had no use for churches and preaching, and she'd made it hard for him by starting all kinds of little tales, like her favorite one about being surprised at how hungry she was when she woke up after the only sermon of his she ever heard, only to find that was because he'd gone right on through and it was the second Sunday, and he hadn't wound up his argument then, but his voice gave out. And she could imitate him too, his way of talking, his nervous habits with his hands, his Gladstone pose. She always pretended to be friendly, in a hearty way, when she saw him, and the man was afraid of her. But on the other hand she was a lot more than ordinarily set against what she thought was wrong-doing. I missed my guess if she hadn't had a part in driving Gil's Rose out of town. She didn't like women, wouldn't have one in her house, not even for one night's sleep. In ways, I think she was crazy, and that all her hates and loves came out of thinking too much about her own past. Sometimes I even wondered if the way she mistreated her own body, with dirt and more work than she needed to do and long hunts and rides she didn't want to make and not much rest or sleep, when about everything else she was a great joker and clean and orderly, wasn't all part of getting even with herself, a self-imposed penance. The other side of that, I thought, was another little trait. She was fond to foolishness of mountains and snow, just of looking at them, but of going up in them too, though snow-shoeing nearly killed her with her weight. She said she'd settled in Bridger's just to look at mountains; that they brought out what little was good in her. Most of the time, though, she was big and easy, and she had the authority of a person who knew her own mind and was past caring what anybody else thought about anything, and a way of talking to us in our own language so we'd laugh and still listen, the style Judge Tyler would like to have had.

I knew that, at least until she had seen the victims in the flesh, she'd be as much for lynching a rustler as Winder or Bartlett. The only thing that made me wonder how she'd turn was that she liked Davies quite as much

76

as she didn't like Osgood. She wasn't given to thinking very far, but she did a lot of intelligent feeling.

She was greeted right and left when she joined us, and she spoke to Gil and me with the others, calling me "boy" as she had when I'd stayed at her place, and we stood a lot better with the rest just on that. Then she started asking questions, and they told her what they knew, which she saw right off, from the different versions, wasn't straight. She set out to straighten it. It wasn't that she was trying to be boss. She simply wanted things in order in her mind when she had anything to do, and in putting them in order she just naturally took over. When some of them were all for starting without Bartlett she checked that. When they told her about Davies she just looked down at him standing on the walk and grinned and asked him if he wasn't going. Davies said he was if they went right, if anybody really needed to go. Ma looked at him, not grinning now, and he explained that Risley was already down at Drew's, and that Drew had a dozen men down there, and that he thought it would be just good sense not to go unless we were sent for, sent for by Risley, who would really know what was going on. There was muttering around him at that. I was surprised myself. So that was why he'd thought that little fact could do a lot; he believed he could use it to stop them from going at all.

Ma said, "Art, you read too many books," to him, and began to dig into young Greene, calling him son, and acting as if what he thought was just as important as what he knew. At that she boiled it down better than anybody else had. Kinkaid had been killed way down in the southwest corner of the valley, eight miles below the ranch. They didn't know just when, but it must have been noon or earlier, because a couple of the riders had picked up his horse clear over by the ranch road, and at about two o'clock had found Kinkaid lying on his back in the sun in a dry wash over under the mountains. Greene didn't know if there were any more cattle gone; they hadn't been able to distinguish the rustlers' tracks. Too many cattle had been working over the range there, and there were still a lot of horses' prints from the roundup. She kept him toned down except on that one thing, that Kinkaid had been shot through the head. That was the one thing he seemed to have clear without question. He had kept on saying that to the men too. It impressed him that Kinkaid had been shot through the head, as if he could feel it more, as if he would have felt better if Kinkaid had been shot in the belly or in the back, or anywhere but in the head. When Ma asked him, he admitted that he hadn't seen Kinkaid, but that the man who told him had. No, he hadn't seen the sheriff down there; it must have been three o'clock before they sent him to Bridger's and he hadn't seen the sheriff all day.

Ma said to Davies, "I guess we're goin', Art; as quick as Bartlett gets here."

Somebody said, "He's comin' now."

The men who weren't mounted climbed up, Gil and I with them. Only Davies and Osgood and Joyce were left standing on the walk, and Canby on the steps. Sparks was back too, on an old and sick-looking horse with a wheat sack for a saddle.

Davies said to Ma, "At least wait for Judge Tyler. He's coming. I sent word for him." He sounded stubborn and defeated now, nearly as bad as Osgood. Riders looked at him contemptuously, and some started to tell him off, but Ma made them grin at him instead.

"Art, you're gettin' worse every day," she said. "First you let the reverend there give you prayin' faith, and then you let Tyler argue you into drummin' up business for him. It's them books, Art, them books. You better lay off them."

And then, "Not the reverend and you *and* Tyler. I couldn't stand it, Art. I'm only a woman, and I'm gettin' on toward my time." The men laughed.

Bartlett came up at a lope, his son Carl, the blond one, with him. The other one, Nate, was dark, but that was the only difference between them. They were both tall, thin, silent and mean. I wondered if Nate had got too drunk to sit in a saddle, the way he did, and they'd had to leave him. Carl stayed behind his father, away from the men, and after the first glance didn't look at them.

"Carl was riding," Bartlett explained. "We had to get him in."

"Tetley not here?" he asked, looking around. And then, louder, "We'll have to wait for Tetley. Nate's gone for him."

"What do we need with God-Almighty-Tetley," Winder said. But he didn't say it loudly; if I hadn't been right next to him, I wouldn't have heard it at all. All the men were uneasy, but not loud. They were irritated at the further delay, but they were quiet about it, nearly sullen. It was news if Tetley was coming. It would make a difference; even Ma was afraid of Tetley.

Excepting Drew, Tetley was the biggest man in the valley, and he'd been there a lot longer than Drew, the first big rancher in the valley, coming there the year after the Civil War. On the west edge of town he'd built a white, wooden mansion, with pillars like a Southern plantation home, and big grounds around it, fenced with white picket fence. The lawns were always cut, and there were shrubbery and flower beds, a stone fountain where birds drank, and benches set about under the trees. Tetley was like his house, quiet and fenced away; something we never felt natural with, but didn't deride either. Except for the servants, he had only his son Gerald living with him now, and they didn't get on. Tetley had been a Confederate cavalry officer, and the son of a slave owner, and he had that kind of a code, and a sharp, quiet head for management. Gerald was always half sick, kept to himself and the big library as much as his father would let him, hated the ranching life and despised yet feared the kind of men Tetley had to deal with now. Things had been better between them before Mrs. Tetley had died; she had acted as a go-between, and even as a shield for Gerald, and had been such a charming little thing herself, beautiful, intense and cheerful, yet gentle, that nothing could be very unpleasant around her. But when she died each of them had become only more what he was. People who had been there said the house was like it never had the dustcovers off the furniture now, and Tetley, though he wouldn't tolerate a word about the boy from anyone else, was himself ashamed of him, and a hard master. Sparks, who worked there quite often, had said once, when he was more off his guard than usual, that he had seen things between them that made him sure Tetley would have killed the boy if he hadn't looked so much like his mother. He did, too, as much as a sullen, sick boy can look like a woman with all her spirit and knack for being happy.

It looked like Bartlett thought he had talked himself into something when he had to get Tetley. I knew that

79

if Tetley came he'd take over. Wherever he came things always quieted down, and nothing sounded important except what Tetley had to say. Partly, I think, that was because nothing else seemed important to Tetley either. A man so sure of himself can always sound important if he isn't a windbag, and Tetley was no windbag. He didn't talk often, and usually it was short then. When you happened to meet him on the street, which was seldom, he would only nod, and nobody ever started a talk with him. It wasn't that he was impolite or superior acting either. He had more real manner than any other man in the valley, or than any I'd ever met. You just couldn't get close to him. I don't think it would have mattered who you were.

The word that Tetley was coming gave Davies a little more time, if that could do him any good now, but it looked to me like a reprieve for a man that knew he had to swing at the end of it, anyway. Tetley wouldn't be coming to do Bartlett a favor, and if he objected to the lynching on principle, which wasn't likely, he still wouldn't be coming down himself to stop it. There was only one reason that I could see for Tetley's interest, that he wanted that lynching.

Davies must have figured the same way, but he was still going to make a try. I saw him talking hard and quickly to Joyce again, and then Joyce, looking more frightened than ever, went off down the street at a run, and Davies went out, keeping it casual, to talk to Bartlett. Bartlett wasn't so wild any more, just touchy, the way a man is who feels strongly about something, but is a muddy thinker. He answered a bit short, but didn't blow off. He kept looking at his watch, a big silver turnip, and then at the sky, and only paid a fretful half-attention to Davies. Davies knew better than to argue the soul of society with Bartlett, and even held out on his notion of the men not going at all, and just stuck to legal deputation and trying to get a promise Bartlett wouldn't act without Risley. And he stayed friendly while he made his points, always seeming to be making just suggestions, and asking Bartlett's opinion, and Ma's, and even Winder's. The men let him talk because they had to wait, anyhow, though I noticed a few, close to him, seemed to be listening. Bartlett, though, wouldn't hear more than once about bringing prisoners in. Short justice was the kind he wanted. And Ma kept taking the point out of Davies' talk by making jokes. He hadn't got anywhere when the Judge and Mapes appeared, the Judge, by the way his free hand was waving, still arguing it hot and heavy with Mapes, who wasn't even answering now.

When they pulled up, just on the edge of the crowd of riders, everything was silent, even the people on the walks waiting to see what the Judge would say. They didn't have much respect for the Judge, but he was the law, and they waited to see what line he would take. The Judge felt the hostility and was nervous about the quiet; he made a bad start, taking off his hat by habit, like he was starting an oration, and raising his voice more than he had to.

"I understand how it is, men," he began, and went on about their long tolerance, and their losses, and the death of a dear friend, a long apology for what he was working up to.

Mapes, beside him, took off his sombrero solemnly, the way the Judge had taken his off, and began slowly and carefully to improve the crease in it.

The men grinned, and Smith called, "Cut the stumping, Judge," and when the Judge hesitated, "It's all been said for you, Tyler. All we want's your blessing."

Davies didn't want the Judge to get into an oration any more than the rest did. He came over beside the Judge's horse before the Judge could start again, and said something. Osgood trailed out too.

"Certainly, certainly, Mr. Davies," the Judge said, but still in his platform voice, "just the point I was coming to.

"Men," he addressed us, "you cannot flinch from what you believe to be your duty, of course, but certainly you would not wish to act in the very spirit which begot the deed you would punish."

"By the time you got us ready to act, Tyler," Smith shouted, "the rustlers could be over the Rio." There was agreement; others called ribald advice. Ma leaned on her saddle directly in front of the Judge and grinned at him. The Judge's neck and jowls began to swell slowly and turn red.

"One more word out of you, Smith," he bellowed, "and I'll have you up for impeding the course of justice and connivance in an act of violence."

It was a bad move after his weak start. The joking rose to shouting. There were jeers, and men made signs of his insignificance at the Judge. Ma said, still grinning, "Judge, you can't impede what don't move anyway."

"And you, a woman," the Judge shouted at her, "to lend yourself to this . . ." He couldn't describe us, but just waved a hand over us, choking, and then suddenly put his hat back on and yanked it down, and glared at us.

In the general roar you could still hear Farnley's voice, so furious it was high and breaking, "For Christ's sake, Butch, let's get out of this."

Horses began to mill and yank, and the riders chose to let them. A woman, holding onto a post of the arcade with one hand, leaned out and shrieked at us. She was a tall, sallow, sooty-looking woman, with black hair streaming down and blowing across her face, and her sunbonnet fallen back off her head so she looked wild. She kept screaming something about Kinkaid. Smith called out salaciously to know what Kinkaid was to her.

"More than he was to any of you, it looks like," she screamed back at him.

Some of the other women too called out at us then, laughing angrily and jibing. Others, who had men in the street, were quiet and scared-looking. One small boy, being yanked about by his mother, began to cry. This scared others of the children.

Moore rode over, holding his horse close, and spoke to the wild-looking woman. "We can take care of this, Frena," he told her, then said to the others, "Get those kids out of here; this is no place for a kid."

The woman he called Frena ran into the street beside him, as if she'd like to pull him off and throw him around. "Why ain't it?" she shrieked up at him. "There isn't anything going to happen, is there?" Moore didn't say anything, or even look at her, but just waited there until the women with children began to lead them away. Two of them stopped at the corner, though, and watched again.

Davies hadn't paid any attention to the uproar, but talked up earnestly to the Judge. He got the Judge calmed a little. He nodded and said something.

"Where's Greene?" Ma Grier called back. Things quieted a little. "Greene," she called to him, "come on up here. The Judge wants to talk to you."

The rest of us wanted to hear, and tried to bunch around the talkers, but the horses kept sidling out, and were blowing and hammering and making leather squeal. We couldn't hear much, but only catch glimpses of young Greene on his horse facing the Judge on his and making answers. They didn't appear to be getting anywhere; the kid grinned sardonically a couple of times and the Judge, though pompous, was flustered again. Then, apparently, Davies took over again. They were both looking down and not saying anything. The kid began giving answers again, and not looking so sure. The men right around them had quieted down a lot. Once most of them, all together, and the Judge, too, looked up at the sky, and the Judge, when he looked down, nodded. The Judge, then, was apparently putting in a word here and there for Davies. Greene looked ready to cry. Only once, when he'd stood about all he could, we heard him cry out, "Olsen told me so. I've told you that twenty times already." Mapes ceased pretending to look bored, and began glancing around the circle of men. Once he said something, but the Judge, a lot surer of himself now, turned on him and made a quick reply. The only thing I caught was the word "constituted" which sounded as if the Judge was in his usual line of blather. But Mapes didn't say anything further, only stuck out his chin and looked surly and stared for a moment at his saddle horn. But though we couldn't hear anything, we could feel that the drift was changing. Men close in began to look at each other, just quick glances, or look down. The temper was out of them. When, after four or five minutes, the woman Frena had waited as long as she could with her mouth closed, and wanted to know if they were holding a prayer meeting, one of the men angrily called to her to shut up.

It became quiet enough to hear the voices, the kid's choky and stubborn, Davies' easy in short even questions, or sometimes a longer remark, and then the Judge, his voice being so heavy, we could catch a word here and there from him. Then the kid was let out of the ring. His face was red, and he wouldn't look at any of us, or answer when Winder asked him a question, only shrug his shoulders. The riders who had heard pulled their horses back so that we had to pull away to give them room. Davies and Osgood came through them toward the arcade. Osgood looked happy, and kept chattering beside Davies in an excited way, Davies just nodding. Under the edge of the arcade Davies climbed up onto the tie rail and stood there, holding onto a post to steady himself. He didn't call out, but just waited until it was quiet. Most of us reined around to listen to him; only Farnley and young Greene stayed clear out, as if they didn't want to hear. Farnley started to curse us for listening to more such talk, which he called lily-livered, but Moore quieted him, saying that Davies didn't want to stop them, and that they had to wait for Tetley anyhow.

"If you guys get careful of yourselves," Farnley told him, as if he meant it, "I'm going myself. Don't forget that." Then he was quiet too, and Davies started to talk. When the woman Frena tried to interrupt him, and twice Smith also, he didn't talk back to them, but just waited, as you would until a door was closed that was letting in too much noise, and then went on the same reasonable way, just loudly enough to be heard.

"We don't know anything about those rustlers, boys," he told us, "or whether they were rustlers, or who shot Kinkaid. Young Greene there wasn't trying to make trouble; he was doing what he thought he ought to do, what he was told to do. But he got excited; he was sent for the sheriff, but on the way up he got excited thinking about it, and forgot what he should do, and did what seemed to him like the quickest thing. Really, he doesn't know anything about it. He didn't see any rustlers or any killer. He didn't even see Kinkaid. He only heard what Olsen told him, and Olsen was in a hurry. All that Olsen actually told him, when we get down to the facts, was that Kinkaid had been shot, that they'd found him in the draw, and that he was to come to town for the sheriff. That's not much to go on.

"Then there's another thing. It's late now. If it was a gang that Kinkaid ran into, they must have gone out by the south pass, as they did before." He went on to show us that it was twenty miles to that pass and would be dark before we got there, that the rustlers had at least a five or six hour start of us. He showed us that the sheriff had been down there since early morning, that there were a dozen men there if he wanted them, and pointed out that it wasn't the sheriff who had sent for us, that nobody had sent for us, that Greene had been sent only for the sheriff, and that if the sheriff had wanted more men we'd have heard from him by now.

He argued that although he could understand our feelings, there certainly was no use in acting in a way that might get us into trouble, or lead us to do something we'd regret for a long while, when the matter was probably being taken care of legally as it was.

"It's my advice, men, for what it's worth," he concluded, "that you all come in and have a drink on me . . ."

"Drinks," said Canby from the door, "on the house. But only one round, by God. I'm not filling any bucket bellies."

"Our friend Canby offers the drinks," Davies said, "and I'll make it two. I guess I owe it. Then, I'd say, we'd all better go home and have supper, and get a good night's sleep. If we're wanted, we'll hear. I sent Joyce down to the ranch to find out what the sheriff has to say. If any of you want to stay in town, Mrs. Grier can put you up, or Canby, or the Inn, if they can still get the doors open."

"I told you the money was all he thought about," Smith cried.

"And I can bed two myself," Davies went on, grinning down at Smith, "and no charge. I'd be glad of the company."

"I can take six," Canby said, "if they don't mind sleeping double. And no charge either; not for those beds, when I know I'm bound to see the guys again."

"I can take care of two, and more than welcome," Osgood said. He sounded really hearty for the first time.

Canby said, "About those drinks, though. The offer don't go for any man that's had more than five free ones already. Monty, I'll stand you to a cup of coffee. It won't make you more than a little sick." There was some grudging laughter.

Ma, feeling defeated, was a bit surly, but she had to offer rooms too. "Only," she told them belligerently, "any lazy puncher that holes up with me is going to pay for his grub. I'm no charity organization." They jeered her more cheerfully, and she seemed to feel better. Still they didn't break up, though, or get off their horses. Neither did I; I didn't want to look like I was anxious to quit; not any more than anybody else.

Sparks really limbered things up. In the hesitation he said, in that mournful voice of his, "I'd ce'tainly admiah to have any gen'lmun that wishes spend the naght at mah qua'tahs too." They laughed. One of them asked, "Where you sleeping tonight, Sparks?"

"In Mistah Davies' shed foh storin' things, but it'll be all raght with him."

"It's not like you were giving up, boys," Davies told us. "It's just good sense. If it's a short chase it's over by now. If it's a long one the sheriff will let you know, and you'll have time to get ready."

"I'm settin' 'em up, boys," Canby called.

The riders closest in began to dismount. They felt foolish, and didn't look at each other much, and made bad jokes about how old they were getting. But I guess they felt chiefly the way I did. I hadn't had much stomach for the business from the beginning. I got down too. Gil tied up beside me.

"Well, the little bastard pulled it," he said. "Jees, and just when I thought for once there'd be something doin'." But he wasn't sore.

We heard the Judge calling, "Going home, Jeff?" We looked. Others who had started in, stopped and looked back too. Farnley was riding off down the street. Winder was with him, and of course Gabe. He didn't pay any attention, and the Judge called again. Davies told the Judge to let him alone, he'd have to go to the ranch, anyway, but I guess the Judge was tired of playing second fiddle. He bellowed this time, and wasn't asking, but ordering Jeff to come back.

Jeff came back. When the Judge saw his face he explained, "You might as well have a shot with us, Jeff. It'll be cold riding. You don't need to worry. This business will be taken care of." He explained it heartily, and at a distance. The woman Frena, who was still hanging around, laughed.

Farnley rode his horse straight in until it was shouldering the Judge's. Winder waited where he had stopped down the street, and Gabe with him. In the Judge's face, as if spitting on him, Farnley told him, "Yeh, but I know now who's going to take care of it. The bastard

86

that shot Larry Kinkaid ain't comin' in here for you to fuddle with your damned lawyer's tricks for six months and then let him off because Osgood or Davies, or some other whining women, claim he ain't bad at heart. He ain't comin' in anywhere. Kinkaid didn't have six months to decide if he wanted to die, did he?"

"Now look here, Jeff," the Judge began.

Davies went out and stood by Jeff's horse, as he had before, but didn't, at first, touch him. "Jeff," he said, and then again, "Jeff," until Farnley quit staring at the Judge and slowly looked down at him. Then he said, "Jeff, you know nobody in this country is going to let a thing like this go. Risley is a good man, Jeff; he'll get him. And there aren't twelve men in the West that wouldn't hang him." Then he put his hand on Jeff's knee again. Jeff's face looked to me like he couldn't understand what was being said. But he'd heard it. "You can see that, can't you, Jeff?" Davies asked him.

"No," Farnley said, "when I look at you, any of you," he said, looking around at us slowly, "I can't see anything. Not one damned thing." He knocked Davies' hand off his knee with the back of his own hand, and began to rein around, nearly riding Moore down. Moore was trying to talk to him too.

The rest of us were keeping out of it, except Gil. He was unhitching again. "By God," he told me, with pleasure, "if he goes, I'm going. That won't be no hanging; that'll be a fight." Even Moore was afraid of Farnley, the way he was feeling now, he ran along beside him, still trying to talk to him.

We'd all been watching this business so close that we hadn't seen Tetley coming until Farnley pulled around to look because Winder was pointing. Even then it didn't seem to matter, except that there'd be more explaining, which we wanted to escape. We'd been pulled back and forth enough. We were already chilled with sitting in the wind; there was a storm coming on, you could feel that definitely now. All I wanted right now was a drink, a meal and a smoke. Most of us were in this mood; there were more men on the walk than mounted, and their attention to Tetley was more curious than anything else. He was so obviously ready to go somewhere. With military rigidity he was riding alone on his tall, thin-legged palomino with the shortened tail and clipped mane like those of a performing horse. He wore a Confederate field coat with the epaulets, collar braid and metal buttons removed, and a Confederate officer's hat, but his gray trousers were tucked into an ordinary pair of cowboy's shin boots. There was a gun belt strapped around his waist, over the coat. It had a flap holster, like a cowboy would never wear, which let show just the butt of a pearl-handled Colt. He didn't have a stock saddle either, but a little, light Mc-Lellan.

Behind him, like aides-de-camp, almost abreast, were three riders, his son Gerald, his Mex hand called Amigo, and Nate Bartlett.

When he had drawn up, his three riders stopping behind him too, he looked us over, his small, lean, gray-looking face impassive; no, he reviewed us, and was amused without expression. Irony was the constant expression of Tetley's eyes, dark and maliciously ardent under his thick black eyebrows. His hair, even gray, was heavy and of senatorial length, cut off straight at his coat collar, and curling up a little. There were neat, thin sideburns of the same gray from under his campaign hat to the lower lobes of his ears, and a still thinner, gray mustache went clear to the corners of his mouth, but didn't cover the upper lip of his mouth, which was long, thin, inflexibly controlled, but as sensitive as a woman's. He was a small, slender man who appeared frail and as if dusted all over, except his eyes and brows, with a fine gray powder. Yet, as he sat quietly, rigidly, his double-reined bridle drawn up snugly in his left hand in a fringed buckskin glove, his right arm hanging straight down, we all sat or stood quietly too. He addressed Tyler as the man who should be in authority.

"Disbanding?"

Tyler avoided the condemnation. "Davies convinced us, Major Tetley."

"So?" Tetley said. "Of what, Mr. Davies?" he asked him.

Even Davies was confused. He began an explanation that sounded more like an excuse than a plea. Nate Bartlett cut him short, drawing up cautiously beside Tetley, and speaking to him cautiously.

"I guess they don't know about their having gone by the pass, sir."

Tetley nodded. Davies looked from one to the other of them uncertainly.

"You were acting on the supposition that the raiders left by the south draw, I take it, Mr. Davies?"

"Yes," Davies said, doubtfully. He didn't know where he stood.

"They didn't." Tetley smiled. "They left by the pass."

We knew what he meant, Bridger's Pass, which went through the mountains to the west; it was part of the stage-road to Pike's Hole, the next grazing range over, which had a little town in it, like Bridger's Wells. It was a high pass, going up to about eight thousand; snow closed it in the winter, and with the first thaws the creek came down beside it like a steep river, roaring and splashing in the narrows, until it bent south in the meadows and went brimming down toward Drew's and through the draw at the south. The west road from Drew's came up along the foothills and joined the stage-road right at the foot of the pass. It was only a little off this west road that Greene thought Kinkaid had been found. If the rustlers had gone by the pass, it changed the whole picture. Then it was the sheriff who was off the track. If he'd gone to the draw, toward that branding camp Kinkaid had found, he'd be twenty miles off. We began to really listen.

"By the pass, from the south end," Davies said, "that would be crazy." He didn't sound convinced. He sounded as if he had a lump in his throat. It wasn't which way they'd gone that mattered to Davies.

Tetley still smiled. "Not so crazy, perhaps," he said, "knowing how crazy it would look; or if you lived in Pike's Hole."

"You seem pretty sure," Ma said.

"Amigo saw them," Tetley said.

A half a dozen of us echoed that, "Saw them?" Farnley came back in, Winder and Gabe with him.

"He was coming back from Pike's, and had trouble getting by them in the pass."

"Trouble?" Mapes asked importantly. The Judge was just sitting in his saddle and staring at Tetley. Osgood, I thought, was going to cry. It was hard, when it had all been won. And Davies was standing there as if somebody had hit him but not quite dropped him.

"Si," Amigo said for himself. He was grinning, and had very white teeth in a face darker than Sparks'. He liked the attention he was getting. Tetley didn't look around, but let him talk.

"Heem not see me, I theenk," Amigo explained. "Eet was low down, where I can steel get out from the road. I take my horse into the hollow place so they can get by. At first I theenk I say hello when they come; I have no to smoke left by me. Then I theenk it funny to drive the cattle then."

"Cattle," Moore said sharply.

"But sure," Amigo said. He grinned at Moore. "Why you theenk I have to get out of hees road?"

"Go on," Moore said.

"Well," Amigo said, "when I theenk that, I be quiet. Then, when I see what marks those cattle have, I be veree quiet; veree slow I take my horse behind the bush, and we be still." He explained his conduct. "See, I have not the gun with me." He slapped his hip.

"What were the marks?" Mapes asked.

"What you theenk? On the throat, sweenging nice, three leetle what-you-call-heems—" He didn't need to say any more. We all knew Drew's dewlap mark.

"Why, the dirty rats," Gil said. It sounded as if he half admired them. "To kill a man," he said, "and still risk a drive."

"I told you, didn't I?" old Bartlett cried. "Let them get away with it a few times, I said, and there's no limit to what they'll try."

Davies was looking at Amigo. "Were they all Drew's?" he asked him.

"You can't get around it that way," Bartlett yelped at him. "With roundup just over they'd still be bunched, wouldn't they? And Drew was branding down his own end; he just cut out at the main camp. Ain't that right, Moore?"

"That's right," Moore said.

"How many of them?" Farnley asked Tetley.

"About forty head," Tetley said.

"That's what you said, isn't it, Amigo?" he asked over his shoulder.

"Si," said Amigo, grinning.

"No; I mean rustlers."

"Three, eh, Amigo?"

"Si, they was three."

"Did you know any of them?" Ma asked Amigo.

The grin disappeared from Amigo's face. But he shook his head. "I not evair see heem before," he said, "not any of heem."

"Well, you can't find a way out of this one, can you?" Farnley asked. But he didn't look at Davies. He seemed to be asking us all. Davies was looking at the Judge, but the Judge couldn't think of anything to say. I thought Davies was going to cry. He looked whipped. Until then I hadn't known how hard he was taking this; I'd felt it was just a kind of contest between his ideas and our feelings. Now I saw he was feeling it too. But I knew that I, for one, wasn't with him. I untied and mounted. Others were doing the same. Some slipped in to claim their drink from Canby, but came right out again.

Davies, without much conviction, tried Tetley. "Major Tetley," he said, "it's late. You can't get them tonight."

"If we can't," Tetley told him, "we can't get them at all. It's going to storm; snow, I think. We have time. They will move slowly with those cattle, and in the pass there is no place for them to branch off."

"Yes," admitted Davies, "yes, that's true." He ran a hand through his hair as if he was puzzled. He was smiling shakily.

"What time did Amigo see them?" Ma asked.

"About four o'clock, I believe. Wasn't it, Amigo?"

"Si."

"In the lower pass at four," said Farnley. "Sure we can get 'em."

"You were a long time bringing the word, Major," the Judge said. I was surprised to hear him still sounding like a friend of Davies.

Tetley looked at him with that same smile. It had a different meaning every time he used it.

"I wanted my son to go along," he said. "He was out on the range."

Young Tetley was sitting with his bridle across the saddle horn, pulled tight between his hands. His face got red, but he gave no other signs of having heard.

We all had the same notion, I guess, that young Tetley hadn't been on the range at all. But nobody would have said so, and it didn't matter now.

Davies made one more try. "The sheriff should be here," he protested.

"Isn't he?" Tetley asked. "We must do what we can, then," he said.

"Major Tetley," Davies pleaded, "you mustn't let this be a lynching."

"It's scarcely what I choose, Davies," Tetley said. His voice was dry and disgusted.

"You'll bring them in for trial then?"

"I mean that I am only one of those affected. I will abide by the majority will."

Ma grinned at Davies. "There's your majority stuff right back at you, old man," she said.

Davies didn't argue that. He looked around again, but he didn't find friends. I didn't look at him myself. We knew what we were after now, and where, and it encouraged us to know there were only three rustlers. We'd thought, perhaps, being bold to work right in daylight on a small range, there might be twenty of them.

When Davies tried to speak again, Winder and Farnley told him to shut up.

The Judge expanded and said, "Tetley, you know what's legal in a case like this as well as I do. Davies is only asking what any law-abiding man should choose to do without the asking. He wants the posse to act under a properly constituted officer of the law, and as a posse, not a mob."

"Risley made me deputy," Mapes said loudly.

The Judge went on: "This action is illegal, Major," he blew. Tetley stared at him without any smile. "But in a measure I sympathize with it," the Judge admitted. "Sympathize. The circumstances make action imperative. But a lynching I cannot and will not condone."

"No?" Tetley inquired.

"No, by God. I insist, and that's all Davies asks too, that's all any of us ask, that you bring these men in for a fair trial."

"The Judge ain't had anything bigger to deal with than a drunk and disorderly Indian since he got here, Major,"

Ma said, with a sympathetic face. "You can see how he'd feel about it."

"That attitude," shouted the Judge, waving a hand at Ma, "that's what I must protest, Major. Levity, levity and prejudice in a matter of life and law."

"Regrettable," said Tetley, smiling at Ma.

"We shall observe order and true justice, Judge," he told him.

"Are we going, or aren't we?" Farnley wanted to know. Tetley looked at him. "In time," he said.

"Mapes," he said, turning to Butch.

"Yes, sir?"

"You said Risley had made you deputy?"

"Yes, sir," said Butch.

"Then suppose you deputize the rest of us."

"It's not legal," Tyler told him. He appeared infuriated by Tetley's smiling, elusive talk. "No deputy has the right to deputize."

"It'll do for me, Butch; go head and pray," Smith yelled.

Butch looked at Tetley. Tetley didn't say anything or even nod. He just smiled, that thin little smile that barely moved the corners of his mouth.

"How about it, boys?" Butch asked us.

"Mapes," Tyler bellowed at him, "It's ineffective. You're violating the law yourself, in such an act."

Men called out to Mapes: "Go ahead, Butch"; "I guess it will take as well with you as any, Butch"; "Fire away, sheriff."

"Raise your right hands," Butch told us. We did. He recited an oath, which he seemed to have not quite straight. "Say 'I do,'" he told us. We said it together.

Farnley had already ridden out of the press. We began to swing into loose order after him. Davies was standing alone in the middle of the road with a stricken face. When the Judge bellowed after us in a sudden access of fury, "Tetley, you bring those men in alive, or, by God, as I'm justice of this county, you'll pay for it, you and every damned man-jack of your gang," Davies didn't even seem to hear him. Then suddenly he ran down the road, and then was running beside Tetley's horse, talking to him. Then he dropped back and let them go. I called to ask him if he wasn't coming. He looked up at me, and

God, I felt sorry for the man. He'd looked funny, an old man running stiffly in the road after armed men on horses who wouldn't pay any attention to him. But now he wasn't funny. He didn't say anything, but nodded after a moment. When I was going to pull up to wait for him, he made a violent gesture to me to go on.

Looking back I saw him standing with Osgood in the street. The Judge had dismounted, and was talking to them, waving his hands rapidly. Canby hadn't come down, but was watching them and us, from the door. I could see the white towel he still had in his hand.

Davies didn't catch up with us until we had passed Tetley's big and secret house behind its picket fence and trees and were out in the road between the meadows. The meadows were really marshes close to the road, and the road was only a kind of ranch lane, with deep wheel ruts in the mud and a high, grassy center and edges. The road had been built up, like a railroad embankment, to keep it out of the spring flood, and every few hundred yards there was a heavy plank bridge where the water flowed under from one part of the marsh to the other, and the chock of the horses in the mud, or the plop-plop on the sod, deepened into a hard, hollow thunder for a moment.

Davies was riding a neat little sorrel with white socks and small feet. His saddle was an old, dark leather which had turned cherry color and shiny. He'd put on a plaid blanket coat to keep warm, but he had no gun. He still looked hard bitten in the matter, but not the way he had in the street.

I asked him, "Still aiming to cure us?" and he shook his head and smiled.

"I guess not," he said.

Davies and I were riding last, and up ahead we could see the whole cavalcade strung out by ones and twos. Right ahead of us was Sparks, slowly singing something about Jordan to himself. We could hear sad bits of it now and then in the wind. He looked queer, elongated and hunched, saddleless astride that tall old mare with joints that projected like a cow's. His pants had inched up on him and showed his brown shanks like dark bones going down without socks into big, flat shoes that bobbed of their own weight when the mare jogged.

Ahead of him young Tetley and the Mex were riding together, Tetley silent and not looking around, Amigo pleased with himself, talking a lot and illustrating with his bridle hand while he rolled a cigarette against his chaps with the other. When he had lit the cigarette he talked with the hand that held it. The smell of his heavy Mex tobacco, stronger than a cigar, was still hot when it got to us. His horse, a red and white pinto, like Gil's but smaller and neater, had to take two steps to every one of Tetley's horse, a long-legged, stable-bred black that picked each foot up with a flick, as if he wanted to dance.

We counted twenty-eight of us in all, with a little bunch riding separately up at the head, Tetley, Mapes, Farnley, Winder, Bartlett and Ma, with Gabe and Smith not far behind them.

Old Pete Snyder's board shack with one window and one door, set well out by itself on a high spot among the tules, was the last place west of town. There was smoke coming out of its tin chimney with a conical cap, but Pete's horse, with a saddle on, was baiting on the west side of the shack, and Pete himself was sitting on the step, his big, bare arms hanging over his knees, and his short pipe nestled down in his gray club beard. Pete raised a hand to us as if he didn't care and found it a foolish effort. Pete had had a wife once, but not since he'd lived here, and he'd been alone so long he'd got to thinking differently from the rest of us. It's queer how clearly I remember the way Pete just sat there and let us go. To see him just sit and go on with his own thoughts, made me understand for the first time what we were really going to do, so my breath and blood came quicker for a minute.

Beyond Pete's we opened out into a lope. The horses, after so much standing and fidgeting, were too willing, and kept straining to gallop, moving up on each other until the riders had to pull them to escape the mud and clods of soggy turf they were throwing. Blue Boy was nervy from being with all those other horses, but tired too, from roundup and two days of riding, with a lot of climbing. He kept slipping and coming out of it stiff-legged and snorting, but then wanting to lay out again. Others were having trouble too, and we pulled to the jog again, and held it, all the hoofs trampling squilch-squelch, squilch-squelch, and little clods popping gently out to the side and rolling toward the water. The black-birds, usually noisy this time of day, were just taking short flights among the reeds, and out farther, in the meadows, the cattle weren't feeding, but moving rest-lessly in small bunches, and the grass they were plow-ing through was flattened by the wind. I looked for a meadow lark. Usually about sunset you can see them playing, leaping up and fluttering for a moment, and then dropping again, suddenly, as if they'd been hit; then, after they're down again, that singing will come to you, thin and sweet, chink-chink-a-link. But there was too much wind. Probably all over the big meadow they were down flat in the grass and ruffled. They could feel the storm coming too. Ahead of us the shadowy mountains, stippled all over by their sparse pelt of trees, and piebald with lingering snow, loomed up higher than they were, right against the moving sky.

"It'll be dark before we're out of the pass," I said to Davies.

He looked up at the mountains and at the clouds and nodded. "Snow too," he said. We didn't say anything more. That was enough to show I wasn't unfriendly. He was thick with the same feeling of mortality I had, I guess. We were all feeling it some, out in the great spread of the valley, under the growing mountains, under the storm coming. Even Amigo wasn't talking any more, and had quit trying to smoke in that wind.

We rode that way across half the valley until, right

under a steep foothill, we came to the fork where the road bent right to go into the draw, and the west lane from Drew's came into it.

There, while the rest of us jockeyed in a half circle, waiting and watching him, Tetley rode a ways into the lane and pulled up and sat there like he was carefully looking over a field to be fought. Mapes stopped beside him, Ma and Winder behind him. Tetley and Mapes said a few words together; then Mapes got off his horse, and drawing it on the bridle after him, went slowly down one side of the lane, looking down at the lane and at the spongy grass beside it. This lane was even less of a track than the one across the valley. On the valley side of it, perhaps fifty yards down, was the creek winding south, with willows, aspens and alders forming a screen along it; here and there a big, half-leafed cottonwood rose above this serpent of brush. On the other side, quite close in places, began the pine forest of the mountain. Through the trees, black in the shadow, showed patches of snow which hadn't melted yet. The forest rose steeply from there, and when you could no longer see the shape of the mountain leaning away from you, you could feel it rolling on up much higher. On the east side of the valley the tops of the mountains had disappeared above the plane of cloud.

Amigo was saying, in a clear, explanatory voice, "Eet was thees branding, si. What for you theenk I have the eyes, not to know heem; like thees," and he held up the thumb and forefinger of his right hand, with the second finger curved out and touching the forefinger at the nail, and placed a finger of his left hand across the space between the thumb and forefinger of the right. This made a fair figure of Drew's joined H brand. "I theenk I not mees heem," he said contemptuously, and spit and started to roll a cigarette to make his hands feel natural again. The mountain cut off the wind there.

"Look," he said, pointing while he licked the cigarette, "he have made beeg track all the way, like the army." He seemed to feel this halt was to test his word. He talked to Gil because Gil was beside him, but he didn't care who heard.

He was right enough about the tracks; you didn't have to ride out and scout to see them. The lane was churned with the sharp marks, fresh, the new grass crushed down into the mud still.

Mapes went about thirty or forty yards, then crossed the lane and came back up the other side in the same way. When he got back to Tetley he said something and mounted. Tetley nodded. I could guess he was smiling his I-knew-it-all-the-time smile. They rode back to us and Tetley said, "Amigo's right. They're fresh tracks, the first made this spring. We can't tell how many head, of course . . ."

"Forty," Amigo said, looking around at us.

"Possibly," Tetley said. "There were three riders. They left tracks going both ways." We nodded like that settled it.

Tetley rode around us to get ahead again. Mapes and Ma Grier and Winder followed him, and Gabe Hart. Farnley had ridden farther up the main road and waited alone, watching, below him, Tetley and Mapes playing field officers, but he let them pass him now, and turned in with the rest of us. I was nearer the middle of the bunch now, and when we strung out I was riding with young Tetley.

In the shadow under the mountain we felt hurried because of the lateness. We stepped up to the jog again until we came around the bend where the pass opened above us. There the road began to climb stiffly from the start and we had to walk. The soft lane of the meadow turned into a mountain track, hard and bouldery, with loose gravel and deep ruts made by the water, but already dry. The horses clicked and stumbled, climbing with a clear, slow, choppy rhythm. Where, at the side of the road, it was still muddy from seepage, the mud was already stiffening for the night.

Behind us Sparks began one of his hymns; it came in lonely fragments through the sounds of the horses and the rushing of the creek below us on the right. When I first heard him, I saw too that young Tetley shivered and bent a little, drawing his shoulders together. But that might have been only the wind. It sucked rapidly and heavily down this draw.

I looked back at Sparks. No one was riding with him, and he was grasping his horse's shoulders and gripping the barrel with his long legs to keep from sliding back off. But he didn't know he was having so much trouble;

99

he was thinking about something else. Behind him were Davies, the two Bartlett boys, Moore and Gil riding together, and two men I didn't know, except that one of them had been playing poker at the back table in Canby's. I believe I looked back to keep from looking too much at young Tetley. But I looked at him again. He was riding easily, but too slumped for a cowboy. He was a thin, very young-looking fellow. In this light his face was a pale daub with big shadows for eyes. His black hair came out over his shirt collar in the back. I'd noticed before, in better light, how heavy and shining it was, as if oiled. He looked lonely and unhappy. I knew he didn't know me.

"Cold wind," I began.

He looked at me as if I'd said something important. Then he said, "It's more than wind," and stared ahead of him again.

"Maybe," I said. I didn't get his drift, but if he wanted to talk, "maybe" shouldn't stop him.

"It's a lot more," he said, as if I'd contradicted him. "You can't go hunting men like coyotes after rabbits and not feel anything about it. Not without being like any other animal. The worst animal."

"There's a difference; we have reasons."

"Names for the same thing," he said sharply. "Does that make us any better? Worse, I'd say. At least coyotes don't make excuses. We think we can see something better, but we go on doing the same things, hunt in packs like wolves; hole up in warrens like rabbits. All the dirtiest traits."

"There's still a difference," I said. "We've got it over wolves and rabbits."

"Power, you mean," he said bitterly.

"Over your wolves, and bears too."

"Oh, we're smart," he said, the same way. "It's the same thing," he cried; "all we use it for is power. Yes, we've got them scared all right, all of them, except the tame things we've taken the souls out of. We're the cocks of the dungheap, all right; the bullies of the globe."

"We're not hunting rabbits tonight," I reminded him.

"No; our own kind. A wolf wouldn't do that; not a mangy coyote. That's the hunting we like now, our own kind. The rest can't excite us any more."

"We don't have to hunt men often," I told him. "Most

100

people never have. They get along pretty well together."

"Oh, we love each other," he said. "We labor for each other, suffer for each other, admire each other. We have all the pack instincts, all right, and nice names for them."

"All right," I said, "what's the harm in their being pack instincts, if you want to put it that way? They're real."

"They're not. They're just to keep the pack with us. We don't dare hunt each other alone, that's all. There's more ways of hunting than with a gun," he added.

He'd jumped too far for me on that one. I didn't say anything.

"Think I'm stretching it, do you?" he asked furiously. "Well, I'm not. It's too nice a way of putting it, if anything. All any of us really want any more is power. We'd buck the pack if we dared. We don't, so we use it; we trick it to help us in our own little killings. We've mastered the horses and cattle. Now we want to master each other, make cattle of men. Kill them to feed ourselves. The smaller the pack the more we get."

"Most of life's pretty simple and quiet," I said. "You talk like we all had knives out."

"Your simple life," he said. "Your quiet life. All right," he said, "take the simplest, quietest life you know. Take the things that are going on around us all the time, so we don't notice them any more than old furniture. Take women visiting together, next-door neighbors, old friends. What do they talk about? Each other, all the time, don't they? And what are the parts they like, the ones they remember and bring home to tell to the men?"

"I don't know anything about women," I said.

"You don't have to," he said. "You know anyway. Gossip, scandalous gossip, that's what wakes them up, makes them talk faster and all together, or secretively, as if they were stalking enemies in their minds; something about a woman they know, something that can spoil her reputation: the way she was seen to look at a certain man, or that she can't cook, or doesn't keep her parlor clean, or can't have children, or, worse, could but won't. That's what wakes them up. And do you know why?" He turned the white shape of his face toward me sharply.

101

I didn't like the way the talk was getting to sound like a quarrel. I tried to ease it off.

"No," I said. "Why?" as if I was really curious.

"Because it makes them feel superior; makes them feel they're the wolves, not the rabbits. If each of them had it the way she wants it," he said after a moment, "she'd be the only woman left in the world. They can't manage that, so they do the best they can toward it."

"People can be pretty mean sometimes," I admitted, "picking on the weak ones." It was no good.

"It's not always the weak ones," he said angrily. "They're worse than wolves, I tell you. They don't weed out the unfit, they weed out the best. They band together to keep the best down, the ones who won't share their dirty gossip, the ones who have more beauty or charm or independence, more anything, than they have. They did it right there in Bridger's Wells this spring," he blazed.

"How was that?" I asked, remembering what Canby had said about Rose Mapen.

"They drove a girl out. Made a whore of her with talk."

"Why? what did she do?"

"Nothing. That's what I'm telling you. You know what they had against her? You know what was her intolerable sin against the female pack?"

"How would I know?"

"She was better looking than any of them, and men liked her."

"That can make a whore sometimes," I said.

"She wasn't and they knew it."

"There must have been something."

"There was when they got done," he said. "Everything. But not before. They were scared of her, that's all."

"Why should they be?"

"Men. They're the biggest part of a woman's power."

I had to grin; this kid talking about women like he'd had the testing of the whole breed. And he the kind that would fall over himself to do anything for any of them if they asked it, or just looked it.

He didn't say anything more for a moment, and I heard the creek far down, and the horses clicking and heaving on the grade.

Then he asked, "Do you know Frena Hundel?"

102

"No," I said. So far we'd kept it pretty general; anyway, no names.

"The wild-looking woman who was so afraid we wouldn't come out and hunt down these three, the whole heroic thirty of us."

"Yeah," I said. "What about her?"

"You know what's the matter with her?"

"How would I know?" I asked again. It didn't freeze him.

"She wants those men to die."

He'd got beyond me again, chasing his own hate.

"Before you came," I told him, "she was wild because Larry Kinkaid had been killed. That was what she kept yelling about. I thought she was sore about Larry, maybe sweet on him."

"Oh, yes," he said scornfully, "now he's dead, she's sweet on him. She'd take any dead man as her personal grief; it makes her feel important."

"What's the sense in that?" I asked.

"He wasn't anything to her before he was shot. In her heart she's glad he's dead."

That still didn't make sense to me. I waited, twisting a hand in Blue Boy's mane and feeling his big shoulders working under it.

"Frena can't get a man," he explained, "so she wants to see them all die. Yes, all of them. She's glad Kinkaid's dead. She doesn't know these men we're after, doesn't know anything about them, but she's wild to have us kill them. And she's wild to get the rest of us the same way, too, to push us into something that will kill our souls, if we have any; that will make us afraid to face men again, anyhow. Because she can't get a man."

"It's a big project," I said, "to kill us all because she can't get one of us."

"I don't say she can. I say it's what she wants."

I didn't say anything.

"If there were no men, she could do what she pleased with most women, make them her slaves. Men are the part of power she can't get, and Frena wants power. Frena's got a bigger appetite for power than the pack will tolerate because most of them couldn't stand it themselves. It would tear them to pieces in a week to want anything as much as Frena wants everything."

103

"You don't think much of women, do you?" I said.

"Men are no better," he said. "Men are worse. They're not so sly about their murder, but they don't have to be; they're stronger; they already have the upper hand of half the race, or they think so. They're bullies instead of sneaks, and that's worse. And they're just as careful to keep up their cheap male virtues, their strength, their courage, their good fellowship, to keep the pack from jumping them, as the women are to keep up their modesty and their hominess. They all lie about what they think, hide what they feel, to keep from looking queer to the pack."

"Is there anything so fine about being different?" I asked him.

"Did you ever hear a man tell another man about the dreams he's had that have made him sweat and run his legs in the bed and wake up moaning with fear? Did you?"

"What do you want? Everybody running around telling his dreams, like a little kid?"

"Or any woman tell about the times she's sighed and panted in her sleep for a lover she wasn't married to?"

"For Lord's sake," I said.

"No," he babbled on, "you never did and you never will."

"It's all right with me if I don't."

The white of his face was to me again. "You're like all the rest," he raged. "You've had dreams like that; you know you have. We've all had those dreams. In our hearts we know they're true, truer than anything we ever tell; truer than anything we ever do, even. But nothing could make us tell them, show our weakness, have the pack at our throats.

"Even in dreams," he said, after a bit, as if he was talking to himself, but so I could hear, "even in dreams it's the pack that's worst; it's the pack that we can never quite see but always feel coming, like a cloud, like a shadow, like a fog with our death in it. It's the spies of the pack who are always hidden behind the next pillars of the temples and palaces we dream we're in, watching us go between them. They're behind the trees in the black woods we dream about; they're behind the boulders on the mountains we dream we're climbing,

104

behind the windows on the square of every empty dream city we wander in. We've all heard them breathing; we've all run screaming with fear from the pack that's coming somewhere. We've all waked up in the night and lain there trembling and sweating and staring at the dark for fear they'll come again.

"But we don't tell about it, do we?" he dared me. And said quickly, "No, no, we don't even want to hear anybody else tell. Not because we're afraid for him. No, we're afraid our own eyes will give us away. We're afraid that sitting there hearing him and looking at him we'll let the pack know that our souls have done that too, gone barefoot and gaping with horror, scrambling in the snow of the clearing in the black woods, with the pack in the shadows behind them. That's what makes us sick to hear fear admitted, or lust, or even anger, any of the things that would make the pack believe that we were either weak or dangerous."

He turned his face fully toward me, furious and challenging. "That is what makes you sick now, to hear me," he told me. "That's what makes you so damned superior and cold and quiet." His voice choked him so I thought he was going to cry. "You're just hiding the truth, even from yourself," he babbled.

My hands were twitching, but I didn't say anything.

Then he said more quietly, "You think I'm crazy, don't you? It always seems crazy to tell the truth. We don't like it; we won't admit what we are. So I'm crazy."

I was thinking that. I don't like to hear a man pouring out his insides without shame. And taking it for granted everyone else must be like him. You'd have thought he was God, making everyone in his own pattern. Still, he was a kid and weak and unhappy, and his own father, they said, was his enemy.

"Every man's got a right to his own opinion," I told him.

After a moment he said, "Yes," low and to his saddlehorn.

Having heard myself speak I realized that queerly, weak and bad-tempered as it was, there had been something in the kid's raving which had made the canyon seem to swell out and become immaterial until you could think the whole world, the universe, into the half-darkness

105

around you: millions of souls swarming like fierce, tiny, pale stars, shining hard, winking about cores of minute, mean feelings, thoughts and deeds. To me his idea appeared just the opposite of Davies'. To the kid, what everybody thought was low and wicked, and their hanging together was a mere disguise of their evil. To Davies, what everybody thought became, just because everybody thought it, just and fine, and to act up to what they thought was to elevate oneself. And yet both of them gave you that feeling of thinking outside yourself, in a big place; the kid gave me that feeling even more, if anything, though he was disgusting. You could feel what he meant; you could only think what Davies meant.

I heard him talking again. "Why are we riding up here, twenty-eight of us," he demanded, "when every one of us would rather be doing something else?"

"I thought you said we liked killing?"

"Not so directly as this," he said. "Not so openly. Not many of us, at least. We're doing it because we're in the pack, because we're afraid not to be in the pack. We don't dare show our pack weakness; we don't dare resist the pack."

"What do you want us to do," I asked him, "sit and play a harp and worry about how bad we are while some damned rustler kills a man and cleans out the country?"

"It isn't that," he said. "How many of us do you think are really here because there have been cattle stolen, or because Kinkaid was shot?"

"I'm not wrong about your being here, am I?" I asked him.

Then he was quiet. I felt mean. The thing that made me sorest about this whole talk was that I knew the kid was just scared. I knew he didn't want to quarrel; but he talked so you couldn't do anything else.

"No," he said finally. "I'm here, all right." He had dug himself up by the roots to say that.

"Well?" I said, easier.

"I'm here because I'm weak," he said, "and my father's not."

There wasn't anything a guy could say to that. It made me feel as I had once listening to a man describing just how he'd got to a woman, undressing her, so to speak, right in front of us, even telling us what she'd said; a woman we all knew at that. But at least he'd been drunk.

"That doesn't help, does it?" young Tetley was asking.

"I'm not claiming to be superior to anyone else," he said. "I'm not. I'm not fit to be alive. I know better than to do what I do. I've always known better, and not done it."

He burst out, "And that's hell; can you understand that that's hell?"

"You kind of take it for granted nobody else is as smart as you are, don't you, kid?" I asked him.

He hunched over the saddle, twisting the front of his coat, I thought, with one hand. It was too dusky to be sure. After a while he answered, as if he had forgotten what I'd said, and then remembered it again.

"I didn't mean it that way," he said. He sounded far away and tired; ashamed he'd said so much. It was as if he'd been on a jag, but it was over now and he was feeling sick. He couldn't let it drop, though.

"Maybe I am crazy, in a way," he said very quietly.

"You take it too hard, son," I told him. "You didn't start this."

"But I know this," he said, "if we get those men and hang them, I'll kill myself. I'll hang myself."

Louder he said, "I tell you I won't go on living and remembering I saw a thing like this; was part of it myself. I couldn't. I'd go really crazy."

Then he said, quietly again, "It's better to kill yourself than to kill somebody else. That settles the mess anyway; really settles it."

I'd had enough. I'd heard drunks talk like this and it was half funny, but the kid was cold sober.

"We haven't hung anybody yet," I told him. "You can go home and keep your own hands clean."

"No, I can't," he said.

"I can't," he said again; "and if I could it wouldn't matter. What do I matter?"

"You seem to think you matter a lot," I said.

I could see the pale patch of his face turned toward me in the dusk, then away again.

"It does sound that way, doesn't it?" he asked, as if I was wrong.

I began humming the "Buffalo Gal" to myself. He didn't say anything more, but after a bit dropped back and rode beside Sparks. They didn't talk, because I stopped humming and heard Sparks still singing to himself.

At the first level stretch in the road we stopped to breathe the horses. It was dark now, and really cold, not just chilly. There was frost on my blanket roll when I went to get my sheepskin out. The sheepskin was good, cutting the wind right away, and I swung my arms across my chest to get warm inside it. Others were warming themselves too. I could see them spreading and closing like dark ghosts, and hear the thump of their fists.

Gil came up alongside and peered to make sure who it was. Then he said, "Doing this in the middle of the night is crazy. Moore don't like it much either," he added. We sat there, listening to the horses breathe, and some of the other men talking in low voices.

Gil was still worrying about the dark. "If it hadn't clouded up," he said, "there would have been a full moon tonight, bright as day." Gil knew his sky like the palm of his hand. One place and another I'd read quite a lot about the sun and moon and the constellations, but I could never remember it. Gil had never read anything, but he always knew.

When the horses were breathing quietly again, and beginning to stamp, we started on, Gil and I riding together, which felt more natural. Except right in front of us and right behind us, we couldn't see the riders. We could only hear small sounds of foot and saddle and voice from along the line. The sounds were short, flat and toneless, just bits coming back on the rushing of the creek. Gil was quiet, for him. He didn't talk or hum; he didn't change position in his saddle or play with the quirt end of his bridle. He didn't look around. There wasn't much to see, of course, the broken shadows of the forest against the fainter but rearing and uniform shadow that was the mountain rising across the creek; that and the patches of snow, bigger and more numerous, showing at vague distances through the trees, like huge, changing creatures standing upright and seeming to move. Even so a man will usually look around even more when it's dark, unless he's got saddle-sleepy and dazed. Gil wasn't sleepy; he wasn't sitting his horse like a sleepy man. If I knew him, he was thinking about something he didn't like. I should have let him alone, but I didn't.

"Still seeing those three guys reaching for the barrels, Gil?"

"No," he said, coming out of it. "I'd forgot all about them until you mentioned it. Why should I worry about that now?"

"What's eating you?"

He didn't say anything.

"I thought you liked excitement," I said. "I thought you'd be honing for something to do."

"I've got nothing against hanging a rustler," he said loudly. The riders ahead turned in their saddles and peered back at us. One of them hissed at us angrily. That made me sore on account of Gil; we were like that, fight each other a good part of the time, but be happier to pitch in together on somebody else. Though there was a difference between us. Gil really liked to fight, liked to let his temper slip and to feel the sweat and the hitting. I just fought because Gil got so pig headed and insulting when he wanted to fight that I had to or feel yellow.

"Why all the secret?" I said, as loud as Gil had. "Afraid the three of them will round us up?"

The man who had hissed pulled his horse in and reined half around. It was old Bartlett. For a minute I thought he was coming for us. But Gil rode right over toward him, like he would love to mix it, and Bartlett turned back into line, though slowly, to show he wasn't afraid of Gil.

When we were straightened out, Gil said, "It ain't that I don't believe in gettin' a killer, any way you have to. But I don't like it in the dark. There's always some fool will get wild and plug anything that moves; like young Greene there, or Smith, or maybe young Tetley."

"He won't do any shooting," I said.

"Maybe not; but he scares easy; he's scared now. And he's got a gun."

He went on, "That ain't what bothers me most, though. I like to pick my bosses. We didn't pick any bosses here, but we got 'em just the same. We was just herded in. So, and who herded us in? That kid Greene, if I remember, with a wild-eyed story he couldn't get straight, and Smith and Bartlett blowing off, and Osgood because he got us sore. That's a sweet outfit to tell you what you're going to do, ain't it?"

"They didn't really get us in," I said.

"They started us, them and Farnley. Not that Farnley's like them; Farnley's got plenty of sand. But when he's mad he's crazy. He's no kind of a guy to have in this business. When he's mad he can't think at all. He don't rile cool.

"I remember once," he began narrating, "I saw Farnley get mad. We was together in Hazey's outfit over on the Humboldt. It was beef roundup. Some wise guy, trying to improve his stock, had got a lot of long-horns in with his reds that spring. They was big as a chuck-wagon, and wild. Some of 'em you couldn't drive; they was fast as a pony, and didn't want to bunch, like a steer. You had to get 'em one at a time with a rope, like you would for branding.

"Well, in the thick of it, all dust and flurry, one of these long-horns, a big gray-splotched fellow with legs like a horse and nine feet of horns, got under Farnley's pony and ripped him open like splitting a fish; the guts sagged right out in a belch of black blood. The steer pulled loose all right, but he'd got in deeper than it looked at first. The pony, stiff-legged, tried to get away from him, but then, all of a sudden, came red blood, a lot of it, and he went over all at once, his legs folding right under him. Farnley got clear, he's quick as a cat and smooth. But then you know what he done? He took one look at the pony, it was his best one, one he'd had four years, and then he went wild-eyed for that steer. Yes he did, on his feet, no gun or anything; like he thought he could break its neck with his hands. Lucky I saw him, and there was another fellow, Cornwall, Corny we called him, not too far off that I yelled to. We got the steer turned off before he'd more than punched one hole under Farnley's ribs; not too deep, a sort of rip along the side. And even then it wasn't enough for Farnley. He fought us like a wildcat to get at the critter again. I was sore enough to let him go ahead and be mashed, but Corny'd known him a long time, and knew how he got. So Corny climbs down, and says to me, 'Let him come,' and when I let Farnley go he went for Corny milling. Corny just stood there cool and knocked him out with one punch. He folded up like an empty sack, and we had to get water from the chuck-wagon to bring him to.

"You'd think that was enough, wouldn't you? Corny'd

110

risked his own neck plenty, gettin' down in the middle of all that. The steer was near as wild as Farnley was, dodging around us, trying to get in another poke. I had all I could do to keep heading him out. He was blood crazy, and I didn't relish the idea of losing my pony the same way. But do you think Farnley said thanks? He did not. Lying there in the shade of the chuck-wagon, while the cook tied up his side the best he could, he kept looking at us like he wanted to take a knife to both of us. By Godfreys, if he had of tried something I'da let him have it fer a nickel. Corny made me come off.

"It was pretty near the end of roundup before Farnley'd even see us when he went by. And he never did mention the thing, not to this day. That's how long he can stay that way."

I thought Gil was off the track, but he wasn't.

"And that's the guy that's going to do something when it comes to doing something," he said.

"He's had a lot of time to think it over," I reminded him. "It's not the same. Tetley can stop him."

"Not Tetley or anybody else," Gil said. "And that's another thing. Who picked Tetley? He's not our man, the damn reb dude."

"It was Tetley brought us, when it came to the show-down," I said.

"I don't like it," Gil said.

"We can quit," I reminded him. "There's no law makes us be part of this posse."

Gil said quickly, "Hell, no. I'll see this thing out as far as any man will.

"You watch yourself," he added, "don't you let Davies and Osgood, or that loose-mouth Tyler, get to you. There's not a damn thing they can do to us as long as we stick together, and they know it."

"I didn't bring this up," I reminded him.

"Neither did I," he said. "I'm just warnin' you we got to keep an eye on some of these guys. Farnley and Bartlett and Winder and Ma; yes, and Tetley too. No slick-smiling bastard's going to suck me into a job I don't like, that's all."

"Have your own way, whatever way that is."

"Shut up," he ordered.

We rode along saying nothing then, Gil still angry

because he couldn't make his feelings agree, and me laughing at him, though not out loud. He'd have ridden right over me if I'd even peeped.

We came to a steeper pitch, where I could feel Blue Boy's shoulders pump under the saddle and hear his breath coming in jerks. Then we came into a narrows and I knew we were nearly at the top of the pass. The road there just hung on the face of a cliff, and the other wall across the creek wasn't more than twenty feet away. On a night as dark as that you wouldn't think it could get any darker, but it did in that narrows. The wall went straight up beside us, probably forty or fifty feet. The clambering of the horses echoed a little against it even with the wind, and with the creek roaring as if we were on the edge of it. The wind was strong in the slot, and smelled like snow again.

We all hugged the cliff side of the road, not being able to see the drop-off side clearly. I was on the inside, and sometimes my foot scraped the wall, and sometimes Gil and I clicked stirrups, he had pulled over so far. His horse sensed the edge and didn't like it, and kept twisting around trying to face it.

"A nice place for a holdup," Gil said, showing he was willing to talk again.

"In here three men could do in a hundred," I agreed.

"But they won't."

"I wouldn't think so."

After a minute I said, "It's going to snow."

He must have been testing the wind himself; then he said, "Hell. Won't that be just lovely! Still," he said, "it can't be much of a storm this time of year."

"I don't know. I remember trying to get through Eagle Pass the first week in June one year. I had to go back; the horse was up to his belly and we weren't half way to the summit. A fellow bringing the mail across on snow-shoes said there was nine feet at the summit. He had a stick poked in up there with notches on it."

"Yeh, but that wasn't all new snow."

"Every inch of it. The trail had been clear two days before."

"Eagle Pass is higher, though."

"Some. But this is nearly eight thousand. That's high enough."

112

"Maybe they'll have to call it off," Gil suggested.

"Depend on how much of a lead they thought the rustlers had."

"Well, it won't be any picnic," Gil said, "but we'll be making a lot better time than they can. This was a fool way to come with cattle. And they'd have to stop when it got dark, too. You can't drive cattle on this road in the dark."

"By the same sign," I said, "we could go right by them and never know it."

Gil thought. Then he said, "Not unless they stopped in the Ox-Bow. There's no place else from here to the Hole where they could get forty head of cattle off the road."

The Ox-Bow was a little valley up in the heart of the range. Gil and I had stayed there a couple of days once, on the loose. It was maybe two or three miles long and half or three quarters of a mile wide. The peaks were stacked up on all sides of it, showing snow most of the summer. The creek in the middle of it wound back on itself like a snake trying to get started on loose sand, and that shape had named the valley. There was sloping meadow on both sides of the creek, and in the late spring millions of purple and gold violets grew there, violets with blossoms as big as the ball of a man's thumb. Beyond the meadow, on each side, there was timber to the tops of the hills. It was a lovely, chill, pine-smelling valley, as lonely as you could want. Scarcely anybody came there unless there was a dry season. Just once in a while, if you passed in the late summer, you'd see a sheepherder small out in the middle, with his burro and dogs and flock. The rest of the time the place belonged to squirrels, chipmunks and mountain jays. They would all be lively in the edge of the wood, scolding and flirting.

Someone had lived there once, though, and tried to ranch the place. In the shelter of a few isolated trees extending from the forest on the west side, he'd built a log cabin with a steep roof to slide the snow off. There'd been a corral too, and a regular barn with a loft to store hay. But whoever he was, he'd given up years before. The door and windows were out of the cabin, and the board floor was rotten, seedling pines and sagebrush coming up through it. There were only a few posts of

113

the corral left, and the snow had flattened the barn, splitting the sides out and settling the roof right over them. Small circles of blackened stone showed where short stoppers, like Gil and me, had burned pieces of the barn and fences.

We discussed the chances of the rustlers using the Ox-Bow. The road ran right along the edge of it at the south end; there was good grazing and water and wood to be picked up. But then, there was only that one way in and out, at least for men driving cattle. On the other three sides the mountains were steep, heavily timbered at the base, then grown thick with manzanita, then covered with frost-split, sliding shale, and they didn't let you out anywhere except into more mountains. On the other hand there was no other place on the trail where they could have stopped. There was a clearing right at the summit, but the road ran through the middle of it and there was no grass or water. And the road down the other side was like this one, steep and narrow all the way; a few little washes big enough for the coach to get off the track and stand, but none to hold forty head of cattle. We couldn't see anything but the Ox-Bow or keep going.

On the summit the wind hit full force, as if you'd stepped out from behind a wall. It was bitter cold and damp. I thought I felt a few flakes of snow on my face, but my face was already too numb to be sure. Even the horses ducked their heads into the wind.

In the clearing Tetley and Mapes stopped us to breathe the horses again. Also they began arguing what Gil and I had thought about the trail and the Ox-Bow, and some were for turning back. With snow beginning to come, and that wind blowing, they felt sure of a blizzard. Tetley maintained that was all the more reason for pressing the chase. With their trail covered with snow, and a day or two start, time to switch brands, what would we have to go on? Davies, and Moore backed him up this time, was for sending a couple of riders on across to Pike's Hole, and getting the men there to pick the rustlers up. I could see what he wanted. Kinkaid was nothing to most of the Pike's men, and it wasn't their cattle had been rustled. They'd pick the men up on principle, but they'd be willing to hold them for the sheriff and a trial. Winder and Ma sided with

Tetley. Winder was accusing Davies, and even Moore, of being so scared of the job they'd rather let a murderer slip than do it. Davies admitted he'd rather let ten murderers go than have it on his soul that he'd hung an honest man. Tetley said he wasn't going to hang an innocent man; he'd make sure enough of that to suit even Davies. To Farnley, even Tetley's manner smacked of delay. He told them he'd rather see a murderer hanged than shot, it was a dirtier death, but that he'd bush-whack all three of those men before he'd let one of them get out of the mountains free. I tried to shut Gil up when he started, but he went ahead and told Farnley that nobody who wasn't a horse-thief himself would bush-whack any man, let alone three men for one, and the one a man he hadn't seen do it. Farnley was going to climb Gil, for which I couldn't blame him, but they couldn't pick each other out in the dark, and others held them down. I tried to talk Gil quiet, but he said, "Aw, hell," in disgust, and spit as if it was on the whole bunch of us, and rode farther out by himself. It looked as if it might be another long squabble. I'd been walking Blue Boy back and forth along the edge so I could hear some of the talk, but still keep him from cooling too fast. Cold as it was, the climb had sweated him. Other punchers were doing the same.

Now I eased him over to the edge of the clearing where the trees broke the wind a little, and got down and wiped him over with a few handfuls of old, softened, damp pine needles. They pricked him, and he was restless, but he liked it fine when I finished him off with snow from a little drift at the top of the creek bank. The snow was hard and granular, and brought the blood back into my hands. I listened for the talk to end, but took my time. It felt good to be on my feet and moving around; I'd stiffened to the saddle.

Somebody in the middle of the clearing sang out, "Scatter, boys, there's horses coming." Tetley didn't seem to like the order, for I heard him giving others quickly, but not loud enough so I could understand. The group was already scattering to both sides of the clearing. I could see the shadowy huddle in the middle fanning out toward the edges. In the wind I couldn't hear them, any more than I'd heard anything coming. They were so many shadows floating off slowly, like a cloud breaking up in

115

front of the moon. The middle of the clearing became just a gray, open space waiting for something to come into it. I could see why Tetley hadn't liked that order, besides its being yelled that way. There wasn't a man among us, in the edge of the woods, that could risk a shot into the clearing in the dark and with others right across from him. Four or five riders stayed together and disappeared into the shadow where the road entered the clearing. Tetley was with them, I thought. He kept his head in this sort of thing. I listened hard, but still couldn't hear the running horses I expected from that shout. All I could hear was the wind, roaring on and off in the pines, and higher up booming at intervals, as if clapping in space; and faintly, like a lesser wind, the falling of the creek. Those, and right behind me the trunks of the taller pines complaining.

One of the shadows, on foot and leading his horse, came toward me and disappeared under the trees very near. Then I was listening for him too. A man hates to have somebody near him in the dark when he doesn't know who it is. I felt the animal advantage of being there first.

A voice from the other side of me, Mapes I thought, called out, "Stay where you are till I give you the hail. Then circle out slow if it's anything we want. Don't do any shooting."

It struck me that in that darkness and wind, unless Tetley's bunch stopped him, a rider could be across the clearing and into the narrows before we were sure he was there. And on that down grade, riding alone, he'd have a big advantage on us. I told myself that was none of my worry, but the thought kept me tense.

The man near me was coming closer. I could hear the slow, soft thuds of his horse plodding on the thick blanket of pine needles.

"Who is it?" I asked.

The thudding stopped. "It's jus' me, Spahks," a voice finally said. "Who ah you, suh?"

"Art Croft," I told him.

He seemed to think that over. For some reason I thought of my history since this business had begun; what I found made me feel humble but irritated. Then he asked,

"Don't mahnd if ah come ovah a bit closah, do you, Mistah Croft?"

"No, come on. I'm findin' it lonesome myself."

He stopped right beside me. It was black in there though; I still couldn't see him. He reached out and touched me, just light and quick, to make sure I was there.

"Theah you ah," he said.

Then, apologizing, "Ah wasn't quite cleah you was with us, Mistah Croft. Guess ah wasn't noticin' all that was goin' on. Ah did see you fren' Mistah Cahtah."

"I wasn't mixin' in much," I admitted.

"It's mortal cold, ain't it?"

I remembered that he had on only a thin shirt and jeans. He was a heat-loving nigger anyway, not used to this mountain country yet.

"I've got a blanket if you want it."

"Thank you jus' the same, Mistah Croft," he said. He had a sad little chuckle. "It takes all mah hands to keep on this ole hoss."

I'd noticed that Sparks never called me "sir" when he knew who I was. Not that I wanted to be called sir, and not that Sparks was ever anything but polite, but it did nettle me that he wouldn't be as careful of me as he would of a sponge like Smith, or a weak sister like Osgood. And even if you don't believe in them, you pick up feelings about darkies from men you work with. I'd worked in outfits with a lot of Southern boys, mostly Texas. They'd drop a white man who played with a nigger even faster than they would a nigger, and they had a sharp line about niggers. They wouldn't condescend about them, the way some of us did, but they wouldn't eat or drink where black men did, or sleep in blankets a nigger had used, or have anything more to do with a house where a nigger had been let in the front door. They didn't condescend, I thought, just because they never even considered a nigger the same kind of creature enough to make comparisons. I'd picked up just enough of this crude habit to make me feel guilty whenever I had such thoughts. I did now.

"I've got some whisky in my canteen," I said; "better have a couple of shots."

"No, thanks, Mistah Croft, ah guess not."

"Go on," I said, "I've got plenty."

"Ah don't drink it, Mistah Croft." He didn't want to sound like a temperance lady. "There's devil enough in me bah mahself," he explained.

"In this cold you could drink the whole canteen," I told him.

"No, thanks."

I shut up, and he felt I was a little stiff, I guess.

"Ah wish we was well out of this business," he said.

"It's a way of spendin' time," I told him.

"It's man takin' upon himself the Lohd's vengeance," he said. "Man, Mistah Croft, is full of error." He said it jokingly, but he wasn't joking.

I suppose I think as much about God as the next man who isn't in the business. I spend a lot of time alone. But I'd seen, yes and done, some things that made me feel that if God was worried about man it was only in large numbers and in the course of time.

"Do you think the Lord cares much about what's happening up here tonight?" I asked him, too sharply.

Sparks took it gently though. "He mahks the sparrow's fall," he said.

"Then He won't miss this, I guess."

"God is in us, Mistah Croft," he pleaded. "He wuhks th'ough us."

"Maybe, then, we're the instruments of the divine vengeance," I suggested.

"Ah can't fahnd that in mah conscience, Mistah Croft," he said after a moment. "Can you?" he asked me.

"I'm not sure I've got a conscience any more."

He persisted, taking another angle. "Mistah Croft, if you had to hold the rope on one of those men with your own hands, could you fohget it raght away aftahwahds?" he asked me.

"I don't suppose I could," I admitted.

"And wouldn't it trouble you to think of it, even a long time aftah?"

"Not with a rustler," I lied.

When Sparks didn't say anything I felt I'd let another good man down, the way I had about Davies.

"I haven't heard anything yet," I said. "Did you hear anything out there?"

"Ah didn't," Sparks said, as if he wasn't interested. "It was Mistah Mapes and Mistah Windah."

118

"It don't seem to me the rustlers would double back when there's only one trail," I said.

"No, suh." That "sir" had the politeness of a grievance. It annoyed me.

"You seem to be taking this pretty personal."

"It's like ah was sayin', Mistah Croft," he answered after a moment. "There's some things a man don't fohget seein'."

You can't ask a man to talk about such things, so I didn't say anything. Perhaps on account of the darkness Sparks decided to tell me anyway.

"Ah saw mah own brothah lynched, Mistah Croft," he said stiffly. "Ah was just a little fella when I saw that, but sometimes ah still wakes up from dreamin' about it."

There was still nothing for me to say.

"And pahtly ah was to blame," Sparks remembered.

"You were?"

"Ah went to find Jim where he was hidin' and they followed me and got him."

"How old did you say you were?"

"Ah'm not shuah; a little fella, six or seven or eight."

"You couldn't have been much to blame then," I said.

"Ah've ahgued that with mahself, Mistah Croft, but it don't help the feelin'," Sparks said. "That's what ah mean," he added.

"Well, had he done what they picked him up for?"

"Ah don't know; we didn' any of us evah know foh shuah. But it still don' seem lahk anythin' ah evah knew about Jim."

"They wouldn't lynch him without knowing," I said.

He thought for a while before he answered that. "They made him confess," he admitted. "But they would have anyhow," he protested. "It wouldn't have done him any good not to, and confessin' made it shortah. It was still bad, though; awful bad," he added. "Ah wouldn' lahk to see a thing lahk that again, Mistah Croft."

"No," I said.

We were quiet and I could hear his teeth chattering.

"I'll tell you," I said, as if I was joking, "a drop or two more whisky can't do my soul any harm. You take my coat and I'll take the drink."

"No, thanks, Mistah Croft." I was afraid he was going to feel responsible for my drinking too, but he went on,

119

"Ah'm all used to it now, an' you'd catch youah death o' cold takin' that coat off." He wanted that coat, though; it wasn't easy for him to object.

"I've gone in my shirt sleeves when it was colder than this," I said, "and my shirt's flannel."

I took off the coat. He protested, but I talked him down cheerfully and he put it on.

"Sure a fahn coat," he said happily. "Ah'll get me warmed up a mite in it, then you take it. Ah get awful cold around the heart," he said seriously. "Seems like ah always feel it most there. This woolly'll warm me up in no tahm. Then you take it again."

"I don't even feel it," I said, which wasn't true. "You keep the coat, Reverend." I'd been cold again from standing around, even before I'd taken the coat off, and there was more snow in the wind now, blowing in even under the trees. There was no question about its being snow. Still I felt more cheerful than I had since morning, which seemed a long way back now, and like another life.

I found the canteen on my saddle and had two long swallows. It was rotten stuff of Canby's all right, but it was hot in the mouth and warming in the belly. It gave me a good shiver, then settled broadly in my middle and began to spread through my body like a fire creeping in short grass. I stood there and let her spread for a minute; then I had another, corked the canteen, tied it back on the saddle and rolled a cigarette. I offered Sparks the makings, but he didn't smoke either. I turned my back to the clearing to cover the flare I'd make; two or three voices called at me though, low and angry. Having started, I held the flame until my cigarette was going. The smoke was good, drawn in that cold air, and after the whisky in my mouth.

I could hear somebody leading his horse, and stopping close on my right.

"You damn fool," he said in a low, hostile voice, "want to give us away?" I thought it was Winder. I knew I was in wrong, which made me even sorer.

"Who to?" I asked him out loud.

"You guys have been hearing things," I told him, the same way. "Let's get moving before we freeze stiff and can't. Or are we giving this up?"

I heard his hammer click; the sound brought me awake,

120

quick and clear. I kept the cigarette in my mouth, but didn't draw on it, and got hold of my own gun.

"You chuck that butt," he ordered, "or I'll plug you. You've been a lily since this started, Croft." He must have seen my face when I lit up.

"Start something," I told him. "For every hole you make, I'll make two. Anybody who'd ride a mule couldn't hit a barn in the daylight, let alone a man in the dark."

I was scared though. I knew Winder's temper, and he wasn't more than five steps off. When I'd talked the cigarette had bobbed in my mouth too, in spite of my trying to talk stiff-lipped; he'd know where it was. I made a swell target; he could judge every inch of me. When he didn't say anything, my back began to crawl. I wouldn't have thought I could feel any colder, but I did, all under the back of my shirt. Still, after the way he'd put it, I couldn't let that cigarette go either. I drew my own gun slowly, and kept staring hard to see what he was doing, but couldn't. I wanted to squat, but it was no use with that cigarette. The best was to hold still and let the ash form.

I jumped when Sparks spoke behind me, but felt better at once. My mind was beginning to freeze on the situation, and his voice brought me to my senses, though I didn't move after the first start, or look away.

"It looks like you'll have a lot of shootin' to do, Mistah Bahtlett," Sparks said. So he thought it was Bartlett. That idea made me feel a lot happier. I looked along the edge of the woods and saw what Sparks meant. Half a dozen men were lighting up. They felt the same way I did, I guess, foolish about waiting so long. The closest man was Tetley's Amigo. He had his hands cupped around the match, and I could see his brown, grease-shining face before he flipped the match out and drew deeply, making the cigarette glow and fade.

"Damned fools," the man said, whoever he was. Then I heard him let the hammer down again, and his horse following him off.

"Let's go," I said to Sparks. Other shadows were moving out into the clearing again.

It was a thick dark, even out there. You couldn't have told it was snowing except by the feel. I didn't get used to the feel; it kept on being a surprise. I could see shapes moving when they crossed against a snow bank, but that was about all, except the cigarettes. Once in a while one of these made a brief shower of sparks when a man turned across the wind.

In the huddle somebody, Mapes I thought, said, "Reckon we must have been hearing our own ears, boys."

"We heard it, and it warn't no ears," a voice told him. That was Winder I was sure, and I thought again that it must have been Winder under the trees.

"To hell with it," somebody said. "This is no kind of a night for the job." His voice was nervous from waiting blind.

"You're right there," another agreed.

"This snow will be three feet deep by morning," the first man said.

There was a lot of muttering in agreement. After trying to see into the clearing all that time the job did look ridiculous. Also, unseasonable winter takes the heart out of men the same as it does out of animals. You just get used to the sun and the limber feeling, and when they go you want to crawl back into your hole.

Tetley spoke up. You could tell his voice without any question. That superior smile was in the tone of it. "It's either now or not at all," he said. "The entrance to the Ox-Bow is less than a mile from here."

"Let's get at it," Ma said cheerfully. "Boys," she told us, "we'd be the laughing stock of the country if we went home on account of a little snow, and it turned out we'd been right there within a mile of the men we wanted all the time."

"Well, then, let's go," Smith said. His voice was big and hearty and empty as ever. You couldn't mistake it. "This rope will have to be thawed out now, before it's fit to use." He added, "I'm stiff enough myself. Got a drink, anybody?"

"Hey," a man in back of us yelled, "look out!"

"Jesus," said the man next to me. He was scared. So was I. That yelp had been loud. At first I didn't see, the horses milling some, what he was yelping about. Then I saw it. It was the stagecoach. It wasn't coming fast, but it was already close. The trees and bank had hidden it till it was nearly on us. We scattered out to the sides, some of the horses wheeling and acting up.

"Stop him," Mapes yelled.

"He can tell us," Ma called.

Others were shouting too, and some of them rode back toward the coach, calling at the driver to stop.

Caught by surprise, the driver started to pull up; his lead horses reared and the brakes squealed a little. Then he changed his mind. There was a lantern swinging off the seat on the road side. It made a long narrowing shadow of the coach and driver up a snow bank on the far side. By its light I saw the driver stand straight up and let his whip go out over the horses. The tip exploded like a pistol shot. The horses yanked from side to side, then scrambled and dug and got under way. Checked and then yanked forward again like that, the coach rocked on its straps like a cradle, and the lantern banged back and forth. The driver was huddled down as much as he dared with that hill coming. When the lantern swung up I could see over him that there was another man. He was trying to stick with the bucking seat and get himself laid over the top to shoot. There were four horses, and by the middle of the clearing that whip, which the driver kept snaking out the best he could, had them stretching together, bending away right for that grade in the narrows. We all yelled at him then, but there were too many yelling. There were passengers too. A woman screamed, and behind the flapping curtain a light went out. The guard shouted from the roof.

"Keep down," he yelled at the people inside. "Stickup. Keep down, I tell you, they'll shoot."

I saw the driver reaching for the lantern to throw it away, but he couldn't get to it and keep his lines. All the time he was staring ahead, trying to see where the dip started.

A man's voice from inside was yelling at the driver to stop, and the woman was still screaming almost every time the coach lurched.

Several riders had started out to come alongside but, seeing the guard, had pulled away, yelling at him. Winder, though, didn't seem to see him. That was his coach heading for the narrows and the creek below. He kept calling, "Hey, Alec, hey, Alec; hey, Alec, you goddamned fool," but his mule couldn't keep/ beside the coach. We were all yelling at the driver and at Bill now. I saw it wasn't doing any good, and touched Blue Boy up, intending to turn Winder anyhow, before he was drilled. It was all serious enough, God knows, and yet so crazy, all that commotion suddenly, and the driver and the guard playing hero, that I was nearly laughing too, while I yelled.

I was hit in the shoulder, so unexpectedly it nearly drove me out of the saddle. At once I heard the bang of the guard's carbine, and then somebody scream and keep moaning for a moment while I pulled straight in the saddle. The report was a flat sound in the clearing, but distinct above all the others. The yelling stopped at once, and then, even in the wind, the explosion echoed faintly in the narrows.

Distantly, with the sounds of the coach, I heard Ma Grier's big voice calling her name at the driver; then saw the horses dip suddenly onto the steep down grade and the coach yank over after them. One instant the lantern was there, flying like a comet gone loco, and the next it had winked out. There was a long screeching and wailing of brakes which echoed so I couldn't tell which was brakes and which echo.

Blue Boy was still trying to bolt with the others following the coach, but for some reason I was pulling him. On the edge of the pitch-over I got him stopped. Then I just sat there. I was hanging onto the saddlehorn, and my stomach was sick and I was trembling all over. It wasn't until I reached up and felt of my shoulder because it was hot and tickling, and found my shirt wet, and that it slipped greasily on my flesh, that it got through to me that I'd been shot. The guard had meant to get Winder, but he'd got me behind him. I understood then, with shame, that I'd done the moaning too.

I wondered how bad it was, and started to get down, but couldn't. After trying, I started making a silly little chattering, whining noise, which I couldn't stop. I thought, by God, if he's killed me, what a fool way to die; what a damn fool way to die!

The driver had got the coach stopped at the foot of the first pitch; I don't know how. It was standing on the level-off just before the first turn, which would have put it into the creek. The lantern settling made a big shadow of the coach moving back and forth slowly on the wall of the gorge. The driver was leaning out to look back, and the guard was standing up beside him, watching, over the baggage on the roof, the riders come down in the dark and spit of snow. He wasn't sure yet, and was holding the carbine ready in both hands. Most of the riders passed me and went down to the coach. Those that didn't want to delay any longer hesitated, but then slowly went down too. I felt like crying when they all left me. It was the jolt, I suppose; it hadn't begun to hurt yet, but I felt shaken to pieces, like I'd been hit by a big rock instead of pierced by a little slug. I heard Tetley asking who'd been hit, but couldn't seem to tell him. I wanted to wait until I was steadier before I tried talking. I was holding onto my shoulder with some idea of stopping the bleeding, but I could tell by the warm tickle down my ribs that I didn't have it stopped.

One rider passed me, but turned in the saddle and peered at me, then pulled around and came back. It was Gil.

"That you, Art?" he asked, still peering.

"I guess so," I said, trying to pass it off.

He came alongside, but facing me. "What's the matter?" I told him.

"Where?" he asked.

"In the shoulder, I think; in the left shoulder." It seemed important to me that he knew it was the left shoulder.

"Lemme see," he said.

"Hell," he said after a moment, "can't tell a thing here. How do you feel?"

"All right."

"Can you make it down to the coach? We can see something there."

When we started down he steadied me in the saddle, but I was already a lot clearer. The shoulder was beginning to hurt, so the dizziness was gone and I didn't feel so much like throwing up. I told him I could make it.

There was a lot of talk around the coach. The driver, who was white, and still trembling in the knees from his close call and standing on the brakes, was hanging onto the edge of the seat and repeating, "I thought it was a stickup. God, there was a lot of you. I thought it was a stickup." He was Alec Small, a little, thin, blond man with a droopy mustache, a nice fellow, but not tough, and not the driver Winder was. Winder was bawling him out and telling him he was lucky by turns, and looking at the horses' ankles between curses. The horses were trembling and restless; they kept turning their heads toward the drop-off and wanting to sidle into the cliff. Gabe was getting down to quiet them. Small didn't seem to hear Winder. He was drunk, and the mob dazed him.

I knew the guard too, Jimmy Carnes, a big, black-bearded man with a slouch hat and a leather coat. He'd been a government hunter for the army and then for the railroad while it was building. It had been a good thing for Winder, if not for me, that it was dark and the coach rocking.

Carnes was saying, "I hope I didn't get him too bad."

"Get who?" Ma asked him.

"I got somebody," he said. "I heard him yell. You know," he went on, "you hadn't ought to have come barging out like that, in the dark especially. It's only lucky if I haven't killed somebody. You hadn't ought to have come barging out like that." He shook his head heavily. He'd been drinking too, and was thick, and his face was worried. "I was pretty near asleep when Alec yelled at me," he said. "I couldn't see who you was, and everybody yelling.

"I didn't kill anybody, did I?" he asked.

Now Winder was wanting to know what the hell the stage was doing on the pass at night anyway. For a minute Gil and I couldn't get through the press; I didn't care if we got through; I felt far away, like watching a picture. Gil was getting angry though, and trying to be heard and to push a way to the light.

The passengers were getting out while everybody watched them. They were two women and a man, and they'd been thrown around, by their looks. Their stylish clothes were askew, and the ladies, after they got down shakily, were trying to straighten themselves without being too obvious about it. They looked around haughtily. They'd been well scared. The man was young, tall and thin, and had red mutton-chop whiskers, and was elegant in the way young Tetley might have been if he had noticed things more. He was laughingly accepting it all as a joke, although his beaver was badly bent. This made the men around them grin too.

When the shorter woman turned around I saw she was Rose Mapen. You could understand why young Tetley was so hot about the hens running her out, and why Gil had talked about her all winter like a boy about his first love. She had dark hair showing out from under her bonnet, which was lacy, a broad-cheeked face with big, dark eyes and a big, full-shaped mouth that was beginning to smile inclusively, and yet personally. She had big, full but firm breasts too, and a round-limbed, strong, fiery figure. Her dress was cut as far down between her breasts as she dared. When she recognized some of the riders she began to charm them at once; it was a habit with her. Right then I wasn't much interested, but I could see how I might have been. Her manner wasn't that of handing out cheap promises though. Nobody but a drunk or a jealous woman would take it for that.

Or a jealous man. When Gil saw her he stopped shoving and sat still on his horse. The man with the red whiskers was holding Rose's elbow to show she was his property. Winder stopped chewing, and we could hear Rose's voice too, a voice such as I thought Ma Grier's must have been once. She was introducing the man to Tetley and Gerald and Davies, and to the rest of us in the pack, as Mr. Swanson of San Francisco, and her husband. Tetley managed a compliment to Swanson and a joke about Rose being in such a hurry to show the women what could be done, all in one. Even Tetley was willing to be delayed further to have a look at Rose and hear her talk. She laughed at his joke, but I don't think it was altogether funny to her; she bridled with an air of purpose. Davies was pleased by her too, and congratulated her and shook hands with Swanson, but chiefly he was watching the men. They were all congratulating Rose too, some, who couldn't get closer, calling out to her, and only Smith was a little bit ribald, asking Swanson had they only been married that day that he was still able to get around. The others went no farther than saying to Rose they thought it was mean of her to do it secretly and where they couldn't interfere, and telling Swanson he could thank his stars it was all done and beyond help before he came to Bridger's Wells. They were all cheerful and lively seeming, as men always

127

were with Rose, but some of them had moments of being a bit stiff too. They were embarrassed at this pleasantry when they thought of the job they were supposed to be on. They didn't know what to say when Rose asked them back to Canby's to have a celebration for the Swansons. They looked at Tetley or at Davies, and just grinned. It was a temptation, in their doubt and on such a night. Only young Tetley didn't offer any congratulations or even smile, but stared at her with big serious eyes and kept swallowing as if about to say something. Rose tried to ignore him to keep cheerful. She was curious about what we were doing up there at night too, but didn't ask, and nobody wanted to tell her.

The other woman was introduced too, but nobody paid any attention to her after the first polite murmur and hat-lifting. She was Swanson's sister, a tall thin woman, older than he was I thought, dressed in dark silk with a cape around her shoulders. Her face was long and thin too, with heavy lines under the eyes, hollow cheeks, and heavy, unhappy grooves down from her mouth. In the lantern-light her complexion was powdery white. She stood there while they talked, playing with the coach door with one hand and looking from face to face, quickly and nervously, as the men spoke, yet not as if she really expected them to do anything. She wanted to get back into the coach and be sheltered from the spit of snow and all the unknown faces.

Then Gil recovered enough to stop glaring at Rose and her red-whiskered man. There was no change of expression on his battered face, but I could tell he was furious. He shouldered his horse through to the lantern without even making a sign to the men, and I followed him. None of the men said anything though; they thought he was going to make trouble about Rose. Tetley must have thought so too, for he stopped talking to Rose and Swanson and watched Gil, and didn't understand him for a minute when he said, "Art's shot. Carnes got him in the shoulder."

But Davies understood right away, and helped me down, telling Gil to get a trunk from the coach for me to sit on. Gil did this without saying anything to Rose or even looking at her, though he passed right in front of her. If he hadn't been too busy about what he was doing, you

128

couldn't have told he knew she was there. Rose watched him, though, and stopped smiling, expecting him to speak. When he didn't she began to smile again at once, and was all worried over what had happened to me. I didn't notice her. Rose and I had never got on, and I wasn't going to help her out now. Swanson noticed this act. He studied Gil while Gil was getting the trunk down, and then looked at Rose and then at Gil again. He was still smiling, but not the same way. I'd figured him for a weak sister at first, something Rose had got hold of because she could handle it, but now I wasn't so sure.

I sat down on the trunk, and Sparks brought the lantern over and held it while Davies began to take my shirt off, being too gentle where it was beginning to stick.

"It's nothing," I told him.

"Do the women have to watch this?" I asked him. I was going to feel sick again, and it made me angry, with everybody watching.

The women offered to help, Rose saying she was good at that sort of thing. I told Davies I didn't want their help, and Rose stopped smiling and encouraging me. She and Gil looked at each other for the first time, and Gil grinned. Rose turned around quickly and got into the coach. Swanson also stopped smiling and stared at Gil at the same time he helped his sister into the coach with Rose. Gil was standing with his legs apart and his thumbs hooked in his gun belt, which was a bad sign. He stared back at Swanson and continued to grin the way he had at Rose. It wouldn't take much to set him off, but when Swanson closed the coach door he leaned in the window and talked to Rose for a moment, and nothing happened.

Carnes climbed down from the box, and came over with that worried look on his face, and kept asking me in his thick voice if I was all right, and telling me that he hadn't meant to get me, that he was sorry, that he was sure sorry it had happened, until I was tired of assuring him, while Davies was picking at the wound, that it was all right and how could he tell who we were. The picking around the edge of the wound made me faint, and I didn't think I could stand much more of Carnes' apology. Gil finally saw how it was, and told Carnes to

129

shut up. Again I thought there'd be a scrap, but Carnes was really feeling so guilty he did shut up, looking as if he were going to cry.

I'd spilled quite a lot of blood already. That side of my jeans, under the chaps, was soaked with it too. But the wound itself wasn't so much. The bullet had just gone through the flesh of my chest, and ripped on out at the back, lower down, Davies told me. He thought maybe it had nicked a rib, but nothing much more. He pressed me along the side to see if it had nicked the rib, and it hurt all right, but I couldn't be sure. Davies was careful, but too slow. I had to go out to the edge of the road and throw up, with Gil holding onto me. Then Moore gave me a stiff drink, and another when Davies was done picking the threads of shirt out of the hole, and I felt strong enough, just light-headed. All that bothered me was that I continued to tremble all over, as if I had a chill or was all nerves, but Davies said that was probably just from the impact; that it would take a long time for the shock to wear off from being hit from a heavy rifle that way. He washed the wound clean with whisky, but told me they'd have to fire it to prevent infection. They took the lantern into the coach to get it out of the wind, and slowly heated a pistol barrel red hot in the flame. Then Gil and Moore held me down while the wound was burned. I got through the front side well enough, just holding my breath and sweating, but on the back I passed out.

When I next knew where I was Davies had me bandaged up tightly with strips of somebody's shirt, my sheepskin was on me again, and Moore was trying to pour another drink into me. I felt shaky and empty, but angry too, because so many people had watched me pass out.

The men pretended they hadn't seen any weakness; they were going about their business, remounting and forming above the coach. Gil lit me a cigarette, and when I looked at the men forming and then at him, he nodded. I felt weak, all washed out, and it was snowing harder than before, a thin cover of snow showing on the ground in the light around the circular shadow of the bottom of the lantern. I wasn't interested any longer, not either way; the voices talking were like those of people in another room, heard through the wall. They didn't concern me. But when Davies told me that "the fools still meant to go on," but there was room for me in the coach, and I'd better go back and rest at Canby's and get some hot food and get out of the wind, I told him hell no, there was nothing the matter with me. He argued a little, and Ma came and joked at me but helped him argue, and I got to feeling stubborn and just sat there smoking my cigarette and saying no, and finally just smoking. When I had to stand up so they could put the trunk back on the coach, Rose got out and came over and took hold of my elbow and tried to charm me into going down with them. Somehow I could tell from her talk that she knew what we were doing now. That only made me all the surer; I didn't want to ride down with her and the spinster sister and red-whiskers all interested and pumping me about it. I liked her hand holding me affectionately by the arm as if I were an old, dear friend she was worried about, but even so it only made me more stubborn, because I knew she didn't mean it. Then Winder came and told me not to be a damned fool, to get in the coach and go on home, where I wouldn't be in the way. Gil told Winder to mind his own business, that he'd look after me himself if I needed any looking after. Winder turned his head slowly and stared at Gil like he couldn't believe he'd heard anyone speak to him that way, but Rose broke it up this time by letting go of my arm and telling Winder to let the idiot, meaning me, go ahead and act like an idiot if he wanted to, it was none of their funeral. That made Gil grin at her again. She stared at him for an instant too, but thought better of what she was going to say, and turned her back on him and got back into the coach with a flourish of her skirts. She slammed the door after her, although her husband wasn't in. He'd been standing by the back wheel of the coach all this time, once in a while brushing the snow from his front, and talking with Tetley, Small and Carnes. Again he hadn't missed anything. He took his part in the talk, so quietly I couldn't hear him, but he watched Gil all the time, very steadily. He didn't even stop watching Gil when Rose slammed into the coach, but kept looking at him like he wanted to remember everything about him.

Out of the corner of my mouth I told Gil, "Red-whiskers is measuring you for a coffin, my friend."

131

Gil looked at Swanson, and then returned his stare, grinning. "Yeah?" he said to me, and then, still staring at Swanson, "What have I said? I didn't say anything."

"That's his wife, now," I reminded him, "and kind of new."

"It does look that way, don't it?" Gil said, as if it didn't. He said it too loudly, and from the way Swanson stared more intently for just a moment, I thought he'd heard. But then he turned away from Gil and looked at Tetley again, answering a question of Tetley's. Gil relaxed, his little grin changing so it meant he knew he'd won.

Swanson and Carnes and Small had been telling Tetley about some men they'd seen, four, Carnes and Swanson thought, but Small thought three, who had a fire in the mouth of a ravine five miles the other side of the summit. They had seen horses, but no cattle, but Swanson said the ravine was so black they couldn't have told past the fire. Small said, if there'd been any cattle, there couldn't have been many. He knew the ravine, used the mouth of it as a turn-out to rest his horses, and it was too small. No, he was sure they couldn't have got forty head in there; not even ten or fifteen without their showing. Yes, he was sure about the place. He'd had it in his mind to stop there to breathe the horses, but the men were so quiet he hadn't liked it; he'd changed his mind and gone right by and breathed the team at Indian Springs, farther up.

Swanson agreed that the men had not seemed friendly. They'd stood up when the coach came by, and when Alex had hailed them they hadn't said anything, and only one of them had raised a hand. He was sure there'd been a fourth man, just beyond the firelight, and that he'd stood up too. Alec admitted he might have missed him; he'd been busy with the team, to keep them from turning in there, where they expected to. No, neither Small nor Carnes had recognized any of the men. Carnes thought they'd kept their faces out of the light on purpose. He thought also that all the men except the one who had raised his hand had been ready to draw, but Carnes must have been drunk then, and now his imagination was working from the story about Kinkaid. Swanson didn't think they were going to draw; he merely thought they were very watchful and too quiet. But yes, he agreed with Carnes and

132

Small that the men were wearing guns. He couldn't be sure whether the men were really camped for the night. Carnes said they weren't. The fire, he said, was a small one, and the horses weren't hobbled or tethered, but just standing at one side of the fire with their bridles trailing and the saddles still on. When Tetley asked him, Small repeated exactly where the place was and what you came to before you got there. He tried to remember just what marks you could still tell by in the snow, and then Winder, who had joined them, told Tetley he knew the place, and could warn them long enough before they got there, even if the fire was out. There were marks you couldn't miss, he said, and mentioned trees and boulders, and the shape of the road, and Tetley was satisfied.

He thanked Swanson, as if Swanson had told him everything and the other two hadn't even been along. He told Swanson that he and the sheriff were very grateful that Swanson had been so observant, that it let them know more clearly what to expect; they could figure on four men, armed and wary. I looked at Gil and Gil looked at me and grinned just a little. It tickled us, in an ornery way, that even Tetley didn't like the idea of Swanson knowing that this was a lynching party instead of a posse. Then Tetley complimented Swanson again on his fortune in wedding, and hoped he might have the pleasure of entertaining Swanson and his bride and his sister in his own poor way, if they were going to be in Bridger's Wells for a while. From all the anxiety Tetley let show you'd have thought they were two men passing the time of day in a hotel lobby, with nothing coming up but a good night's sleep. Then Tetley turned toward his horse, and Winder with him, and Carnes and Small climbed up onto the high seat.

Gil was just going to help me into the saddle when there was Swanson standing in front of us. It surprised us, and Gil let go of me quickly to get his hands free. It made him sore that he had been surprised into moving quickly.

Swanson smiled a little. He spoke very politely and quietly. "I take it," he said, "that yours was the privilege of knowing Miss Mapen before she became my wife?"

"Yeah," Gil said slowly, "that's right."

"And that possibly you imagined, at the time, that there was something between you?"

"I didn't have to imagine it," Gil said.

"No?" Swanson asked him. "Possibly not," he continued. "My wife is a very impulsive woman, given naturally to regarding everyone as a friend."

He stopped and looked at Gil, still smiling. Gil didn't say anything. He was slow in understanding what to make of that kind of talk.

"Needless to say," Swanson went on, "I am pleased to regard any friend of my wife as a friend of my own." He smiled at Gil, but didn't offer his hand. Gil still just looked at him.

"However," Swanson said, "I needn't remind you, of course, that the pleasure of such an acquaintance depends somewhat upon the recognition by all parties of the fact that Miss Mapen is now my wife. She must be given a little time," he continued, "to become accustomed to her new responsibilities. As yet, I must confess, I am peculiarly jealous of even her least attentions. You will forgive me, I know. A bridegroom is prone to be overly susceptible for a time.

"Later," he concluded, "when we have had time to become accustomed to our new relations, I will be most anxious, if it is still my wife's desire, to welcome you, and others of my wife's friends, at our home in San Francisco.

"Until then," he nodded pleasantly, still smiling, turned around, walked to the coach, got in, and closed the door quietly. He relighted the lamp inside the coach, and as it started on down we could see him sitting beside Rose. She had her hands joined through his arm and was smiling up at him, but he wasn't smiling any more.

Gil had it all straight by then. "The damned superior son-of-a-bitch," he said softly, looking after the coach. He'd never got a taking down like that in his life before.

He mounted silently, but turned his horse to look after the coach again. I got up too, making more fuss than I had to, so he'd help me. Then I said, "It looks to me like Rose had caught herself a load of trouble."

We started up after the others, just feeling the snow in the dark again.

"Yeah?" Gil said. "Maybe she ain't the only one. Rose is no stable filly."

I didn't answer. I was glad enough we'd come out of it without any more trouble than the talk. We were up in the clearing again before Gil said, "If that bastard's got her all roped and tied the way he talks, what are they doing up here at all? I'll bet a dollar to a doughnut hole that wasn't his idea."

"Forget it," I told him.

"Sure, for now," he said.

Then he said, "If you get to feelin' it, fellow, sound off. This still ain't any of our picnic."

"I will."

"I should have made you go down in the coach," he apologized later, "but with all of them raggin' you, I didn't think."

I told him I was all right. In a way I was, too. The whisky was working good, like I had all the blood back, and somehow being hit like that, now that I was patched up, made me feel like I had a stake in the business.

We rode across the clearing and under the trees on the other side. The snow was right in our faces, and we couldn't tell where we were farther than the rumps of the horses ahead. We went slowly, but even so the procession kept stopping while Tetley and Mapes made sure we were still on the road, and nearly every time we stopped, Blue Boy rammed his nose on the horse ahead and brought up short, throwing his head. My shoulder would jerk then, and finally I got to swearing softly. Just sitting there in the dark, with nothing else to think about, I began to feel that shoulder. It felt hard and drawn together, like it was crusted, and would tear if I moved it. They'd put my shirt back on me too, and it was stiff and scratchy down that side where the blood had dried in it. Twice I had a drink from my canteen to keep my head from getting light. But my head got even lighter, and, besides, it was so much work trying to twist around and get the canteen that I quit that too. Between the whisky and the pain I must have been getting dopey, because at first I didn't hear Gil trying to say something to me. Then the wind was so strong and muffled with snow that I had to ask him twice what he'd said before he heard me.

"I said that damned Small and his free-shootin' friend Carnes were drunk." They were generally a little drunk, and I said so.

"Well," Gil said, "they oughtn'ta be drivin' when they're like that. Winder oughta know better'n to let them on like

135

that." Then I lost a few words in the wind. Then he was saying, "Can you imagine any guy damned fool enough to start down that grade like that? He didn't know where he was, that's all. He just got scared and saw an open place and let drive. He couldn't have known where he was, to drive like that. If his horses hadn't been a sight smarter than he was, that coach would be all piled up at the bottom of the creek right now, and everybody in it with a broken neck."

"What do you care?" I asked him. "There's nobody there makes any difference to you now, is there?" I didn't like being drawn out of my shell just when I was beginning to forget myself.

"Not a damned bit," he said. And then, "Let her go ahead and break her neck. It's none of my worry. What was she in such a hell of a hurry to get back up here for, anyway? Wouldn't her delicate friend keep overnight?"

"All right," I agreed, "let her break her neck. That's what I say too."

I knew that would make him sore, but it would shut him up about Rose Mapen too.

We rode some distance then without any halt, the trees being even on the two sides so the road was plain. Then there came another, and I knew I'd nearly fallen asleep. I felt unreal and scared. Ahead, men were exclaiming about something in low voices. I saw what they were talking about. To the right, far through the trees through the snow, was a fire burning. It looked very small, and sometimes disappeared when the trees moved in the wind. Then I realized we were at the end of the Ox-Bow valley, and that the fire must be way out toward the center. I judged that when it disappeared it must have been flattening in the wind, and then I decided it was partially concealed by the cabin, and we only saw it when it blew back. But it must have been a big fire at that, because even when it was out of sight I thought I could see a kind of halo of light from around it, like the moon through the thin edges of clouds. It was easy, though, to see how the men on the stage missed it. Having our minds set on those men in the gully on the down-grade, we didn't know quite what to make of it. Then, with a turn of the wind, we heard a steer bellowing. You couldn't trust it, of course. Nobody said anything, or moved, and we heard it a second time.

Word came back along the line that we were turning down into the valley, and then to bunch up for last orders. I recovered the sensation that our business was real, instead of everybody being crazy and just wandering in the mountains. Previously, in my dozing, I'd been remembering a story I'd heard once about the Flying Dutchman, and wondering vaguely if that was the way we were getting. It made a fine picture, twenty-eight riders you could see through on twenty-six horses and two mules nothing but bones, riding around forever through snowstorms in the mountains, looking for three dead rustlers they had to find before their souls could be at peace.

We had passed the turn-off into the valley, and had to slide and scramble down a bank. Even in the wind you could hear the horses snort about it, and the slap of leather and the jangle of jerked bits. They didn't like it in the dark. By the time I got to the slide it was a long black streak torn down through the snow. Blue Boy smelled the rim, tossed his head two or three times, and pitched over. He descended scraping and stiff-legged, like a dog sitting down, and the wrenching made me sick to my stomach again.

When we were grouped among the cottonwoods in the hollow, Tetley gave us our marching orders. We were underneath the wind, and he didn't have to talk very loudly. First he said maybe the stage men had been mistaken, that this was a better place for men with cattle to hide, and that anyway it was our job to make sure before we went on. He cautioned us about playing safe, and against any shooting or rough work until we were sure.

"They must have an opportunity to tell it their way," he said. "Mapes and I will do the talking, and if there's any shooting to do I'll tell you. The rest of you hold your fire unless they try to break through you. We'll divide to close in on them.

"Where is Croft?" he asked.

"Here," I said.

"How do you feel, Croft?" he asked.

"I'm all right."

"Good. But you stay with my group. We'll go the most direct way."

Farnley said, "The son-of-a-bitch that got Kinkaid is mine, Tetley. Don't forget that."

137

"He's yours when we're sure," Tetley told him.

"Well, don't forget, that's all."

"I won't forget," was all Tetley said, and that quietly.

Then, like an officer enjoying mapping out a battle plan that pleases him because the surprise element is with him, he directed our attack. But I noticed he put Farnley in his own group, and his son Gerald too. He picked Bartlett and Winder and Ma Grier to lead on the other three sides, and divided the rest among the four parties. Winder's party was to work around through the woods and come down back of the cabin, Bartlett's to circle clear around and come in by the far side, Ma Grier's to come up from the valley side. They were to fan out so they'd contact by the time they got close to the firelight and make a closed circle. He didn't say so, but you could tell by his care that he thought either the rustlers trusted too much to the snow to stop us, or there were a lot more than three of them; others waiting up here maybe, to support them and hurry the branding.

"They're least likely to break for the valley or the side away from this," he continued. "The unarmed men, then, unless they'd rather wait here, had best go, one with Mr. Bartlett and one with Mrs. Grier."

"Give them guns," Winder said; "lots of us have a couple."

"Will you take a gun, Davies?" Tetley asked.

Davies answered from the other side of him, "No, thanks. I'll go with the Bartletts."

"Just as you choose," Tetley said. His voice was even, but the scorn was there.

"Sparks?" he asked.

"No, suh, Cun'l Tetley, thank you jus' the same."

"With Mrs. Grier, then."

"Yessuh."

"Keep your eyes and ears open," Tetley warned us. "They may have pickets out. And if you come on the cattle ride easy, don't disturb them.

"If any party does spring a picket," he added, "and he gets away, shoot into the air once. All of you, if you hear the shot close in as quickly as you can, but keep spread."

"This is no battle, you know," Farnley said. "We're after three rustlers, not an army."

"We don't know what we're after until we see. Unnecessary risk is simply foolish," Tetley told him, still evenly.

"And don't fire," he told the rest of us, "unless they fire first, except if they should break through. Then stop them any way you have to. The quicker and cleaner this job is, the less chance we'll have anything to regret. A surprise is what we want, and no shooting if we can help it.

"All clear?" he asked, like he was getting ready to roll up the maps again.

We said it was.

"All right," Tetley said, "my group will wait here until we judge the rest of you have had time to move into position.

"Good luck, boys," he said.

Winder and his outfit started off, working single file into the woods. In a moment you couldn't tell which was riders and which trees. The snow blurred everything, and blotted up sound too, into a thick, velvety quiet. Ma Grier and Bartlett led off at an angle toward the valley. They were heading for the shallows of the creek, where there weren't any banks but an easy incline, a cross gully worn by sheep and cattle going down to drink. I'd seen deer drinking there too, but only in the early spring, and then warily. It would take time to find that crossing in this kind of a night.

Gil came alongside me.

"How you feeling now, fellow?" he asked.

"Good," I said.

"Take care of yourself," he said. "This still don't have to be our picnic."

"It looks like it was," I said.

"Yeah," he agreed, "but it ain't."

He went away from me, stepping his pinto a little long to catch up with his gang.

The rest of us, in Tetley's outfit, didn't talk much. There was nothing to do but wait, and none of the arguing ones were left with us. Only Mapes tried a little of his cottoning-up, he-man talk on Tetley, but since Tetley didn't want to talk, that stopped too. We weren't a friendly gang anyway; no real friends in the lot. Tetley, I thought, was short with Mapes because he was trying to count in his mind, or some such system, to keep track of the time. Through the trees we watched the fire out by the cabin. Once it began to die down, and then a shadow went across it, and back across, and the fire darkened and flattened completely. At first we thought they had wind of us, but the fire gradually grew up again, brighter than ever. It was just somebody throwing more wood on.

The snowing relaxed for a spell, then started again with a fresh wind that whirled it around us for a minute or two, even in the woods, and veiled the fire, probably with snow scudding up from the open meadow. Then the wind died off and the snow was steady and slanting again, but thinner. It didn't feel any longer as if it might be a real blizzard. The branches rattled around us when the wind blew. Being in the marshy end of the valley they weren't pines, but aspens, and willow grown up as big as trees. When the horses stirred, the ground squelched under them, and you could see the dark shadow of water soaking up around their hoofs through the snow. In places, though, the slush was already getting icy, and split when it was stepped on.

Several times we heard the steers sounding off again, hollow in the wind, and sounding more distant than they could have been.

After a time Tetley led us out to the edge of the aspens to where the wind was directly on us again. We waited there, peering into the snow blowing in the valley, and the dark gulf of the valley itself, but unable to see the other riders, of course, or anything but the fire. It felt to me as if it must be one o'clock at least, but I learned early that I couldn't tell within four hours on a cloudy night unless I was doing some work I did every night, like riding herd in the same valley.

Finally Tetley said, as if he had been holding a watch

141

before him all the time, and had predetermined the exact moment to start, "All right, let's go."

As we started Mapes asked, "Want us to spread out now?"

"No, we'll ride in on them in a bunch, unless they get wind of us. If the fire goes out, or there's any shooting, then spread and work toward the fire. In that case, you on the wings, don't tangle with Mrs. Grier or Winder."

So we went out in a group, plowing a wide track through the half-frozen sponginess. Tetley and Farnley and Mapes rode abreast ahead. They didn't any of them want another to get there ahead of him. Young Tetley and I came behind them, and there were two other riders following us. We all watched toward the fire steadily.

But even when we came much closer there was nothing to see but the fire, beginning to die again, and the little its light revealed of the cabin wall and the trunks of the closest pines on the other side. I got to wondering if they had built the fire up as a blind and had already run out on us, or even were lying up somewhere ready to pick us off. My head came clear again and I didn't even notice my shoulder. Only the snow annoyed me, though it was falling light and far spaced now. It made me feel that my eyes were no good. The four of us in back kept watching out to the sides, feeling that we didn't have our side of the square covered, but the three in front continued abreast and seeming to watch only the fire and the clearing right around it, though I could tell by the way they sat that they were as wide awake as we were.

When we began to climb the little rise the cabin was on, I could see the three silhouetted clearly against the fire. Mapes reached under his arm pit and got a gun out into his hand. Farnley's carbine moved across his saddle, and I thought I heard the hammer click. Tetley, though, just rode right ahead.

I reached my gun out too. There was a twinge in the injured shoulder when I raised the right one, and I didn't want to have to make a fast draw and get sick and dizzy as I had riding down the pitch. My head was clear, all right; I thought of every little thing like that. And my senses were up keen too. Without even looking around I could tell how the men behind me were getting set. I was excited, and peculiarly happy. It seemed to me that if the rustlers were concealed I could pick the trees they'd gone behind. Only young Tetley was wrong. I risked a look, and we were so close to the fire I could see his face. He was staring ahead, but blindly, and he wasn't getting any gun out. Now I can see that he was perhaps still having a struggle with himself that he was here at all, but then it just angered me that one of us failed to be alert; then it just seemed to me that he was too scared to know what to do, and I got furious at him for a moment, the way you will when you think another man's carelessness is risking your neck. I pulled over and jogged him, though jogging him wrenched my shoulder so my breath whistled. He turned his head and looked at me, and I could see he wasn't blanked out. He was awake, all right, but he still didn't look any better.

We were really into the edge of the firelight before Tetley stopped us. I had my mind made up they were laying for us, so what I saw surprised me. Between Tetley and Mapes I could see a man asleep on the ground in a blanket with a big pattern on it. His head was on his saddle and toward the fire, so his face was in the shadow, but when we looked at him he drew an arm up out of his blanket and laid it across his eyes. He had on an orange shirt and the hand and wrist lifted into the light were as dark as an old saddle. Not Indian, either; at least not thick and stubby like the hands of Washoes and Piutes I'd seen, but long and narrow and with prominent knuckles. We were so close that I could see on his middle finger a heavy silver ring with an egg-shaped turquoise, a big one, in it; a Navajo ring. By the bulk of him he was a big man, and heavy.

There were two other men asleep also, one with his side to the fire and his head away from me, the other on the far side with his feet to the fire. I couldn't make out anything but their shapes and that they had dark bluish-gray blankets with a black stripe near each end, the kind of blankets the Union had used during the rebellion.

I guess Tetley figured as I did, that they were strangers, at least, if nothing else, because he only waited long enough to be sure they were not playing possum, and then rode into the light, and right up to the feet of the man with the ring. We followed him, spreading around that

143

edge of the fire as he motioned us to. After looking down at the man for a moment he said sharply and loudly, "Get up."

The other two stirred in their blankets, and began to settle again, but the man with the ring woke immediately and completely, and when he saw us said something short to himself and twisted up out of his blanket in one continuous, smooth movement, trailing one hand into the blanket as he came up.

"Drop it," Farnley ordered. He was holding the carbine at his thigh, the muzzle pointing at the man. The man had heavy black hair and a small black mustache. He looked like a Mex, though his hair was done up in a club at his neck, like an Indian's, and his face was wide, with high, flat cheeks. He looked to me like a Mex playing Navajo.

He looked quickly but not nervously around at all of us, sizing us up, but didn't move the hand which had come up behind him.

"I said drop it," Farnley told him again, and nudged the carbine out toward him, so he wouldn't make any mistake about what was meant.

The Mex suddenly smiled, as if he had just understood, and dropped a long-barreled, nickel-plated revolver behind him onto the blanket. He was an old hand, and still thinking.

"Now put 'em up," Farnley told him.

The smile died off the Mex's face, and he just stared at Farnley and shrugged his shoulders.

"Put 'em up; reach, you bastard."

The Mex shrugged his shoulders again. "No sabbey," he said.

Farnley grinned now. "No?" he asked. "I said reach," he repeated, and jerked the muzzle of the carbine upward two or three times. The Mex got that, and put his hands up slowly. He was studying Farnley's face all the time.

"That's better," Farnley said, still grinning, "though some ways I'd just as soon you hadn't, you son-of-a-bitch." He was talking as quietly as Tetley usually did, though not so easily. He seemed to be enjoying calling the man a name he couldn't understand, and doing it in a voice like he was making an ordinary remark.

"No sabbey," the Mex said again.

"That's all right, brother," Farnley told him, "you will."

The other two were coming out of their sleep. I was covering the one on the cabin side, and Mapes the other. Mapes' man just sat up, still in his blanket. He was still fumed with sleep; a thick, wide-faced old-timer with long, tangled gray hair and a long, droopy gray mustache. He had eyebrows so thick they made peaked shadows on his forehead. The way he was staring now he didn't appear to be all there.

My man rose quickly enough, though tangling a little with his blanket. He started to come toward us, and I saw he'd been sleeping with his gun on and his boots off.

"Take it easy, friend," I told him. "Stay where you are and put your hands up."

He didn't understand, but stared at me, and then at Tetley, and then back at me. He didn't reach for his gun, didn't even twitch for it, and his face looked scared.

"Put your hands up," I told him again. He did, looking as if he wanted to cry.

"And keep them there."

The old man was out of his blanket now too, and standing with his hands raised.

"Gerald, collect their guns," Tetley said.

"What are you trying to do? What do you want? We haven't got anything." It was my man babbling, half out of breath. He was a tall, thin, dark young fellow, with thick black hair, but no Indian or Mex.

"Shut up," Mapes instructed him. "We'll tell you when we want you to talk."

"This is no stickup, brother," I explained to him. "This is a posse, if that means anything to you."

"But we haven't done anything," he protested. "What have we done?" He wasn't over his first fright yet.

"Shut up," Mapes said, with more emphasis.

Young Tetley was sitting in his saddle, staring at the three men.

"Gerry," Tetley said, in that pistol-shot voice he'd used to wake the men.

The boy dismounted dreamily and picked up the Mex's gun from the blanket. Then, like a sleepwalker, he came over to my man.

"Behind him," said Tetley sharply.

The boy stopped and looked around. "What?" he asked.

"Wake up," Tetley ordered. "I said go behind him. Don't get between him and Croft."

"Yes," Gerald said, and did what he was told. He fumbled around a long time before he found the old man's gun, which was under his saddle.

"Give the guns to Mark," Tetley ordered, jerking his head at one of the two riders I didn't know. Gerald did that, handing them up in a bunch, belts, holsters and all.

It made me ashamed the way Tetley was bossing the kid's every move, like a mother making a three-year-old do something over that he'd messed up the first try.

"Now," he said, "go over them all, from the rear. Then shake out the blankets."

Gerald did as he was told, but he seemed to be waking a little now. His jaw was tight. He found another gun on the Mex, a little pistol like the gamblers carry. It was in an arm-sling under his vest. There was a carbine under the young fellow's blanket. He shrank from patting the men over, the way he was told to, and when he passed me to give Mark the carbine and pistol, I could hear him breathing hard.

Tetley watched Gerald, but spoke to my prisoner while he was working.

"Are there any more of you?"

The young fellow was steadier. He looked angry now, and started to let his arms down, asking, "May I inquire what business . . ."

"Shut up," Mapes said, "and keep them up."

"It's all right now, Mapes," Tetley said. "You can put your hands down now," he said to the young man. "I asked you, are there any others with you?"

"No," the kid said.

I didn't think the kid was lying. Tetley looked at him hard, but I guess he thought it was all right too. He turned his head toward Mark and the other rider I didn't know.

"Tie their hands," he ordered.

The young fellow started to come forward again.

"Stay where you are," Tetley told him quietly, and he stopped. He had a wide, thick-lipped mouth that was

146

nonetheless as sensitive as young Tetley's thin one, and now it was tight down in the corners. Even so you would have said that mouth was beautiful on some women, Rose Mapen for instance, the fiery or promising kind. And his eyes were big and dark in his thin face, like a girl's too. His hands were long and bony and nervous, but hung on big, square wrists.

He spoke in a husky voice. "I trust that at least you'll condescend to tell us what we're being held for."

Mapes was still busy being an authority. "Save your talk till it's asked for," he advised.

Tetley, though, studied the young man all during the time the two punchers were tying the prisoners on one lass rope and pushing them over to the side of the fire away from the cabin. He looked at them still when they were standing there, shoulder to shoulder, the Mex in the middle, their faces to the fire and their backs to the woods and the little snow that was still falling. It was as if he believed he could solve the whole question of their guilt or innocence by just looking at them and thinking his own thoughts; the occupation pleased him. The Mex was stoli now, the old man remained blank, but the kid was humiliated and angry at being tied. He repeated his question in a manner that didn't go well with the spot he was in.

Then Tetley told him, "I'd rather you told us," and smiled that way.

After that he signaled to the parties in the dark in the woods and behind the cabin, dismounted, giving the bridle to his son, and walked over to the fire, where he stood with his legs apart and held out his hands to warm them, rubbing them together. He might have been in front of his own fireplace. Without looking around he ordered more wood put on the fire. All the time he continued to look across the fire at the three men in a row, and continued to smile.

We were all on foot now, walking stiff-legged from sitting the saddle so long in the cold. I got myself a place to sit near the fire, and watched the Mex. He had his chin down on his chest, like he was both guilty and licked, but he was watching everything from under his eyebrows. He looked smart and hard. I'd have guessed he was about thirty, though it was hard to tell, the way it is with an Indian. The lines around his mouth and at the corners of his eyes and across his forehead were deep and exact, as if they were cut in dark wood with a knife. His skin shone in the firelight. There was no expression on his face, but I knew he was still thinking how to get out. Then all at once his face changed, though you couldn't have said what the change was in any part of it. I guess in spite of his watchfulness he'd missed Tetley's signal, and now he saw Ma and her gang coming up behind us. He looked around quickly, and when he saw the other gangs coming in too he turned back and stared at the ground in front of him. He was changed all over then, the fire gone out of him; he was empty, all done.

The old man stood and stared, as he had from his first awakening. He didn't seem to have an idea, or even a distinct emotion, merely a vague dread. He'd look at one of us and then another with the same expression, pop-eyed and stupid, his mouth never quite closed, and the gray stubble sticking out all over his jaws.

When the young fellow saw the crowd he said to Tetley, "It appears we're either important personages or very dangerous. What is this, a vigilance committee?" He shivered before he spoke though. I thought the Mex elbowed him gently.

Tetley kept looking at him and smiling, but didn't reply. It was hard on their nerve. Ma Grier had ridden up right behind us, and said, before she got down, "No, it ain't that you're so difficult, son. It's just that most of the boys has never seen a real triple hangin'."

There wasn't much laughter.

Everybody was in now except the Bartlett boys. Some stayed on their horses, not expecting the business to take much time, and maybe just as glad there were others willing to be more active. Some dismounted and came over to the fire with coils of rope; there was enough rope to hang twenty men with a liberal allowance to each.

As if it had taken all that time for the idea to get through, the young fellow said, "Hanging?"

"That's right," Farnley said.

"But why?" asked the kid, beginning to chatter. "What have we done? We haven't done anything. I told you already we haven't done anything."

Then he got hold of himself and said to Tetley, more

148

slowly, "Aren't you even going to tell us what we're accused of?"

"Of course," Tetley said. "This isn't a mob. We'll make sure first."

He half turned his head toward Mapes. "Sheriff," he said, "tell him."

"Rustling," said Mapes.

"Rustling?" the kid echoed.

"Yup. Ever heard of it?"

"And murder," said Farnley, "maybe he'll have heard of that."

"Murder?" the kid repeated foolishly. I thought he was going to fold, but he didn't. He took a brace and just ran his tongue back and forth along his lips a couple of times, as if his throat and mouth were all dried out. He looked around, and it wasn't encouraging. There was a solid ring of faces, and they were serious.

The old man made a long, low moan like a dog that's going to howl but changes its mind. Then he said, his voice trembling badly, "You wouldn't kill us. No, no, you wouldn't do that, would you?"

Nobody replied. The old man's speech was thick, and he spoke very slowly, as if the words were heavy, and he was considering them with great concentration. They didn't mean anything, but you couldn't get them out of your head when he'd said them. He looked at us so I thought he was going to cry. "Mr. Martin," he said, "what do we do?" He was begging, and seemed to believe he would get a real answer.

The young man tried to make his voice cheerful, but it was hollow. "It's all right, Dad. There's some mistake."

"No mistake, I guess." It was old Bartlett speaking. He was standing beside Tetley, looking at the Mex and idly dusting the snow off his flat sombrero. The wind was blowing his wispy hair up like smoke. When he spoke the Mex looked up for a second. He looked down again quickly, but Bartlett grinned. He had a good many teeth out, and his grin wasn't pretty.

"Know me, eh?" he asked the Mex. The Mex didn't answer. Farnley stepped up to him and slapped him across the belly with the back of his hand.

"He's talking to you, Mister," he said.

149

The Mex looked wonderfully bewildered. "No sabbey," he repeated.

"He don't speak English," Mapes told Bartlett.

"I got a different notion," Bartlett said.

"I'll make him talk," Farnley offered. He was eager for it; he was so eager for it he disgusted me, and made me feel sorry for the Mex.

The young fellow appeared bewildered. He was looking at them and listening, but he didn't seem to make anything of it. He kept closing his eyes more tightly than was natural, and then opening them again quickly, as if he expected to find the whole scene changed. Even without being in the spot he was in, I could understand how he felt. It didn't look real to me either, the firelight on all the red faces watching in a leaning ring, and the big, long heads of horses peering from behind, and up in the air, detached from it, the quiet men still sitting in the saddles.

When Farnley started to prod the Mex again, Tetley said sharply, "That will do, Farnley."

"Listen, you," Farnley said, turning on him, "I've had enough of your playing God Almighty. Who in hell picked you for this job anyway? Next thing you'll be kissing them, or taking them back for Tyler to reform them. We've got the bastards; well, what are we waiting for? Let them swing, I say."

Smith put in his bit too. "Are you going to freeze us to death, Tetley, waiting for these guys to admit they shot a man and stole a bunch of cattle? Maybe you know somebody who likes to talk his head into a noose."

"There's the fire. Warm yourself," Tetley told him. "And you," he said, looking at Farnley, "control yourself, and we'll get along better."

Farnley's face blanched and stiffened, as it had in the saloon, when he'd heard the news about Kinkaid. I thought he was going to jump Tetley, but Tetley didn't even look at him again. He leaned the other way to listen to something Bartlett was saying privately. When he had heard it he nodded and looked at the young fellow across the fire.

"Who's boss of this outfit?" he asked.

"I am," the young fellow said.

"And your name's Martin?"

"Donald Martin."

"What outfit?"

"My own."

"Where from?"

"Pike's Hole."

The men didn't believe it. The man Tetley called Mark said, "He's not from Pike's, or any place in the Hole, I'll swear to that."

For the first time there was real antagonism instead of just doubt and waiting.

"Mark there lives in Pike's," Tetley told the kid, smiling. "Want to change your story?"

"I just moved in three days ago," the kid said.

"We're wasting time, Willard," Bartlett said.

"We'll get there," Tetley said. "I want this kept regular for the Judge."

Not many appreciated his joking. He was too slow and pleasurable for a job like this. Most of us would have had to do it in a hurry. If you have to hang a man, you have to, but it's not my kind of fun to stand around and watch him keep hoping he may get out of it.

Tetley may have noticed the silence, but he didn't show it. He went on asking Martin questions.

"Where did you come from before that?"

"Ohio," he said angrily, "Sinking Spring, Ohio. But not just before. I was in Los Angeles. I suppose that proves something."

"What way did you come up?"

"By Mono Lake. Look, Mister, this isn't getting us anywhere, is it? We're accused of murder and rustling, you say. Well, we haven't done any rustling, and we haven't killed anybody. You've got the wrong men."

"We'll decide as to that. And I'm asking the questions."

"God," the kid broke out. He stared around wildly at the whole bunch of us. "God, don't anybody here know I came into Pike's Hole? I drove right through the town; I drove a Conestoga wagon with six horses right through the middle of the town. I'm on Phil Baker's place; what they call the Phil Baker place, up at the north end."

Tetley turned to Mark.

"Phil Baker moved out four years ago," Mark said.

151

"The place is a wreck, barns down, sagebrush sticking up through the porch."

Tetley looked back at Martin.

"I met him in Los Angeles," Martin explained. "I bought the place from him there. I paid him four thousand dollars for it."

"Mister, you got robbed," Mark told him. "Even if Baker'd owned the place you'da been robbed, but he didn't. He didn't even stay on it long enough to have squatter's rights." We couldn't help grinning at that one. Mark said to Tetley, "Baker's place is part of Peter Wilde's ranch now."

Martin was nearly crying. "You can't hang me for being a sucker," he said.

"That depends on the kind of sucker you are."

"You haven't got any proof. Just because Baker robbed me, doesn't make me a murderer. You can't hang me without any proof."

"We're getting it," Tetley said.

"Is it so far to Pike's that you can't go over there and look?" Martin cried. "Maybe I don't even own the Baker place; maybe I've been sold out. But I'm living there now. My wife's there now; my wife and two kids."

"Now that's really too bad," Smith said, clucking his tongue in a sound of old-maid sympathy. "That's just too, too bad."

The kid didn't look at him, but his jaw tightened and his eyes were hot. "This is murder, as you're going at it," he told Tetley. "Even in this God-forsaken country I've got a right to be brought to trial, and you know it. I have, and these men have. We have a right to trial before a regular judge."

"You're getting the trial," Tetley said, "with twenty-eight of the only kind of judges a murderer and a rustler gets in what you call this God-forsaken country."

"And so far," Winder put in, "the jury don't much like your story."

The kid looked around slowly at as many of us as he could see, the way he was tied. It was as if he hadn't noticed before that we were there, and wanted to see what we were like. He must have judged Winder was right.

"I won't talk further without a proper hearing," he said slowly.

"Suit yourself, son," Ma said. "This is all the hearing you're likely to get short of the last judgment."

"Have you any cattle up here with you?" Tetley asked him.

The kid looked around at us again. He was breathing hard. One of the men from Bartlett's gang couldn't help grinning a little. The kid started to say something, then shut his mouth hard. We all waited, Tetley holding up a hand when the man who had grinned started to speak. Then he asked the question again in the same quiet way.

The kid looked down at the ground finally, but remained silent.

"I'm not going to ask you again," Tetley said. Smith stepped out with a rope in his hands. He was making a hangman's noose, with half a dozen turns to it. The place was so quiet the tiny crackling of the burned-down wood sounded loud. Martin looked at the rope, sucked in his breath, and looked down again.

After a moment he said, so low we could hardly hear him, "Yes, I have."

"How many?"

"Fifty head."

"You miscounted, Amigo," Tetley remarked. Amigo grinned and spread his hands, palms up, and shrugged his shoulders.

"Where did you get them, Mr. Martin?"

"From Harley Drew, in Bridger's Valley."

When he looked up, there were tears in his eyes. Most of the watchers looked down at their boots for a moment, some of them making wry faces.

"I'm no rustler, though. I didn't steal them, I bought them and paid for them." Then suddenly he wanted to talk a lot. "I bought them this morning; paid cash for them. My own were so bad I didn't dare try to risk bringing them up. I didn't know what the Mono Lake country was like. I sold them off in Salinas. I had to stock up again."

He could see nobody believed him.

"You can wait, can't you?" he pleaded. "I'm not likely to escape from an army like this, am I? You can wait till you see Drew, till you ask about me in Pike's. It's not too much to ask a wait like that, is it, before you hang men?"

Everybody was still just looking at him or at the ground.

"My God," he yelled out suddenly, "you aren't going to hang innocent men without a shred of proof, are you?"

Tetley shook his head very slightly.

"Then why don't you take us in, and stop this damned farce?"

"It would be a waste of time," Farnley said. "The law is almightly slow and careless around here."

The kid appeared to be trying to think fast now.

"Where do you come from?" he asked.

"Bridger's Valley," Farnley told him. There were grins again.

Martin said to Tetley, "You know Drew then?"

"I know him," Tetley said. You wouldn't have gathered it was a pleasure from the way he spoke.

"Well, didn't you even see him? Who sent you up here?"

"Drew," Tetley said.

"That's not true," Davies said. He came out from the ring and closer to the fire. He looked odd among the riders, little and hunched in an old, loose jacket and bareheaded.

"Don't let him get started again," Smith said in a disgusted voice. "It's one o'clock now."

Davies didn't pay any attention to him. "That statement is not true," he repeated. "Drew didn't send us up here. Drew didn't even know we were coming."

Tetley was watching him closely. There was only a remnant of his smile.

"As I've told you a hundred times," Davies told us all, "I'm not trying to obstruct justice. But I do want to see real justice. This is a farce; this is, as Mr. Martin has said, murder if you carry it through. He's perfectly within his rights when he demands trial. And that's all I've asked since we started, that's all I'm asking now, a trial." He sounded truculent, for him, and was breathing heavily as he spoke. "This young man," he said, pointing to Martin and looking around at us, "has said repeatedly that he is innocent. I, for one, believe him."

"Then I guess you're the only one that does, Arthur," Ma told him quietly.

Tetley made a sign to Mapes with his hand. Mapes stepped out and took Davies by the arm and began to shove him back toward the ring of watchers. Davies did not struggle much; even the little he did looked silly in Mapes' big hands. But while he went he called out angrily, "If there's any justice in your proceedings, Tetley, it would be only with the greatest certainty, it would be only after a confession. And they haven't confessed, Tetley. They say they're innocent, and you haven't proved they aren't."

"Keep him there," Mapes told the men around Davies after he'd been pushed back.

"Indirectly, Drew," Tetley said, as if Davies had not spoken.

"Now, if you're done," he went on, "I'd like to ask another question or two." Martin seemed to have taken some hope from Davies' outburst. Now he was looking down again. It was clear enough what most of the men thought.

"First, perhaps you have a bill of sale for those cattle?"

Martin swallowed hard. "No," he said finally. "No, I haven't."

"No?"

"Drew said it was all right. I couldn't find him at the ranch house. He was out on the range when I found him. He didn't have a bill of sale with him. He just said it was all right, not to wait, that he'd mail it to me. He told me it would be all right."

"Moore," Tetley said, without looking away from Martin.

"Yes?" Moore said. He didn't want to talk.

"You ride for Drew, don't you?"

"You know I do."

"In fact you're his foreman, aren't you?"

"Yes, what of it?"

"How long have you been riding for Drew?"

"Six years," Moore said.

"Did you ever know Drew to sell any cattle without a bill of sale?"

"No, I can't say as I ever did. But I can't remember every head he's sold in six years."

155

"It's customary for Drew to give a bill of sale, though?"

"Yes."

"And Moore, did you ever know Drew to sell any cattle after spring roundup, this year, or any other year?"

"No," Moore admitted, "I don't know that he's ever done that."

"Was there any reason why he should make a change in his regular practice this spring?"

Moore shook his head slowly. Young Greene shouted from over in front of Davies, "I heard him myself, say, just a couple of days ago, that he wouldn't sell a head to God himself this spring."

"Well?" Tetley asked Martin.

"I know it looks bad," the kid said, in a slow tired voice. He didn't expect to be believed any more. "I can't tell you anything else, I guess, except to ask Drew. It was hard to get them from him, all right. We talked a long time, and I had to show him how I was stuck, and how nobody wanted to sell this spring because there were so few calves. He really let me have them just as a favor, I think. That's all I have to tell you; I can't say anything else, I guess, not that would make any difference to you."

"No," Tetley agreed, "I don't believe you can."

"You don't believe me?"

"Would you, in my place?"

"I'd ask," Martin said more boldly. "I'd do a lot of asking before I'd risk hanging three men who might be innocent."

"If it were only rustling," Tetley said, "maybe. With murder, no. I'd rather risk a lot of hanging before too much asking. Law, as the books have it, is slow and full of holes."

In the silence the fire crackled, and hissed when the snow fell into it. The light of it flagged up and down on the men's serious faces, and Ma turned to observe Tetley. The mouths were hard and the eyes bright and nervous. Finally Ma said mildly, "I guess it would be enough, even for Tyler, wouldn't it, Willard?"

"For Martin, perhaps," Tetley said.

"The others are his men, ain't they?" Farnley inquired.

Others quietly said it had been enough for them. Even Moore said, "It's no kindness to keep them waiting."

156

Still Tetley didn't say anything, and Ma burst out, "What you tryin' to do, play cat and mouse with them, Tetley? You act like you liked it."

"I would prefer a confession," Tetley said. He was talking to Martin, not to us.

Martin swallowed and wet his lips with his tongue, but couldn't speak. Besides Smith, Farnley and Winder were knotting ropes now. Finally Martin groaned something we couldn't understand, and abandoned his struggle with himself. The sweat broke out on his face and began to trickle down; his jaw was shaking. The old man was talking to himself, now and then shaking his head, as if pursuing an earnest and weighty debate. The Mex was standing firmly, with his feet a little apart, like a boxer anticipating his opponent's lunge or jab, saying nothing and showing nothing. It got to Gil even.

"I don't see your game, Tetley," he said. "If you got any doubts let's call off this party and take them in to the Judge, like Davies wants."

This was the first remark that had made any impression on Tetley's cool disregard. He looked directly at Gil and told him, "This is only very slightly any of your business, my friend. Remember that."

Gil got hot. "Hanging is any man's business that's around, I'd say."

"Have you a brief for the innocence of these men?" Tetley asked him. "Or is it merely that your stomach for justice is cooling?"

"Mister, take it easy with that talk," Gil said, swinging out of line and hitching a thumb over his gun belt. A couple of men tried to catch hold of him, but he shook them off short and sharp, without looking at them or using a hand. He was staring at Tetley in a way I knew enough to be scared of. I got up, but I didn't know what I'd do.

"No man," Gil said, standing just across the corner of the fire from Tetley, "no man is going to call me yellow. If that's what you mean, make it plainer."

Tetley was smooth. "Not at all," he said. "But we seem to have a number of men here only too willing to foist the burden of a none too pleasant task onto others, even when those others, as we all know, may well never perform it. I was just wondering how many such men.

It would be a kindness, in my estimation, to let them leave before we proceed further. Their interruptions are becoming tiresome."

Gil stood where he was. "Well, I'm not one of them, get that," he said.

"Good," Tetley said, nodding as if he were pleased. "We have no quarrel then, I guess."

"No," Gil admitted, "but I still say I don't see your game. Hanging is one thing. To keep men standing and sweating for it while you talk is another. I don't like it."

Tetley examined him as if to remember him for another time. "Hurry is scarcely to be recommended at a time like this," he said finally. "I am taking, it seems to me, the chief responsibility in this matter, and I do not propose to act prematurely, that's all."

I could see Gil didn't believe this any more than I did, but there wasn't anything to say to it, no clear reason that you could put a finger on, for doubt. Gil stood there, but said nothing more. It was a hard spot for him to retreat from. Martin was watching him, hoping to God something would break. He sagged again, though, and closed his eyes and worked his mouth, when Gil just stood balanced and Tetley said, "Since they will not ease our task directly, we'll get on."

"We've had enough questions," Winder said. "They aren't talking."

Tetley said to Martin, "You called the old man Dad. Is he your father?"

"No," Martin said, and again added something too low to hear.

"Speak up, man," Tetley said sharply, "you're taking it like a woman."

"Everybody's gotta die once, son. Keep your chin up," Ma said. That was bare comfort for him, but I knew Ma wasn't thinking of him so much as of us. His weakness was making us feel as if we were mistreating a dog instead of trying a man.

The kid brought his head up and faced us, but that was worse. The tears were running down his cheeks and his mouth was working harder than ever.

"God Almighty, he's bawlin'," said Winder, and spit as if it made him sick.

158

"No," said Martin, thick and blubbery, but loudly, "he works for me."

"What's your name?" Tetley asked, turning to the old man. The old man didn't hear him; he continued to talk to himself. Mapes went and stood in front of him and said loudly in his face. "What's your name?"

"I didn't do it," argued the old man. "No, how could I have done it? You can see I didn't do it, can't you?" He paused, thinking how to make it clear. "I didn't have anything in my gun," he explained. "Mr. Martin won't let me have any bullets for my gun, so how could I do it? I wasn't afraid to, but I didn't have any bullets."

"You didn't do what?" Tetley asked him gently.

"No, I didn't, I tell you. I didn't." Then his wet wreck of a face seemed to light up with an idea. "He done it," he asserted. "He done it."

"Who did it?" said Tetley, still quietly, but slowly and distinctly.

"He did," burbled the old man, "Juan did. He told me so. No, he didn't; I saw him do it. If I saw him do it," he inquired cutely, "I know, don't I? I couldn't have done it if I saw him do it, could I?"

The Mex didn't stir. Farnley was watching the Mex, and even his hard grin was gone. He was holding his breath, and then breathing by snorts.

Martin spoke. "Juan couldn't have done anything. I was with him all the time."

"Yes, he did too do it, Mr. Martin. He was asleep; he didn't mean to tell me, but I was awake and I heard him talking about it. He told me when he was asleep."

"The old man is feeble-minded," Martin said, slowly and quietly, trying to speak so the old man wouldn't hear him. "He doesn't know so what he's talking about. He's dreamt something." He looked down; either it hurt him to say this or he was doing a better job of acting than his condition made probable. "You can't trust anything he says. He dreams constantly; when he's awake he invents things. After a little while he really believes they have happened. He's a good old man; you've scared him and he's inventing things he thinks will save him."

Then he flared, "If you've got to go on with your filthy comedy you can let him alone, can't you?"

"You keep out of this," Mapes shouted, stepping

quickly past the Mexican and standing in front of Martin. "You've had your say. Now shut up."

Martin stared down at him. "Then let the old man alone," he said.

Mapes suddenly struck him across the face so hard it would have knocked him over if he hadn't been tied to the others. As it was, one knee buckled under him, and he ducked his head down to shake off the sting or block another slap if it was coming.

"Lay off, Mapes," somebody shouted, and Moore said, "You've got no call for that sort of thing, Mapes."

"First he wouldn't talk, and now he talks too damned much," Mapes said, but let Martin alone.

We had closed the circle as much as the fire would let us. Tetley moved closer to Martin, and Mapes made room for him, though strutting because of the yelling at him.

"You mean actually feeble-minded?" Tetley asked.

"Yes."

"What's his name?"

"Alva Hardwick."

"And the other speaks no English?"

Martin didn't reply.

"What's his name?"

"Juan Martinez."

"No, it isn't," old Bartlett said.

Tetley turned and looked at old Bartlett. "You seem to know something about this man?" he asked.

"I've been trying to tell you ever since this fool questioning started," Bartlett told him, "but you've got to be so damned regular."

"All right, all right," Tetley said impatiently. "What is it?"

Bartlett suddenly became cautious. "I don't want to say until I'm sure," he said. He went up to the Mex.

"Remember me?" he asked. "At Driver's, last September?"

The Mex wouldn't know he was being talked to. Bartlett got angry; when he got angry his loose jowls trembled.

"I'm talking to you, greaser," he said.

The Mex looked at him, too quick and narrow for not

160

understanding, but then all he did was shake his head and say, "No sabbey," again.

"The devil you don't," Bartlett told him. "Your name's Francisco Morez, and the vigilantes would still like to get hold of you."

The Mex wouldn't understand.

"He talks English better than I do," Bartlett told Tetley. "He was a gambler, and claimed to be a rancher from down Sonora way somewhere. They wanted him for murder."

"What about that?" Tetley asked Martin.

"I don't know," the kid said hopelessly.

"Does he speak English?"

The kid looked at the Mex and said, "Yes." The Mex didn't bat an eye.

"How long's he been with you?"

"He joined us in Carson." Martin looked up at Tetley again. "I don't know anything about him," he said. "He told me that he was a rider, and that he knew this country, and that he'd like to tie up with me. That's all I know."

"They stick together nice, don't they?" Smith said.

"You picked him up on nothing more than that?" Tetley asked Martin.

"Why don't you come to the point?" Martin asked. "Why ask me all these questions if you don't believe anything I tell you?"

"There's as much truth to be sifted out of lies as anything else," Tetley said, "if you get enough lies. Is his name Morez?" he went on.

"I tell you I don't know. He told me his name was Martinez. That's all I know."

Without warning Tetley shifted his questioning to the old man. "What did he do?" he asked sharply.

"He did," mumbled the old man. "Yes, he did too; I saw him."

"What did he do?"

"He said that—he said." The old man lost what he was trying to tell.

"He said . . ." encouraged Tetley.

"I don't know. I didn't do it. You wouldn't kill an old man, Mister. I'm very old man, Mister, very old man."

He assumed his expression of cunning again. "I wouldn't live very long anyway," he said argumentatively.

"You're a big help," Bartlett said.

"Yeah," said Farnley, grinning at Tetley, "he makes it all clear, don't he?"

"What do you know about the old man?" Tetley asked Martin patiently.

"He's all right; he wouldn't hurt anything if he could help it."

"And he's been with you how long?"

"Three years."

"As a rider?"

"I'd rather not talk about this here," Martin said. "Can't you take me in the cabin, or somewhere?"

"It's a better check on the stories if they don't hear each other, at that," Winder put in.

"What stories?" Farnley asked. "One of them don't talk and the other don't make sense. There's only one story."

"We'll do well enough here," Tetley said. "Does the old man here ride for you?"

"Only ordinary driving. He's not a cowboy. He's a good worker if he understands, but you have to tell him just what to do."

"Not much use in this business, then, is he?" Tetley spoke absent-mindedly, as if just settling the point for himself, but he was watching Martin. Martin didn't slip.

"He's a good worker."

"Why did you take him on, if he's what you say?"

Martin was embarrassed. Finally he said, "You would have too."

Tetley smiled. "What did he do before he came to you?"

"He was in the army. I don't know which army; he doesn't seem to be clear about it himself. Maybe he was in both at different times; I've thought so sometimes, from things he's said. Or that might be just his way of imagining. You can't always tell what's been real with him."

"I know," said Tetley, still smiling. "You've made a point of that. But you're sure he was in the army?"

"He was in one of them. Something started him thinking that way."

162

"A half-wit in the army?" Tetley asked, tilting his head to one side.

Martin swallowed and wet his lips again. "He must have been," he insisted.

"Still you say he wouldn't hurt anything?"

"No," Martin said, "he wouldn't. He's foolish, but he's always gentle."

Tetley just stood and smiled at him and shook his head.

"I believe," Martin persisted, "some experience in the war must have injured his mind. There's one he always talks about, and never finishes. He must have been all right before, and something in the war did it to him."

Tetley considered the old man. Then suddenly he drew himself up stiffly and clicked his heels together, and barked out, "Attention," with all the emphasis on the last syllable.

Old Hardwick just looked around at all of us with a scared face, more nervous and vacant than ever because he knew we were all watching him.

Tetley relaxed. "I don't think so," he said to Martin.

"He's forgotten. He forgets everything."

Tetley shook his head, still smiling. "Not that," he said.

"You still don't talk English?" he asked the Mex. The Mex was silent.

Tetley sent two riders to help the Bartlett boys shag in the cattle they'd been holding. At the edge of the clearing, seeing the fire, and the men and horses, and being wild with this unusual night hazing anyway, they milled. But they didn't have to come any closer. As they turned, with the firelight on them enough, we could see Drew's brand and his notches.

"Anything you haven't said that you want to say?" Tetley asked Martin.

Martin drew a deep breath to steady himself. He could feel the set against him that one look at those cattle had brought on if all the talk hadn't.

"I've told you how I got them," he said.

"We heard that," Tetley agreed.

"You have the steers, haven't you?" Martin asked. He was short of breath. "Well, you haven't lost anything

163

then, have you? You could wait to hang us until you talk to Drew, couldn't you?"

"It's not the first time," Tetley said. "We waited before."

He studied Martin for a moment.

"I'll make you a deal, though," he offered. "Tell us which of you shot Kinkaid, and the other two can wait."

Martin half-way glanced at the Mex, but if he was going to say anything he changed his mind. He shook his head before he spoke, as if at some thought of his own. "None of us killed anybody," he said in that tired voice again. "We were all three together all the time."

"That's all, I guess," Tetley said regretfully. He motioned toward the biggest tree on the edge of the clearing.

"My God," Martin said huskily, "you aren't going to, really! You wouldn't really! You can't do it," he wailed, and started fighting his bonds, jerking the other two prisoners about. The old man stumbled and fell to his knees and got up again as if it were a desperate necessity to be on his feet, but as clumsily as a cow because of his bound wrists.

"Tie them separately, Mapes," Tetley ordered.

Many ropes were offered. Smith and Winder helped Mapes. Only Martin was hard to tie. He'd lost his head, and it took two men to hold him while he was bound. Then the three were standing there separately, each with his arms held flat to his sides by a half-dozen turns of rope. Their feet were left free to walk them into position. Each of them had a noose around his neck too, and a man holding it.

In spite of Mapes trying to hold him up, Martin slumped down to his knees. We couldn't understand what he was babbling. When Mapes pulled him up again he managed to stand, but waving like a tree in a shifting wind. Then we could understand part of what he was saying. "One of them's just a baby," he was saying, "just a baby. They haven't got anything to go on, not a thing. They're alone; they haven't got anything to go on, and they're alone."

"Take them over," Tetley ordered, indicating the tree again. It was a big pine with its top shot away by lightning. It had a long branch that stuck out straight on the clearing side, about fifteen feet from the ground. We'd all spotted that branch.

"The Mex is mine," Farnley said. Tetley nodded and told some others to get the rustlers' horses.

Martin kept hanging back, and when he was shoved along kept begging, "Give us some time, it's not even decent; give us some time."

Old Hardwick stumbled and buckled, but didn't fall. He was silent, but his mouth hung open, and his eyes were protruding enormously. The Mex, however, walked steadily, showing only a wry grin, as if he had expected nothing else from the first.

When the three of them were lined up in a row under the limb, waiting for their horses, Martin said, "I've got to write a letter. If you're even human you'll give me time for that, anyway." His breath whistled when he talked, but he seemed to know what he was saying again.

"We can't wait all night," Mapes told him, getting ready to throw up the end of the rope, which had a heavy knot tied in it to carry it over.

"He's not asking much, Tetley," Davies said.

Old Hardwick seemed to have caught the idea. He burbled about being afraid of the dark, that he didn't want to die in the dark, that in the dark he saw things.

"He's really afraid of the dark," Martin said. "Can't this wait till sunrise? It's customary anyway, isn't it?"

Men were holding the three horses just off to the side now. Farnley was holding the hang rope on the Mex. He spoke to Tetley angrily.

"Now what are you dreaming about, Tetley? They're trying to put it off, that's all; they're scared, and they're trying to put it off. Do you want Tyler and the sheriff to get us here, and the job not done?" As if he had settled it himself, he threw the end of the Mex's rope over the limb.

"They won't come in this snow," Davies said.

"I believe you're right," Tetley told Davies. "Though I doubt if you want to be." He asked Bartlett, "What time is it?" Bartlett drew a thick silver watch from his waistcoat pocket and looked at it.

"Five minutes after two," he said.

"All right," Tetley said after a moment, "we'll wait till daylight."

Farnley stood holding the end of the rope and glaring at Tetley. Then slowly he grinned up one side of his face and tossed down the rope, like he was all done. "Why not?" he said. "It will give the bastard time to think about it." Then he walked down to the fire and stood there by himself. He was wild inside; you could tell that just by looking at his back.

In a way none of us liked the wait, when we'd have to go through the whole thing over again anyway. But you couldn't refuse men in a spot like that three or four hours if they thought they wanted them.

"Reverend," Tetley said to Sparks, "you can settle your business at leisure."

It was suggested that we put the prisoners into the cabin, but Tetley said it was too cold, and no stove. The fire was fed up again, and the three men put on different sides of it. It was hard to tell where to go yourself. You wanted to stay near the fire, and still not right around those men.

Martin asked to have his hands untied. "I can't write like this," he explained. The Mex said something too, in Spanish.

"He wants to eat," Amigo told us. "He say," he grinned, "he ees mucho hongry from so mooch ride and so mooch mooch of the talk." The Mex grinned at us while Amigo was talking.

"Let him ask for it himself, then," Bartlett said.

"Untie them all," Tetley said, and appointed Smith and Moore and Winder to keep them covered.

When he was freed, Martin moved to sit on a log on his side. He sat there rubbing his wrists. Then he asked for paper and a pencil. Davies had a little leather account book and a pencil in his vest. He gave them to Martin, showing him the blank pages in the back of the book. But Martin's hands were shaking so he couldn't write. Davies offered to write for him, but he said no, he'd be all right in a few minutes; he'd rather write this letter for himself.

"Will the others want to write?" Davies asked him.

"You can ask Juan," Martin said, looking at the Mex. Whenever he looked at the Mex he had that perplexed expression of wanting to say something and deciding not to. "It's no use with the old man, though," he said, looking up at Davies and remembering to smile to show he was grateful. "He wouldn't know what to say, or how to say it. I don't believe he has anybody to write to, for that matter. He forgets people if they're not right around him."

When Amigo asked him, Juan said no, he didn't care to write. For some reason he seemed to think the idea of his writing to anyone was humorous.

Ma was examining the rustlers' packs, which had been propped against the cabin wall. She was going to get a meal for the Mex. She drew articles out, naming them for everybody to hear as she removed them. There was a lot more than three men could want for a meal or two. There was a whole potato sack of very fresh beef, which had been rolled up in paper and then put in the sack, and the sack put in the lee of the cabin, half buried in an old drift. There was coffee too.

When Ma had called off part of her list Smith yelled to her to fix a spread for everybody. He explained loudly that if they had to freeze and lose sleep because somebody was afraid of the dark, they didn't have to starve too, and that it wasn't exactly robbery because by the time it was eaten that food wouldn't belong to anybody anyway. He also hinted that the beef probably belonged to some of us anyhow. He had managed to bring a bottle along, and now that there was no immediate excitement he pulled on it frequently. He was a good deal impressed with how funny he was.

A few men looked around hard at Smith, but most pretended that they were thinking about something and hadn't heard him. Moore spoke up though, and told Ma he didn't want anything; then others of us told her the same thing. Smith called us queasy, but when nobody answered he didn't go any further. He knew what we meant. You can't eat a man's food before him and then hang him.

When Ma set to cooking it, though, with Sparks helping her, many changed their minds. There was a belly-searching odor from that meat propped on forked sticks and dripping and scorching over the coals. None of us had had a real meal since midday, and some not then, and the air was cold and snowy and with a piny edge. It carried the meat smell very richly.

Gil made me drink some of the coffee because my teeth were chattering. I wasn't really so cold as thinned out by the loss of blood. Coffee was better than the whisky had been, and after it I sneaked a bit of the meat too, being careful that Martin didn't see me eat it. I only chewed a little, though, and knew I didn't want it. I took more coffee.

Sparks took meat and bread and coffee on their own plates and in their own cups to the three prisoners. The Mex ate with big mouthfuls, taking his time and enjoying it. The strong muscles in his jaws worked in and out so the firelight shone on them when he chewed. He washed it down with long draughts of coffee too hot for me to have touched, and nodded his head at Ma to show it was all good. When he was done eating he took a pull of whisky from Gil, rolled and lit a cigarette, and sat cross-legged, drawing the smoke in two streams up his nostrils and blowing it out between his lips in strong jets that bellied out into clouds at the end. He watched the fire and the smoke from his cigarette, and sometimes smiled to himself reminiscently.

Old Hardwick ate his meat and bread too, but didn't know he was doing it. He chewed with the food showing out of his mouth, and didn't stop staring. Sometimes he continued to chew when he had already swallowed. Some of the bread he pulled into little pieces and dropped while he was chewing the meat.

Martin drank some coffee, but refused food and whisky. He was holding the notebook and pencil and thinking. It was a hard letter to write. He would stare at the fire with glazed eyes, wake up with a shiver and look around him, put the pencil to the paper, and then relapse into that staring again. It was a long time before he really began to write, and then he twice tore out a page on which there were only a few words, and began again. Finally, he seemed to forget where he was, and what was going to happen to him, and wrote slowly and steadily, occasionally crossing out a line or so with two slow, straight strokes.

Gil made me lie down with a couple of blankets around me and my back against the cabin, but between Ma and Tetley sitting and eating and smoking and not talking much, I could see Martin's face and his hand busy writing.

The young Bartletts were relieved and came in, but they wouldn't eat either, but drank coffee and smoked. It was very quiet, all the men sitting around except the guards. Tetley insisted that the guards stand up. Some of the men talked in low voices, and now and then one of them would laugh, but stop quickly. Tetley kept looking over at Gerald, who hadn't eaten or even taken any coffee, and who wasn't smoking, but sitting there picking up little sticks and digging hard at the ground with them, and then realizing he had them, and tossing them away. When another squall of wind brought the snow down in waves again, men looked up at the sky, where there wasn't anything to see. The wind wasn't steady, however, and shortly the snow thinned out again. Most of it had shaken from its loose lodging on the branches of the pines. I became drowsy, and felt that I was observing a distant picture. After eating, Gabe Hart had rolled up and gone to sleep just beyond me, but all the others were trying to stay awake, though some of them would nod, and then jerk up and stare around as if something had happened or they felt a long time had passed. Only young Tetley kept the scene from going entirely dreamlike. Between times of playing with his sticks he would rise abruptly and walk out to the edge of the dark and stand there with his back turned, and then suddenly turn and come back to the fire and stand there for a long time before he sat down again. After the third or fourth time his father leaned toward him when he sat down, and spoke to him. The boy remained seated then, but always with those busy hands.

Then I slept myself, after short broken dozes. I woke suddenly, with my shoulder aching badly, my head light again, and my mouth dry. I was scared about something, and tried to get out of my blanket quickly and stand up, but a weight was holding me under. I thought that if it should stop pressing I'd take off like a leaf in the wind. Only the ache seemed real, and the weight.

The weight was Gil. He had a hand on my ribs beneath the bad arm, and was holding me down as gently as he could, but heavily.

"What's eating on you?" he asked.

I told him nothing was, and he helped me to sit up and lean against the cabin. Having slept, I felt weak and miserable. The shoulder was round and tight as a river boulder and the ache reached to my breastbone in front and my spine in back. In the center of it there was a small and ambitious core of fire.

"You were jabbering," Gil said, "and flopping around like a fish out of water. I thought maybe you was out of your head."

"No, I'm all right," I told him.

"You must have been dreaming," Gil said. "You was scared to death when I took hold of you."

I said I couldn't remember.

"I wouldn'ta woke you up," he apologized, "only I was afraid you'd start that shoulder bleeding again."

"I'm glad you did," I told him. I didn't like the idea of lying there talking in my sleep.

"Have I been asleep long?" I asked him.

"An hour or two, I guess."

"An hour or two?" I felt like a traitor, as if I'd wasted the little time those three men had by sleeping myself.

"You didn't miss anything," Gil said, "except Smith working on Ma."

That was still going on. They were sitting in front of us, and Smith had one arm around her thick middle and was holding a bottle up to her. He wasn't making any headway, though. She was solid as a stump.

Martin had finished his letter, and was sitting hunched over with his forehead in his hands. I saw him stare at Smith and Ma once, and then bend his head again, locking his hands behind it and pulling down hard, like he was stretching his neck and shoulders. Then he relaxed again, and put his arms across his knees and his head down on them. He was having a hard time of it, I judged.

Sparks was busy with old Hardwick, squatting in front of him and exhorting and now and then taking hold of him gently to make him pay attention. But the old man was scared out of what little wits he had and wasn't listening, but still staring and talking to himself. Davies was trying to get Tetley to talk about something he was showing him, but failing. The Mex was sitting there drowsily, with his elbows on his knees and his forearms hanging loosely between his legs.

Only two men were standing, one on guard with a carbine across his arm, and Farnley, who had moved

170

around to put his back against the big tree, and was much more awake than the guard.

There was no wind, and no snow falling, but no stars showing either; just thick, dark cold.

I heard Tetley making a retort to Davies. It was the first time either of them had raised his voice, and Davies nervously motioned him to be quiet, but he finished what he was saying clearly enough so I could hear it. "It may be a fine letter; apparently, from what you say, it's a very fine letter. But if it's an honest letter it's none of my business to read it, and if it isn't I don't want to."

Martin had heard. He lifted his head and looked across at them.

"Is that my letter you're showing?" he asked.

"It's yours," Tetley told him. I knew how he was smiling when he said it.

"What are you doing, showing my letter?" Martin asked Davies. His voice had aroused the whole circle to watch them now. He repeated his question more sharply.

Smith gave up his game with Ma and rose unsteadily and came toward Martin, hitching his belt as he stumbled.

"Don't go to raising your voice like that, rustler," he ordered thickly.

"Never mind, Monty," Davies said. "He's right. I told him I'd keep it for him."

Smith stood waveringly and looked around at Davies. His face was knotted with the effort to look disgusted and hostile and to see straight at the same time. "Well," he said, "if you like to suck the hind tit . . ."

"Sit down before you fall down, Monty," Ma advised him.

"Nobody's gonna fall down," Smith assured her. "But I'll be damned," he said, squaring around on Martin again, "if I'd let any yellow, thievin' rustler raise his voice at me for tryin' to do him a favor. It's a little late to get fussy about privacy when you got the knot under your ear already."

This time Tetley told him to shut up, and he did.

Martin paid no attention to Smith. He stood up and spoke to Davies. "If I remember rightly, all I asked was

171

that you keep that letter and make sure it was delivered."

"I'm sorry," Davies said, "I was just trying to prove . . ."

Martin began to move across toward Davies. The veins were standing out in his neck. Several men scrambled to their feet. Davies rose too, defensively. The guard didn't know what to do. He took a step or two after Martin, but then stood there holding his carbine like it was a live rattler. Farnley came down from his stand against the tree. He had his gun out when he got to the fire.

"Sit down, you, and pipe down," he ordered.

Martin stood still, but he didn't show any signs of retreating or of sitting down. He didn't even look around at Farnley.

Mapes was standing up behind Tetley. He ordered Martin to sit down also, and drew his gun when Martin didn't move or even glance at him.

"It's enough," Martin said in a smothered voice to Davies, "to be hanged by a pack of bullying outlaws without having your private thoughts handed around to them for a joke."

"I've said I'm sorry," Davies reminded him, sharply for him. "I was merely doing . . ."

"I don't give a damn what you were doing. I didn't write that letter to be passed around. I wrote that letter to—well, it's none of your business, and it's none of the business of any of these other murdering bastards."

"Take it easy on that talk," Farnley said behind him.

"I made no promise," Davies told Martin.

"All right, you made no promise. I should have known I'd need a promise. Or would that have done any good? I thought there was one white man among you. Well, I was wrong."

Then he became general in his reference. He waved an arm around to take us all in. "But what good would an oath do, in a pack like this, an oath to do what any decent man would do by instinct? You eat our food in front of us and joke about it. You make love publicly in front of men about to die, and are able to sleep while they wait. What good would an oath do where there's not so much conscience in the lot as a good dog has?

172

"Give me that letter," he ordered, taking another step toward Davies.

"I'll see that she gets it," Davies said stiffly.

"I wouldn't have her touch it," Martin said.

Tetley stood up. "That's enough," he said. "You've been told to go back and sit down. If I were you, I'd do that. Give him the letter, Davies."

Still holding the letter, Davies said quietly, "Your wife ought to hear from you, son. None of us could be so kind as that letter; and she'd want it to keep."

Martin stared at him. His face changed, the wrath dying out of it. "Thanks," he said. "I'm sorry. Yes, keep it, please, and see that she gets it."

"Hey, the Mex," Ma yelled. She was pointing up to the edge of the woods, where the horses were tied. There was the Mex, working at the rope on one of the bays, the horse nearest the woods on the road side. There was a general yell and scramble. Somebody yelled to spread, he might have a gun. Several yelled to shoot. They circled out fast, snapping hammers as they ran. They were mad and ashamed at having been caught napping. Tetley was as angry as anyone, but he kept his head.

"Mapes, Winder," he called out, "keep an eye on the other two. You," he said to Davies, "if you're part of this trick—" but didn't finish it, but went around the fire quickly to where he could see better.

Martin stood where he was, and old Hardwick, when he saw the guns come out, put his hands up over his eyes, like a little, scared kid.

The Mex did have a gun. At the first shout he just worked harder on the tie, but when Farnley shot and then two more shots came from off at the side, he yanked the horse around in front of him and shot back. In the shadow you could see the red jet of the gun. I heard the bullet whack into the cabin at the left of me. Everybody broke farther to the sides to get out of the light, and nobody was crowding in very fast. Farnley tried another shot and nicked the horse, which squealed and reared so the Mex lost him. The other horses were scared and wheeled and yanked at the tie ropes, and nobody could see the Mex to shoot again. He must have given up trying to get the horse, though, and made a break for it on foot, because Farnley, who was out in the edge of the woods quit creeping and stood up and shot again. Then he came back running and

173

took the carbine away from the guard, and plunged back into the woods, yelling something as he went. Others fanned out into the woods too.

Then it was quiet for a few minutes, those of us who had stayed behind waiting to hear it happen. Finally it began, somewhere up on the mountain and over toward the road, not too far, from the loudness of the reports. There were three short, flat shots in quick succession, then a deeper one that got an echo from some canyon up among the trees. Then it was quiet again, and we thought it was all over, when there were two more of the flat explosions and after a moment the deeper one again. Then it stayed quiet.

We were all nervous waiting, and nobody talked, just watched around the edge of the woods to see where they'd come out. The wait seemed so long that some of the men, who weren't on guard, began edging cautiously into the woods to see what had happened.

Then we saw the others coming down again. Two of them had the Mex between them, but he wasn't dead; he wasn't even out. They carried him down into the light and set him on the log Martin had been sitting on. He was sweating, but not saying anything, and not moaning.

"Tie the others up again," Tetley ordered.

"That must have been some fine shooting," he said to Farnley. "Where's he hit?"

Farnley flushed. "It was good enough," he retorted. "It was dark in there; you couldn't even see the barrel sometimes, let alone the sights." Then he answered, "I hit him in the leg."

"Saving him for the rope, eh?"

"No, I wasn't. I wanted to kill the bastard bad enough. It was the slope that done it; it's hard to tell shooting uphill."

They were talking like it had been a target shoot, and the Mex right there.

One of the men who had gone in after Farnley came up to Tetley and handed him something. "That's the gun he had," he said, nodding at the Mex. It was a long, blue-barreled Colt six-shooter with an ivory grip. "It's empty," the man said, "he shot 'em all out, I guess."

Farnley was looking at the gun in Tetley's hand. He

174

was staring at it. After a moment, without asking, he reached out and took it away from Tetley.

"Well," he said, after turning it over in his own hands, "I guess we know now, don't we? If there was ever anything to wonder about, there ain't now."

Tetley watched him looking at the gun and waited for his explanation.

"It's Larry's gun," Farnley said. "Look," he said to the rest of us, and pointed to the butt and gave it to us to look at. Kinkaid's name, all of it, Laurence Liam Kinkaid, was inlaid in tiny letters of gold in the ivory of the butt.

Tetley recovered the gun and took it over and held it for the Mex to see.

"Where did you get this?" he asked. His tone proved he would take only one answer. Sweating from his wound, the Mex grinned at him savagely.

"If somebody will take this bullet out of my leg, I will tell you," he said.

"God, he talks American," Ma said.

"And ten other languages," said the Mex, "but I don't tell anything I don't want to in any of them. My leg, please. I desire I may stand upright when you come to your pleasure."

"What's a slug or two to you now?" Farnley asked.

"If he wants it out, let him have it out," Moore said, "there's time."

The Mex looked around at us all with that angry grin. "If somebody will lend me the knife, I will take it out myself."

"Don't give him no knife," Bartlett said. "He can throw a knife better than most men can shoot."

"Better than these men, it is true," said the Mex. "But if you are afraid, then I solemnly give my promise I will not throw the knife. When I am done, then quietly I will give the knife back to its owner, with the handle first."

Surprisingly, young Tetley volunteered to remove the slug. His face was white, his voice smothered when he said it, but his eyes were bright. In his own mind he was championing his cause still, in the only way left. He felt that doing this, which would be difficult for him, must somehow count in the good score. He crossed to

175

the Mex and knelt beside him, but when he took the knife one of the men offered him, his hand was shaking so he couldn't even start. He put up a hand, as if to clear his eyes, and the Mex took the knife away from him. Farnley quickly turned the carbine on the Mex, but he didn't pay any attention. He made a quick slash through his chaps from the thigh to the boot top. His leg, inside, was muscular and thick and hairless as an Indian's. Just over the knee there was the bullet hole, ragged and dark, but small; dark tendrils of blood had dried down from it, not a great deal of blood. Young Tetley saw it close to his face, and got up drunkenly and moved away, his face bloodless. The Mex grinned after him.

"The little man is polite," he commented, "but without the stomach for the blood, eh?"

Then he said, while he was feeling from the wound along his leg up to the thigh, "Will someone please to make the fire better? The light is not enough."

Tetley ordered them to throw on more wood. He didn't look to see them do it. He was watching Gerald stagger out toward the dark in the edge of the woods to be sick.

When the fire had blazed up the Mex turned to present his thigh to the light, and went to work. Everybody watched him; it's hard not to watch a thing like that, though you don't want to. The Mex opened the mouth of the wound so it began to bleed again, freely, but then again he traced with his fingers up his thigh. He set his jaw, and high on the thigh made a new incision. His grin froze so it looked more like showing his teeth, and the sweat beads popped out on his forehead. He rested a moment when the first cut had been made, and was bleeding worse than the other.

"That is very bad shooting," he said. He panted from the pain.

Nonetheless, when he began to work again he hummed a Mexican dance tune through his teeth. He halted the song only once, when something he did with the point of the knife made his leg straighten involuntarily, and made him grunt in spite of himself. After that his own hand trembled badly, but he took a breath and began to dig and sweat and hum again. It got so I couldn't watch it either. I turned and looked for young Tetley instead, and saw him standing by a tree, leaning on it with one hand, his back to the fire. His father was watching him too.

There was a murmur, and I looked back, and the Mex had the bloody slug out and was holding it up for us to look at. When we had seen it he tossed it to Farnley.

"You should try again with that one," he said.

Sparks brought some hot water to the Mex, and after propping the knife so the blade was in the coals, he began washing out the two wounds with a purple silk handkerchief he'd had around his neck. He took care of himself as carefully as if he still had a lifetime to go. Then, when the knife blade was hot enough, he drew it out of the fire and clapped it right against the wounds, one after the other. Each time his body stiffened, the muscles of his jaw and the veins of his neck protruded, and the sweat broke out over his face, but still he drew the knife away from the thigh wound slowly, as if it pleased him to take his time. He asked for some of the fat from the steaks, rubbed the grease over the burned cuts, and bound them with the purple kerchief and another from his pocket. Then he lit a cigarette and took it easy.

After inhaling twice, long and slow, he picked up the knife he'd used and tossed it over in front of the man who had lent it. He tossed it so it spun in the air and struck the ground point first with a chuck sound, and dug in halfway to the hilt. It struck within an inch of where the man's boot had been, but he'd drawn off quickly when he saw it coming. The Mex grinned at him.

Martin and old Hardwick were bound again. Tetley told them they needn't tie the Mex, he wouldn't go far for awhile. The Mex thanked him, grinning through the smoke of his cigarette.

But when Tetley began to question him about the gun, all he'd say was that he'd found it; that it was lying right beside the road, and he'd brought it along, thinking to meet somebody he could send it back with. When Tetley called him a liar, and repeated the questions, the Mex at first just said the same thing, and then suddenly became angry and stubborn-looking, called Tetley a blind fool, lit another cigarette, and said no sabbey as he had at first. Martin told the same story about the gun, that they'd found it lying by the west lane when they came out from Drew's place, that all the cartridges had been in it, that he'd told the Mex to leave it because it was too far back to the ranch to take, but that the Mex had thought they might meet somebody who could return it. There wasn't anything else to be had out of either of them.

The Mexican's courage, and even, in a way, young Martin's pride in the matter of the letter, had won them much sympathy, and I think we all believed now that the old man was really a pitiful fool, but whatever we thought, there was an almost universal determination to finish the job now. The gun was a clincher with us.

All but Davies. Davies was trying to get other men to read the letter. He maintained stronger than ever that young Martin was innocent, that Martin was not the kind of a man who could either steal or kill. He worked on those of us who had shown some sympathy with his ideas before. He tried hard not to let Tetley notice what he was doing, to stand naturally when he talked, and not to appear too earnest to a person who couldn't hear him. But he didn't make much headway. Most of the men had made up their minds, or felt that the rest had and that their own sympathy was reprehensible and should be concealed. That was the way I felt. None of us would look at the letter. When he came to us, telling us to read the letter, Gil said, "I don't want to read the letter. It's none of my business. You heard the kid; you ought to remember if anybody does."

"Do you suppose it matters to his wife who sees this letter?" Davies said. "In her place which would you rather have, a live husband with some of his secrets with you revealed, or a dead husband and all your secrets still?

"I don't like to pry any more than you do," he insisted, "but you can't put a life against a scruple. I tell you, if you'll read this letter you'll know he couldn't have done it; not any of it. And if the letter's a fake we have only to wait to know, don't we?"

It wasn't long until daylight, and the men hadn't really settled down again, but were moving around in groups, talking and smoking. Still, I thought Tetley was watching us.

"That must be some letter," Gil was saying.

Davies held it out to him. "Read it," he pleaded.

"You get Martin to ask me to read it and I will," Gil told him, grinning.

"Then you read it," Davies said, turning to me. Gil was watching me, still grinning.

"No," I said, "I'd rather not." I was curious to read that letter, but I couldn't, there, like that.

Davies stood and looked from one to the other of us, despairingly.

"Do you want that kid to hang?" he asked finally.

"You can't change rustlin' and murder," Gil said.

"Never mind that," Davies said. "Don't think about anything but the way you really feel about it. Do you feel that you'd like to have that kid hanged; any of them, for that matter?"

"My feelings haven't got anything to do with it," Gil said.

Davies began to argue to show us that feelings did; that they were the real guide in a thing like this, when Tetley called out to him by name. Everyone looked at Tetley and Davies, and stopped moving around or talking.

"Don't you know a trick when you see one, Davies?" Tetley asked him, for all of us to hear. "Or are you in on this?"

Davies retorted that he knew a trick as well as the next man, and that Tetley himself knew that this wasn't any trick; yes, and that Tetley knew he'd had no part in any such games himself. He was defiant, and stated again, defiantly, his faith in the innocence of the three men. But he talked hurriedly, defensively, and finally stopped of his own accord at a point that was not a conclusion. Whatever else was weakening him, I believe he felt all the time that it was ugly to talk so before the men themselves, that his own defense sounded no prettier there than Tetley's side. Then too, he had little support, and he knew it. He knew it so well that, when he had faltered to silence, and Tetley asked him, "Are you alone in this, Davies?" he said nothing.

"I think we'd better get this settled," Tetley said. "We must act as a unit in a job like this. Then we need fear no mistaken reprisal. Are you content to abide by a majority decision, Davies?"

Davies looked him in the face, but even that seemed to be an effort. He wouldn't say anything.

179

"How about the rest of you men?" Tetley asked, "Majority rule?"

There were sounds of assent. Nobody spoke out against it.

"It has to," Ma said. "Among a bunch of pigheads like this you'd never get everybody to agree to anything."

"We'll vote," Tetley said. "Everybody who is with Mr. Davies for putting this thing off and turning it over to the courts, step out here." He pointed to a space among us on the south side of the fire.

Davies walked out there and stood. Nobody else came for a moment, and he flushed when Tetley smiled at him. Then Sparks shambled out too, but smiling apologetically. Then Gerald Tetley joined them. His fists were clenched as he felt the watching, and saw his father's sardonic smile disappear slowly until his face was a stern mask. There was further movement, and some muttering, as Carl Bartlett and Moore stood out with them also. No more came.

"Five," said Tetley. "Not a majority, I believe, Mr. Davies."

He was disappointed that anyone had ventured to support Davies; I'm sure he hadn't expected as many as four others. I know I hadn't. And he was furious that Gerald had been among them. But he spoke quietly and ironically, as if his triumph had been complete.

Davies nodded, and slowly put Martin's letter away in his shirt pocket, under his waistcoat.

It was already getting light; the cabin and the trees could be seen clearly. There was no sunrise, but a slow leaking in of light from all quarters. The firelight no longer colored objects or faces near it. The faces were gray and tired and stern. We knew it was going to happen now, and yet, I believe, most of us still had a feeling it couldn't. It had been delayed so long; we had argued so much. Only Tetley seemed entirely self-possessed; his face showed no signs of weariness or excitement.

He asked Martin if there was any other message he wished to leave. Martin shook his head. In this light his face looked hollow, pale, and without individuality. His mouth was trembling constantly, and he was careful not to talk. I hoped, for our sake as much as his, that he'd make the decent end he now had his will set on.

Sparks was talking to the old fool again, but he, seeing the actual preparations begin, was frightened sick once more, and babbled constantly in a hoarse, worn-out voice, about his innocence, his age and his not wanting to die. Again and again he begged Martin to do something. This, more than anything else, seemed to shake Martin. He wouldn't look at old Hardwick, and pretended not to hear him.

We were surprised that the Mex wanted to make a confession, but he did. There wasn't any priest, so Amigo was to hear the confession, and carry it to a priest the first time he could go himself. There couldn't be any forgiveness, but it was the best they could do. They went down to the place where the sheds had stood, the Mex limping badly, and Amigo half carrying him along. Bartlett was stationed at a respectful distance as sentinel. We saw the Mex try to kneel, but he couldn't, so he stood there confessing with his back to us. Occasionally his hands moved in gestures of apology, which seemed strange from him. Amigo was facing us; but, when he wants, Amigo has a face like a wooden Indian. If the Mex was saying anything we ought to know now, which was what we were all thinking, we couldn't tell it from watching Amigo. He appeared merely to be intent upon remembering, in order that all the Mex's sins might be reported and forgiven.

In his field-officer manner Tetley was directing. Farnley knotted and threw up three ropes, so they hung over the long branch with the three nooses in a row. Then others staked down the ends of the ropes. The three horses were brought up again, and held under the ropes.

Tetley appointed Farnley, Gabe Hart and Gerald to whip the horses out. It was all right with Farnley, but Gabe refused. He gave no excuse, but stood there immovable, shaking his head. I was surprised Tetley had picked him.

"Gabe's not agin us, Mr. Tetley," Winder apologized,—"he can't stand to hurt anything. It would work on his mind."

Tetley asked for a volunteer, and when no one else came forward Ma took the job. She was furious about it, though. Moore looked at Smith, and so did Tetley, but Smith pretended to be drunker than he really was. Really he was scared sober now.

When it seemed all settled, young Tetley, nearly choking, refused also.

"You'll do it," was all Tetley told him.

"I can't, I tell you."

"We'll see to it you can."

The boy stood there, very white, still shaking his head.

"It's a necessary task," Tetley told him, evenly. "Someone else must perform it if you fail. I think you owe it to the others, and to yourself, on several scores."

The boy still shook his head stubbornly.

Moore, although he had refused on his own account, came over to Tetley and offered to relieve Gerald. "The boy's seen too much already. You shouldn't press him, man."

Tetley's face abruptly became bloodless; his mouth stretched downward, long and thin and hard, and his eyes glimmered with the fury he restrained. It was the first time I'd ever seen him let that nature show through, though I had felt always that it was there. He still spoke quietly though, and evenly.

"This is not your affair, Moore. Thank you just the same."

Moore shrugged and turned his back on him. He was angry himself.

Tetley said to Gerald, "I'll have no female boys bearing my name. You'll do your part, and say nothing more." He turned away, giving the boy no opportunity to reply.

"That must have been a very busy life," he remarked, looking down where the Mex was still confessing to Amigo.

When at last the Mex was done and they came back up, and the three prisoners were stood in a row with their hands tied down, Martin said,

"I suppose it's no use telling you again that we're innocent?"

"No good," Tetley assured him.

"It's not for myself I'm asking," Martin said.

"Other men have had families and have had to go for this sort of thing," Tetley told him. "It's too bad, but it's not our fault."

"You don't care for justice," Martin flared. "You don't even care whether you've got the right men or not. You want your way, that's all. You've lost something and somebody's got to be punished; that's all you know."

When Tetley just smiled, Martin's control broke again. "There's nobody to take care of them; they're in a strange place, they have nothing, and there's nobody to take care of them. Can't you understand that, you butcher? You've got to let me go; if there's a spot of humanity in you, you've got to let me go. Send men with me if you want to; I'm not asking you to trust me; you wouldn't trust anybody; your kind never will. Send men with me, then, but let me see them, let me arrange for them to go somewhere, for somebody to help them."

Old Hardwick began to whimper and jabber aloud again, and finally buckled in the knees and fell forward on his face. The Mex looked straight ahead of him and spit with contempt. "This is fine company for a man to die with," he said.

Martin started to yell something at the Mex, who was right beside him, but Mapes walked up to him and slapped him in the face. He slapped him hard, four times, so you could hear it like the crack of a lash. He paid no attention to protests or to Davies trying to hold his arm. After the fourth blow he waited to see if Martin would say anything more. He didn't, but stood there, crying weakly and freely, great sobs heaving his chest up and making him lift his chin to catch his breath because of the bonds.

Others put the old man back on his feet, and a couple of shots of whisky were given to each of the three. Then they walked them over to the horses. The old man went flabby on them, and they had nearly to carry him.

I saw Davies keeping Amigo behind, holding him by the arm and talking. Amigo's face was angry and stubborn, and he kept shaking his head. Tetley saw it too, and guessed what I had. Smiling, he told Davies that a confession was a confession, and not evidence, even in a court.

"He doesn't have to tell us," Davies said. "All he has to do is say whether we'd better wait; then we could find out."

Amigo looked worried.

Tetley said, "Men have been known to lie, even in

confession, under pressure less than this." Amigo looked at him as if for the first time he questioned his divinity, but then he said, "It wasn't a priest; I don't know."

"Even if it had been," Tetley said, eying the Mex. "I'll give you two minutes to pray," he told the three. They were standing by the horses now, under the branch with the ropes hanging down from it.

Martin was chewing his mouth to stop crying. He looked around at us quickly. We were in a fairly close circle; nobody would face him, man after man looked down. Finally, like he was choking, he ducked his head, then, awkwardly because of the rope, got to his knees. The Mex was still standing, but had his head bent and was moving his lips rapidly. The old man was down in a groveling heap with Sparks beside him; Sparks was doing the praying for him. Moore took off his hat, and then the rest of us did the same. After a moment Davies and some of the others knelt also. Most of us couldn't bring ourselves to do that, but we all bowed and kept quiet. In the silence, in the gray light slowly increasing, the moaning of the old man, Sparks' praying and the Mex going again and again through his rapid patter sounded very loud. Still you could hear every movement of the horses, leather creaking, the little clinks of metal.

"Time's up," Tetley said, and the old man wailed once, as if he'd been hit. The Mex lifted his head and glanced around quickly. His face had a new expression, the first we'd seen of it in him. Martin rose slowly to his feet, and looked around slowly. The moments of silence and the crisis had had the reverse effect on him. He no longer appeared desperate or incoherent, but neither did he look peaceful or resigned. I have never seen another face so bitter as his was then, or one that showed its hatred more clearly. He spoke to Davies, but even his voice proved the effort against his pride and detestation.

"Will you find someone you can trust to look out for my wife and children?" he asked. "In time she will repay anything it puts you out."

Davies' eyes were full of tears. "I'll find someone," he promised.

"You'd better take some older woman along," Martin said. "It's not going to be easy."

"Don't worry," Davies said, "your family will be all right."

"Thanks," Martin said. Then he said, "My people are dead, but Miriam's are living. They live in Ohio. And Drew didn't want to sell his cattle; he'll buy them back for enough to cover their travel."

Davies nodded.

"Better not give her my things," Martin said, "just this ring, if you'll get it."

Davies fumbled at the task. He had trouble with the rope, and his hands were shaking, but he got the ring, and held it up for Martin to see. Martin nodded. "Just give her that and my letter first. Don't talk to her until she's read my letter." He didn't seem to want to say any more.

"That all?" Tetley asked.

"That's all, thanks," Martin said.

They asked the Mex, and he suddenly started speaking very rapidly. He was staring around as if he couldn't quite see us. It had got to him finally, all right. Then he stopped speaking just as suddenly and kept shaking his head in little short shakes. He'd been talking in Spanish. They didn't ask the old man.

The three of them were lifted onto the horses and made to stand on them. Two men had to support old Hardwick.

"Tie their ankles," Mapes ordered.

"God," Gil whispered, "I was afraid they weren't going to." He felt it a great relief that their ankles were going to be tied.

Farnley got up on a horse and fixed the noose around each man's neck. Then he and Ma got behind two of the horses with quirts in their hands. Young Tetley had to be told twice to get behind his. Then he moved to his place like a sleepwalker, and didn't even know he had taken the quirt somebody put in his hand.

The old man, on the inside, was silent, staring like a fish, and already hanging on the rope a little in spite of the men holding him up. The Mex had gone to pieces too, buckling nearly as badly as Hardwick, and jabbering rapid and panicky in Spanish. When the horses sidled under him once, tightening the rope, he screamed. In the pinch Martin was taking it the best of the three. He

185

kept his head up, not looking at any of us, and even the bitterness was gone from his face. He had a melancholy expression, such as goes with thinking of an old sorrow.

Tetley moved around behind the horses, and directed Mapes to give the signal. We all moved out of the circle to give the horses room. In the last second even the Mex was quiet. There was no sound save the shifting of the three horses, restless at having been held so long. A feathery, wide-apart snow was beginning to sift down again; the end of a storm, not the beginning of another, though. The sky was becoming transparent, and it was full daylight.

Mapes fired the shot, and we heard it echo in the mountain as Ma and Farnley cut their horses sharply across the haunches and the holders let go and jumped away. The horses jumped away too, and the branch creaked under the jerk. The old man and the Mex were dead at the fall, and just swung and spun slowly. But young Tetley didn't cut. His horse just walked out from under, letting Martin slide off and dangle, choking to death, squirming up and down like an impaled worm, his face bursting with compressed blood. Gerald didn't move even then, but stood there shaking all over and looking up at Martin fighting the rope.

After a second Tetley struck the boy with the butt of his pistol, a back-handed blow that dropped him where he stood.

"Shoot him," he ordered Farnley, pointing at Martin. Farnley shot. Martin's body gave a little leap in the air, then hung slack, spinning slowly around and back, and finally settling into the slowing pendulum swing of the others.

Gil went with Davies to help young Tetley up. Nobody talked much, or looked at anybody else, but scattered and mounted. Winder and Moore caught up the rustlers' ponies. The Bartlett boys and Amigo remained to drive the cattle, and to do the burying before they started. All except Mapes and Smith shied clear of Tetley, but he didn't seem to notice. He untied his big palomino, mounted, swung him about and led off toward the road. His face was set and white; he didn't look back.

186

Most of the rest of us did, though, turn once or twice to look. I was glad when the last real fall of the snow started, soft and straight and thick. It lasted only a few minutes, but it shut things out.

Gil caught up and rode with me after he and Davies had
helped Gerald. I'd thought, seeing him drop, that the
kid had been killed, but Gil said no, it had been a
glancing blow, that snow on his face and a drink had fixed
him up enough to ride.

We rode slowly because of my shoulder, letting the
others disappear ahead of us, and Gerald and Davies
come up behind us. It was difficult to turn in my saddle,
but I did, to get a look at Gerald. His face had a knife-
edge, marble-white look, and the circles under his eyes
were big and dark, so that he appeared to have enor-
mous eyes, or none at all, but empty sockets, like a skull.
He wasn't looking where he was going, but the trouble
wasn't his injury. I don't think he knew now that he had
it. He was gnawing himself inside again. Passionate and
womanish, but with a man's conscience and pride, that
boy kept himself thin and bleached just thinking and
feeling.

Davies, riding beside him, kept passing his hand over his face in a nerveless way unusual to him, rubbing his nose or fingering his mouth or drawing the hand slowly across his eyes and forehead, as if there were cobwebs on his skin.

We were all tired, even Gil half asleep in his saddle, and we nearly rode into the horses standing in the clearing before we saw them. They were quietly bunched under the falling snow.

"It's the sheriff," Gil said. "It's Risley."

Then he said, "Jesus, it's Kinkaid."

It was too, with a bandage on his head, and a bit peaked, but otherwise as usual, quiet, friendly and ashamed to be there. The other three men, besides the sheriff, were Tyler, Drew and Davies' pimply clerk Joyce. The Judge was red in the face and talking violently, but through the snow his voice came short and flat.

"It's murder, murder and nothing less. I warned you, Tetley, I warned you repeatedly, and Davies warned you, and Osgood. You all heard us; you were all warned. You wanted justice, did you? Well, by God, you shall have it now, real justice. Every man of you is under arrest for murder. We'll give you a chance to see how slow regular justice is when you're in the other chair."

Nobody replied to him, that I could hear.

"My God," Gil said, "I knew it didn't feel right. I knew we should wait. That bastard Tetley," he finished.

Everybody would hang it on Tetley now. I didn't say anything.

The sheriff was stern, but he wasn't the kind to gabble easily, like Tyler. He was a small, stocky man with a gray, walrus mustache and black bushy eyebrows. He had a heavy sheepskin on, with the collar turned up around his ears. His deep-set, hard, blue eyes looked at each of us in turn. Nobody but Tetley tried to hold up against his look, and even Tetley failed.

When he'd made us all look down, he said something we couldn't hear to the Judge. The Judge began to sputter, but when Risley looked level at him too the sputter died, and the Judge just stared around at us belligerently again, thrusting his lower lip out and sucking it in and making a horse, blowing noise.

Risley sat silent for a moment, as if considering carefully, looking us over all the time. Finally he stared into the snow over us and the milky blue shadows of the trees through it and said, "I haven't recognized anybody here. We passed in a snowstorm, and I was in a hurry."

"That's collusion, Risley," the Judge began loudly, getting redder than ever. "I'll have you understand I won't . . ."

"What do you want to do?" Risley cut in, looking at him.

The Judge tried to say something impressive about the good name of the valley and of the state, and the black mark against his jurisdiction and Risley's, but it was no use. Everybody just waited for him to stop; he couldn't hold out against all of us without Risley.

When he was just blowing again, Risley said, "I'm not even looking for the leaders. Nobody had to go if he didn't want to."

He went on in changed tone, as if he had finished unimportant preliminaries and was getting down to business.

"I'll want ten men for my posse."

We all volunteered. We were tired, and we'd had plenty of man hunting and judging to hold us for a long time, but we felt he was giving us a chance to square ourselves. Even Tetley volunteered, but Risley didn't notice him; he passed up Mapes also. But he took Winder, which added Gabe Hart, and he took Moore, and after looking at him for a long time he took Farnley. Kinkaid looked up at that, smiled a little and raised one hand off the horn just enough so Farnley could see it. Farnley straightened as if he'd had half a life given back to him. Farnley was mean with a grudge, but honest. If he didn't like Risley right then, he liked himself a lot less.

When Risley had selected his ten men, he ordered the rest of us to go home. "Go on about your own business," he told us. "Don't hang around in bunches. If you have to tell anybody anything, just tell them I'm taking care of this with a picked posse. You can't stop the talk, but there'll be a lot less fuss if you keep out of it. Nobody knew these men."

He turned to the Judge. "It'll have to be that way," he apologized.

"Perhaps, perhaps," the Judge muttered. "All the same

190

—" and he subsided. Actually, though, he was relieved. We didn't have to worry about him.

Risley and Drew pushed through us, the chosen men falling in behind them. The rest began to drift down toward the valley. Tetley was left to ride by himself this time. But he was iron, that man; his face didn't show anything, not even weariness.

Davies stopped Risley and Drew. Both his manner and his speech were queerly fumbling, as if he were either exhausted or a little mad. While he spoke to them he twisted his bridle, occasionally jerking a length of it between his two hands, and then halting his speech for a moment while he rubbed his forehead and eyes that feeble way. When Drew had questioned him a bit they got it straight. For some obscure reason, connected apparently only with the way he felt, he didn't believe he should take that letter to Martin's wife. He wanted Drew to take it. He wanted Drew to get a woman to help Martin's wife too; he was much impressed by the need of the woman, and repeated it several times, saying it should be an older woman who had had children and wouldn't gush. He insisted that Drew must be able to see why he couldn't take the letter.

You could tell by Drew's face that he couldn't see. He was a big, fleshy man with gray eyes, a yellow tan and a heavy, chestnut beard. He was wearing a gray frock coat and a Spanish sombrero with silver conches on the band, and was smoking a thin Mexican cigar. He talked with the cigar in the corner of his mouth. He was taking the whole thing impatiently, as business to be done. But then, he hadn't seen what we had. And he wasn't totally without concern, because, when Davies asked him, as if, somehow, the answer was very important to him personally, if he had sold the cattle to Martin, he answered only after a delay, and then said, "Yes, poor kid. A lot better for him if I hadn't. It don't do to change your regular ways," he added. "Men get to banking on them."

You could see he thought there was something queer about the way Davies was acting, but he took the letter and the ring from him, assuring him that he would send somebody he could trust if he couldn't take them himself. He promised he would send a woman too, a woman who would take care of things and not be a sympathy monger. When Davies was still fretful, like a man with a very orderly mind who is dying and can't remember if everything is arranged, Drew became short in his answers. But he also thought of the thing which seemed to relieve Davies most for the moment; he hadn't wanted to ask about it.

"I'll give his wife the money he paid me for the cattle, of course," Drew said impatiently. "I have it with me; I haven't even had a chance to get back to the house yet."

Then he got ready to go, but looked hard at Davies, and decided to risk an opinion on something which wasn't strictly any of his business.

"You'd better get some rest," he told Davies. "You're taking this too hard. From what I've heard, you did all you could; there's nothing you or anybody else can do about it now."

Davies looked at him as if Drew were the crazy one. But he didn't say anything, just nodded.

Risley made a come-on motion with his hand to the posse, and they filed off slowly on the snowy road. When they had entered the aisle between the big pines they picked up to a little jog, and finally disappeared, dimming away man by man through the screen of falling snow. In the clearing there was already beginning to be sunlight in the snow.

"Must have been that other bunch after all," Gil said.

"What?" Davies asked.

"The bunch Small and Carnes told us about."

"Oh," said Davies. "Yes, I suppose so."

When we reined around, Gil said, "What the hell's going on now?"

There weren't more than half a dozen riders left in the clearing; they were all bunched on the farther edge, where the ravine pitches down to the creek. Among them were two horses without riders; one of them was young Tetley's black.

We rode over to the edge too, and looked down with the others. About half way up the steep bank, scrambling in the snow and among the loose stones, and slipping on the pine needles, were Smith and Gerald. Smith had one arm around the boy, and was grabbing from bush

192

to bush and at saplings to pull himself up. The kid didn't seem to be hurt, though, he just wasn't doing anything to help himself. Sparks dismounted and went part way down to give a hand to the pair. They came up that way, stumbling and sliding to the top, the kid dragging his feet and not even hanging on.

When they got up he stood by himself all right. Sparks kept a hand on his shoulder.

"What you want to try a thing like that foh, Mastah Tetley?" Sparks asked him. He was trying to prod the kid awake, but console him too. He was scared at what the kid had been doing. The others were scared too, but they were tired and they didn't care so much; they were resentful.

"He's crazy," Ma said, looking down at him.

Gerald didn't say anything. He shook Spark's hand off his shoulder and walked over slowly to his horse and struggled up into the saddle.

"Keep an eye on him," Ma said. "He's crazy. You got the gun?" she asked Smith.

Smith held it up for her to see. "Damned young fool," he said proudly. "I didn't get down there any too soon. Maybe you think that bank isn't steep," he boasted, "and slick. By Godfreys I went down; thought I was gonna dive right in the creek."

"He wouldn't have done it," one of the riders said. He was a thin, middle-aged man with a long, thin nose and a thin, down-turned mouth. He looked sandy, weedy and sour. I didn't know him, or where he came from.

"What was he up to this time?" Gil asked.

Smith was excited and wanted to prove how quick he'd been.

"First thing we just noticed his horse," he said, "and nobody on it." He pointed at the horse, but if young Tetley heard he didn't look at us. "Well, I knew what he was thinking, of course. Who didn't? He hadn't been making any secret about it. Right off I picked the creek canyon as the place. Sure enough, there he was, standing by himself down at the bottom. He was just staring at the water then, but he had this gun in his hand," Smith held the gun up again, "and it didn't take more than one look to know what he was going to do. I tell you, I piled down there in a hurry. Lucky he didn't hear me till I was right on him; noise of the water, I guess. When he did hear me, he was going to do it quick, but I got to him." He looked around at us for admiration.

"He wouldn't have done it," the sour man said again.

"The hell he wouldn't," Smith said, raising his voice.

Young Tetley still didn't look at us, but started his horse for the narrows. Smith didn't notice; he was going right on to prove Gerald would have killed himself.

"We saw it," Ma said. She was watching Gerald.

But Smith had to convince the sour man. He lowered his voice, but went on waving the gun. The sour man was watching the gun; it made him nervous. Smith was going to explain how Tetley had made a fool of his son in front of everybody.

"You're certainly taking a lot of responsibility," the sour man said.

"Somebody had to," Smith yelled at him. "I didn't see you in any hurry."

"He wanted to, maybe," said the sour man, "but he couldn't have done it."

Smith was still going to argue it, but we were all moving away. He stared after the sour man for a minute, then spit and went over to his own horse.

He caught up with us and kept trying to prove Gerald would have shot himself, and on the side that Tetley was responsible for all the trouble. We didn't want to talk, or hear him talk, and finally he gave up and rode on ahead to try it on Ma.

On the way down we just stopped on a few level spots to give me a breather. My shoulder felt stiff and very big. We didn't talk except when I asked Gil for a drink or to light me a cigarette.

By the time we got to the fork at the foot of the grade it had stopped snowing and the sky was beginning to clear, not breaking up, but thinning away everywhere at once and letting pale sunlight through. It was still cold though, and the mountains on both sides of the valley were white to their bases.

On the edge of town Gil asked me, "How do you feel now?"

It seemed to cheer him up when I told him I was coming all right.

"The quicker we get out of this town," he said, "the better I'll feel."

I didn't feel like two days' riding right then. I had my mind set on food and a change of bandage and a bed. I didn't say anything.

He saw what I was thinking, though.

"Still," he said, "I wouldn't mind getting good and drunk and staying that way for a couple of days. We'll lay up at Canby's. Canby's as good as a doctor. And he don't gossip."

"I'll be all set by tomorrow," I told him.

"Sure," he said.

When we went in at Canby's Smith was already there, drinking and arguing. He was working himself up to a fit of righteousness. Canby was standing behind the bar, listening to him, but not showing anything or saying anything. Smith was quiet when he saw us, and began staring down into his drink as if he was thinking hard but keeping his thoughts to himself.

"What'll it be?" Canby asked us, like we'd just come in from work.

"We want a room," Gil said, looking at Smith hunched over his drink.

Canby looked at me. He knew all right. "Go on up," he said, "the front room's empty.

"The whole damn place is empty, for that matter," he continued, looking at Smith, "but the front room's all made up."

Gil put a hand on Smith's shoulder. Smith started to shake it off, but when Gil clinched it he stood still, not even trying to look around.

"Listen, fellow," Gil said, "don't talk so much."

We went up to the front room, which was bare and clean. There was a dresser with a wash bowl and a pitcher of water and a glass on it, a curtain strung across one corner for a closet, one chair, an iron double bed, and a small stove with nickel trimmings. Everything but the stove was painted white, and the curtain was heavy white canvas. The bed had clean but wrinkled linen on it. There was no carpet on the floor and no curtains on the two windows, which made the room seem scrubbed and full of light. Through the eastern window we could see the mountains with the snow on them, and through the other the street, with Davies' store right across from us. But it was cold in there too. While I lay down on the bed Gil built a fire in the stove. There was fresh-cut wood in a heap on the floor beside it. Then he came over and pulled my boots off for me.

"You lay here and take a rest for a while," he said. "I'll take the horses over to Winder's."

When he'd left I could hear Smith talking again downstairs. Then, after a bit, it was quiet. I was half asleep when the door opened and Canby came in. He had another armload of wood for the stove. He dumped it, and started putting some in.

"Monty won't talk for a while," he said, without looking around. "He's back in the poolroom with a whole bottle. Then he'll have to sleep it off."

"It doesn't matter anyway," I said. "Everybody knows."

"Yes," Canby said, straightening up, "but Smith strengthens the facts a bit."

He came over and stood by the bed.

"How's the shoulder?" he asked.

"Not so good," I admitted. "Smith tell you about that too?"

"No," he said, "he was telling me mostly about how he saved young Tetley, and what a first-rate bastard Tetley was, and more about how he saved young Tetley. You didn't walk right," he explained.

"Let me have a look at it," he went on, starting to undo my shirt.

"You a doctor?" I asked him.

"You have to know a little of everything in this business," he said. "Somebody's always getting hurt. They come in to get their courage up, and then they have to prove it."

He peeled me down to my shoulder, and then yanked the rags off. He was neat and quick about it, but they stuck a little before they came away. The shoulder under them was swollen and dark red, the bullet hole looking little and dark in it, like the head of a boil. I had to grind my teeth when he felt around it.

"It could be better," he said. "I'll be back in a minute."

When he came back he had a pitcher of hot water, a jar of some kind of ointment, and some clean strips of white cloth. He squeezed the wound open again, washed

196

it out, and rubbed in the ointment, which burned. Then he bandaged it snugly.

"No," he said while he was finishing up, "Rose Mapen was in for a minute last night, with her new attachment and the duenna. Pretty proper Rose is getting these days. She told me you'd been shot. She said you weren't very polite about their helping either."

"I don't like women around; not the fussy kind anyway," I told him.

"No," he agreed.

"I'll bet Gil was tickled to see them," he said. "I'll bring you up something to eat when Gil gets back."

"I can come down," I said. "There's nothing the matter with my legs."

"No need," he said.

I told him Gil was going to get drunk, and asked him to keep an eye out. He said he would, and went out, closing the door.

I lay there dozing and letting the ointment work. The fire was burning well now, and with that and the sun in the east window the room was getting warm. The sunlight was cheerful too. I didn't feel much connected with anything that had happened, not even my own wound.

I must have fallen asleep, and they didn't want to wake me. The next thing I knew it was afternoon. The room was still warm but there was no sun any more. I forgot about the shoulder and stretched and remembered it. Downstairs I could hear the voices of a number of men. They sounded distant, and didn't interest me. But I was really hungry.

I started to get up to go downstairs and eat, and then I saw Davies. He was sitting on the one chair, looking at the floor. Waking up from a sleep that had freshened me and put the night's business behind me some, I was surprised to see how bad he looked. His hair was tangled from running his hands through it, and he had a little white stubble of beard. He looked tired too, his face slack and really old, with big bruised pouches under the eyes. But that wasn't what made him look so bad. It was his forehead and eyes. His forehead was knotted and his eyes were too steady, like a careful drunk's, but not fogged in that way, but so bright they were mad. The whites of them were bloodshot too, and the rims a raw red, which made that light blue look even crazier. He was so tired he would have keeled over if he'd given up, but he hadn't given up. He was still fighting something.

I sat up as quick as I dared.

"What's wrong?" I asked.

He looked up when he heard the bed creak, but didn't seem to hear me.

"How's the shoulder?" he asked. "You feel better?"

His voice was husky and worn out, as if he'd been arguing for hours.

"It's all right," I said. "Canby fixed it up good."

"You had a long sleep," he said.

"I didn't know you were here."

"It's all right. No hurry. Now or another time; it wouldn't matter."

He wanted to say something, but couldn't get started. I was afraid of it. I didn't want to get mixed up in anything more. But I had to give him a chance to unload.

"You don't look like you'd slept much," I told him.

"I haven't," he said, "any."

I waited.

He got up with slow labor and went to the window where he could look out into the street. Without turning around he said, "Croft, will you listen to me?"

"Sure," I said, but not encouraging him.

"I've got to talk," he protested. "I've got to talk so I can get some sleep."

I didn't say anything.

"I thought about everybody who was up there," he explained, "and I have to talk to you, Art. You're the only one will understand."

Why in hell, I wondered, did everybody have to take me for his father confessor?

"Maybe you'll think I'm crazy," he said, still at the window.

"You sound like you had a confession to make."

He turned around. "That's it," he said, more quickly. "That's it, Croft, a confession."

I still waited.

"Croft," he said, "I killed those three men."

I just stared.

"I told you you'd think I was crazy," he said.

198

Well, I did, and I didn't like a man twice my age confessing to me.

"As much as if I'd pulled the ropes," he was saying.

"Why blame anybody?" I asked him. "It's done now."

"No, it's not done," he said, "it's just beginning. Every act," he began.

I broke in. "If we have to blame somebody," I said, "then I'd say . . ."

This time he stopped me.

"I know," he said, almost angrily, "you'd say it was Tetley. That's what you all say. Smith's been preaching it was Tetley. He has himself all worked up to lynch Tetley."

"Well, wasn't it?"

"No," he said, and then seemed to be making sure of his thought. "No," he said again, after a moment, "Tetley couldn't help what he did."

"Oh, that way," I said. "If you take it that way, nobody can help it. We're all to blame, and nobody's to blame. It just happened."

"No," he said. "Most of you couldn't help it. Most men can't; they don't really think. They haven't any conception of basic justice. They . . ."

"I got all that," I told him. I thought I had too. It seemed to have ironed out while I slept, so I knew right away what he meant by anything he started.

"Yes," he said, smiling hard, and looking down at my sharpness.

"Most people," he went on slowly, "all of those men, see the sins of commission, but not of omission. They feel guilty now, when it's done, and they want somebody to blame. They've chosen Tetley."

"If it's anybody," I began.

"No," he interrupted, "not any more than the rest of you. He's merely the scapegoat. He recognized only the sin of commission, and he couldn't feel that. Sin doesn't mean anything to Tetley any more."

"That doesn't mean he wasn't wrong," I said.

"No," Davies said, "but not to blame."

"If you look at it that way," I said, "only a saint could be to blame for anything."

"There's some truth in that."

I was mean then, but I wanted to shut him up before

199

he'd talked so much he'd be ashamed of it afterwards. You can hate a man you've talked too much to. He's like a man who's seen you show yellow.

"Meaning you're a saint?" I asked him.

He looked at me, but didn't wait even to make sure how I meant it. He was just following his own trouble.

"Something like that," he said without a smile, "by comparison. Or I was before this," he added after a moment. "Oh, God," he said suddenly. "That boy; all night."

He closed his eyes hard and turned back to the window. Holding onto the window sash, he pressed his forehead against his hand and leaned there, trembling all over, like a woman who's been told pretty bad news too suddenly.

I waited until he wasn't shaking, and then asked him, easy as I could, "Meaning this was a sin of omission?"

He moved his head to say yes, but still keeping it against his hand.

"You're thinking about it too much," I told him. "You're making it all up." I was embarrassed that he could show so much emotion. It wasn't natural. Most old men have their feelings so thinned out they can't be much stirred, or their habits so set they can't show it if they are. He was like a boy, or a woman who hasn't had to work much with her body.

He moved his head again, to say no.

I got up off the bed. "You get some sleep," I said. "You can sleep right here. I'm going down and get some grub. I'll tell Canby not to let anybody bother you."

He shook his head, but then turned around slowly, not looking at me.

"You're cutting it too fine," I told him. "This was a sin of commission if I ever saw one. We hung three men, didn't we? Or was that a nightmare I had?"

He looked up at me so I began to hope I was reaching him. All of a sudden I felt awful sorry for that little, bent, old man, ripping himself up about something most of us wouldn't have known was there.

"And if anybody came out of it clean," I said, "you're the one. You and Sparks, and Sparks was just letting it go."

You'd have thought I was offering him his first water

after two days in the dry hills in August. He nearly whispered.

"Do you think so, Croft," he whispered, "really?"

"Sure," I said, "I know so. Now you get some sleep," I said, shaking up the bed to get my own dent out of it.

"You'll see it from the outside when you've slept," I told him.

When I straightened up and looked at him again that light was all gone out of him.

Now what the hell have I said? I wondered.

"Now what's the matter?" I asked him.

He stared at me out of an old and heavy face again, and the eyes dead in it too now. I thought he was going to pass out, and started to give him a hand.

He brushed me off with a short, angry gesture, and stood there swaying like he was drunk.

"For a minute I was going to believe it," he said hoarsely. "Oh, I want to believe it, all right. All day," he went on, "I've been trying to convince myself I was the saint. For a minute," he said, with a little, crazy laugh, "I thought you really knew."

I didn't have anything clear by now.

"If you mean all that about justice," I began.

"Yes, all that about justice," he said.

"I got that," I assured him. "I got that so I could tell what you were thinking every move; like it was me."

"Could you?" he asked.

"Sure. Every move.

"Listen," I argued, "if being able to think of all those things but still not stop it, is all that makes your sin of omission, then I'm as guilty as you are. More, for that matter," I added. "I didn't even try to do anything. Why was it your business any more than mine?"

"You knew what I was thinking?" he insisted.

"Every move. And so did most of the rest, for that matter."

"They couldn't have," he said hopefully.

"They did. They wouldn't have argued it the same way, maybe, but they knew it was there. They could feel it. And they didn't do anything either. Why, if that's all you mean," I burst out when he just kept watching me like I still might say something, "we're all more guilty than you are. You tried. You're the only one that did try. And Tetley's the worst of all. They're right about Tetley."

"Tetley's a beast," Davies said suddenly, with more hatred in his voice than I'd have thought he could have against anybody.

"A depraved, murderous beast," he said, the same way.

"Now," I said, "you're talking sense."

He was quiet at once, as if I had accused him of something, and then said slowly, "But a beast is not to blame."

"He loved it," I said.

Again he searched me, as if to determine how deep my reasons went, and as if it would set him free if they went deep enough.

"Yes," he agreed, "he loved it. He extracted pleasure from every morsel of suffering. He protracted it as long as he could. It was all one to him, the boy's mental torment, the old man's animal fear, the Mex taking that bullet out of his leg. Did you see his face when the Mex was taking that bullet out of his leg?" he asked.

"I saw it. He loved it."

"Yes," he said, "and his son."

"You mean hitting him?"

"And the rest," he said, "clear to the end."

"He's always been like that about Gerald," I said.

"Tetley is a vile man," he said slowly. "That is the only security I have."

I was lost again. He seemed to have some central conception that was the core of the whole thing to him, but to be afraid to get at it, to keep working around it, and losing me all the time.

"Only two things mean anything to Tetley," he said, "power and cruelty. He can't feel quiet or gentle things any more; and he can't feel pity, and he can't feel guilt."

"You know that?" I asked. "Then why be so hard on yourself?"

Davies didn't answer that.

"I keep telling myself," he said, "that I couldn't have changed it; that even though Tetley can't be blamed, I couldn't have made him see."

"That's right," I said.

"And I wouldn't have killed him," Davies said.

"God, no," I said.

202

"And nothing else would have helped."

"No," I said, "nothing else. Maybe," I said, "that's what made us all feel yellow. We didn't think it that way, but just knew we'd have to kill him, that we couldn't stop him any other way. And you can't do that. He was like a crazy animal," I said, remembering, "cold crazy."

"Yes," Davies said, "cold crazy."

Neither of us said anything for a minute, and I heard the voices downstairs in the bar and knew there was a change in them. At first I couldn't figure out what it was. Then I heard a woman laugh, a deep, throaty, pleased laugh, and then her voice saying something, and her laugh again, and a lot of men joining the laugh. Then it was all quiet but one voice, a man's voice, telling something long, and then the woman's laugh again, and the general laugh, as if they were just a little slower than she was to get the point. At first, thinking about Davies still, I couldn't figure what it was that was bothering me about that talk and laughing. Then the man spoke again, and I knew. It was Rose and her husband down there. And Gil had said he was going to get drunk. I didn't know how long I'd been asleep, or whether Gil had already got drunk and passed out and Canby had put him to bed somewhere else, not to bother me, or what. Only I knew Gil wasn't down there now; not with all that laughing, and I didn't like to think what could happen if he did come in drunk and still spoiling for his fight and feeling mean about last night.

I got to feeling mean myself. They laughed again down there. I didn't see how anybody could find anything to laugh at today. They sounded like fools.

Davies had said something.

"What?" I asked.

"He killed the boy, too," Davies repeated.

"Sure," I said, trying to get back to where I'd been. "All three of them."

"No, Gerald," he said.

"Gerald?" I echoed.

"You haven't heard then?" he asked, and that seemed to be another of those peculiar disappointments to him. "I thought you'd have heard."

"I've been right here, sleeping. What would I have heard?"

"That Gerald did kill himself."

"He didn't," I said. I was like the sour man. I still didn't think he'd try again.

Davies sat down slowly in the chair. Then he sat there twisting his hands.

"You didn't think he would?" he asked finally, with that same big question.

"No," I said. "He couldn't have. He talked too much."

"He did, though," Davies said. "He did." And suddenly he put his head down and clung to it with both hands, passing through another seizure like the one at the window.

Then he was quiet again, and looked up, though not at me, and told me evenly, "When he got home his father had locked the house against him. He went out into the barn and hanged himself from a rafter. The hired man found him about noon. I saw him," he said slowly. His hands stopped twisting and gripped together.

"Jeez, the poor kid," I said.

"Yes," he said, "the poor kid."

And then, "The hired man was afraid to tell Tetley. He saw Sparks and told him, and Sparks came for me."

"Did you have to see Tetley then?"

"I didn't want to. I didn't trust myself. But I saw him."

I didn't ask the question, but he answered it anyway.

"It meant nothing to him; not a flicker. Just thanked me as if I'd delivered a package from the store."

The news was like a home punch to me too. I should have known if anybody should, after the way the kid had opened up to me. Also I could see why that might have put Davies off on this spree of blaming himself. It could have been prevented so easily; just somebody to stay with the kid. The sins of omission.

They laughed again downstairs.

Shut up, you brainless bastards, I thought. I guess I half said it, because Davies looked up at me.

"That's not your fault," I said. "With Tetley what he is, it would have happened sooner or later anyway. There's some things you can't butt in on."

"But you didn't think it would happen?"

"No," I said. "Well, I was wrong."

"I did," he whispered. "I knew."

"You couldn't. *I* should have. He talked to me all the way up. I knew then he wasn't straight. But when he didn't, when he let Smith go down and get him like that, I didn't think he'd make another try. You couldn't know."

He suddenly switched our talk again. He couldn't sit still, tired as he was, but got up and went to the window.

"I'm not making a very clear confession, am I?"

"Listen, Mr. Davies," I started, and stopped because the men were laughing again downstairs and the laugh stopped short. I was listening for Gil's voice. But it must have been just a short laugh, the sort you get when the story has to go on. One voice was talking steadily, and though I couldn't hear the words I could hear the way they were clipped off, and the smooth, level tone. Rose's husband. Then he got his big, final laugh, and somebody else started.

I don't think Davies had even heard them. He thought I just couldn't find anything to say, and turned to face me once more, and there was neither that hope or the blind self-torture showing in his face for the moment. There was more a balance, as though he had finally decided exactly what to say and was intent upon my reply. That look brought me back too, so I was only half listening for Gil.

"You say you know what I was thinking all the time?" he asked.

"I could feel it," I said carefully. "We all could."

"Did you believe Martin was innocent?" he asked. "I mean at the time, before we knew. Did you believe he was innocent when they put the rope up over the limb?" he put it.

I stayed careful. "I felt we were wrong," I said slowly, looking right at him, "I felt that he shouldn't hang."

"That's scarcely the same thing," he said. "Nobody wants to see a man hang."

"You couldn't *know* he was innocent," I said. "None of us would have stood there and seen him hang if we'd known."

"No," Davies said. "So you didn't know." He was very quiet saying that.

"You're twisting it again," I told him sharply.

205

"No," he said, "you didn't know, but I did."

Then it struck me so it made the blood come to my own face. He'd known something all along, and been afraid to bring it out, because of Tetley. He'd had a proof, perhaps in that letter, and been afraid for his own skin to bring it out. I could see then why he wanted to believe nothing could have turned Tetley.

"How could you know?" I tried to bluff, but my voice didn't sound right and he caught it.

"Yes," he said. "I knew. I'd read that letter."

He got my question again.

"No," he said, "not that way. There was nothing a court would have called a proof. A court won't take the picture of a man's soul for a proof. But I knew then, beyond any question, what he was like. From the first I felt a boy like that couldn't have done it; not the rustling even; certainly not the murder. And when I'd read that letter I knew it."

So I was wrong again.

"Is that all?" I asked.

"He talked about me in the letter," Davies mooned. "He told his wife how kind I was to him, what I risked trying to defend him. And he trusted me; you saw that. He worked so hard to ease it for his wife, too," he went on, lower. "To keep her from breaking herself on grief or hating us. And he reminded her of things they had done together."

He bent his head in a spasm again. "It was a beautiful letter," he whispered.

"Listen," I said, "that may all make you feel bad, sure. It was a rotten deal, sure. But we all knew we should have brought them in like you said, and if we had, it never would have happened."

"Half an hour," Davies mumbled. "Half an hour would have done it."

"I know," I said. "You think I haven't thought of that too? But there wasn't anything you could do."

"I knew," he repeated. His knowing seemed to be what hurt him most.

"You didn't know," I told him, "any more than the rest of us did. You knew what he was like from that letter, you say. Well, maybe. But we all had a chance to see that letter. That kind of an argument can't stand up

206

against branded cattle, no bill of sale, a dead man's gun, and a guy that acts like that Mex did."

"It could have," he said. "You admit yourself you were ready to be stopped. You admit you thought most of them were."

"There wasn't the proof," I said angrily. "You don't get all set for a hanging and stop for some little feeling you have."

"You might," he said, "when you're hanging on a feeling too."

"You tried to stop it, hard enough and often enough," I said.

"That's the point," he said. This calm and reasonable self-denunciation was worse than when he broke a little. "I tried. I took the leadership, and with it I accepted the responsibility. I set myself up as the power of justice, of common pity, even. I set myself up as the light to oppose Tetley's darkness. And in their hearts the men were with me; and the right was with me. Everything was with me."

"Everything," I reminded him, "except what we all took to be the facts."

"They didn't matter then," he maintained. "They didn't matter."

"God," I said, "if you take any pleasure in feeling responsible for three gang hangings and a suicide."

He closed his eyes like I'd slapped him.

"I'm sorry," I said.

"No, you're right," he said. "I was."

"You get some sleep," I ordered. He'd skirted the point again, if he had one. He was just cutting himself up.

"You'll admit I took it on myself to stand up against Tetley," he persisted.

"All right, you did. There were none of us there hog-tied, or tongue-tied either, for that matter."

He looked at me. I was going to say something more, but suddenly the chatter downstairs stopped, and there was one voice, a new one, had it all; and it was loud and thick and angry. It wasn't till then that I realized how much I was worried about Gil. I had my hand out to take my gun belt off the foot of the bed before I knew it wasn't Gil talking, but Smith. Drunk, too, by the sound.

He had it to himself for a minute. Then I heard the deep, even rumble that was Canby. Then Smith, louder than before, even, and Canby pretty short, and it was quiet. Finally a subdued general talk started again.

I went over to the table by the east window and poured myself a glass of water. My hand was trembling so I slopped water on the floor. The shoulder burned, and I was dizzy. I drank the water off, and felt better, though it was cold and trickling in my empty gut. I was angry at shaking up so easy. I wished Davies would get done. His conscience was getting too big for me. I was used to confessions, but I was lost in this one.

When I turned around Davies was at the window, staring out again. I crossed and sat down on the bed again, to get the dizziness over. He came and stood by the foot of the bed.

"I won't bother you much longer, Art," he said.

"You're not bothering me."

"A man ought to keep things to himself," he said. "Even guilt, unless there's something can be done about it. Confession's no good except for the one confessing. Only I want to be sure," he finished.

"Sure of what?"

"Art, you say you know what I was thinking—" He stopped.

There it was again; that question. And I knew I didn't have the answer this time either. I just sat and waited and didn't look at him.

"Art, just when they were going to hang them, when the ropes were up, what was it I was thinking?"

"How would I know? A man thinks about funny things at a time like that. Every man's would be different. Maybe a song you heard once. I don't know."

"What would you think?" he insisted.

"Like all of us, I suppose. That you wished it didn't have to be done; at least not there in front of you. Or that it was all over, and the poor bastards were dead and happy."

"You didn't think it could be stopped?" he asked.

"It was too late for that."

"You didn't think of using your gun?"

That surprised me. "On what?" I asked.

"Tetley," he said.

"You mean . . ."

"No, just to force him to take them back for trial."

"No," I said finally, "I don't think I did. It was all set-tled. I had a kind of wild idea for a moment, but I didn't really think of it. You get those wild ideas, you know, out of nothing, when you have to do something you don't much like. I didn't really think of it, no," I said again.

"Did you have a feeling it would have worked? That you could have turned the whole thing right then? Or that somebody could have?"

I thought. "No," I said, "I guess not. I guess I just thought it was settled. I didn't like it, but it was settled."

"It should have been stopped," he said, "even with a gun."

"I can see that now."

"I could see it then," he said.

"You didn't even *have* a gun."

"No," he said, "no, I didn't," as if admitting the ulti-mate condemnation of himself.

After a moment I admitted, "I guess you're not twist-ing it; I guess I am. I don't see what you've got to feel bad about."

"I thought of all that," he said. "Do you see? I knew Tetley could be stopped then. I knew you could all be turned by one man who would face Tetley with a gun. Maybe he wouldn't even have needed a gun, but I told myself he would. I told myself he would to face Tetley, because Tetley couldn't bear to be put down, and because Tetley was mad to see those three men hang, and to see Gerald made to hang one of them. I told myself you'd have to stop him with fear, like any animal from a kill."

"You were right," I said. "I wasn't thinking much then; but you were right."

"It doesn't matter whether I was right or not. Do you know what I felt when I thought that, Croft?"

I thought he was going to answer his own question, and let it go. But he didn't.

"Can't you guess, Croft?" he begged.

"No," I said slowly, "I can't. What?"

"I was glad, Croft, glad I didn't have a gun."

I didn't look up. I felt something rotten in what he was saying, or maybe just that he was saying it. It was obscure, but I didn't want to look at him.

"Now do you see," he said triumphantly, like all he had wanted to do was make himself out the worst he could. "I knew those men were innocent. I knew it as surely as I do now. And I knew Tetley could be stopped. I knew in that moment you were all ready to be turned. And I was glad I didn't have a gun."

He was silent, except that I could hear him breathing hard over what he seemed to consider an unmerciful triumph, breathing as if he had overcome something tremendous, and could begin to rest now. I could hear the talking downstairs again too. There wasn't much laughing now, though. For some reason I was relieved that there wasn't much laughing, as if, coming at that moment, even from downstairs, it would have been too much.

But he had to rub it in.

"Yes, you see now, don't you?" he said in a low voice. "I had everything, justice, pity, even the backing—and I knew it—and I let those three men hang because I was afraid. The lowest kind of a virtue, the quality dogs have when they need it, the only thing Tetley had, guts, plain guts, and I didn't have it."

"You take it too hard," I said, still looking at the floor. "You take it too much on yourself. There was no reason . . ."

"Don't trouble yourself," he said hoarsely. "I know what you think. And you're right. Oh, don't you worry," he said, before I could call him, "I've thought of all the excuses. I told myself I was the emissary of peace and truth, and that I must go as such; that I couldn't even wear the symbol of violence. I was righteous and heroic and calm and reasonable."

He paused, and I could feel the bed shaking under his hands.

"All a great, cowardly lie," he said violently. "All pose; empty, gutless pretense. All the time the truth was I didn't take a gun because I didn't want it to come to a showdown. The weakness that was in me all the time set up my sniveling little defense. I didn't even expect to save those men. The most I hoped was that something would do it for me.

"Something," he said bitterly.

Then I thought he was done, but he wasn't. Getting

over the hump, the big fact of what he saw as his cowardice, had just unplugged him. He let it all come. He was so tired he was like a blind man in a strange room, always bumping into something, the chair, the wash stand, the foot of the bed, but he couldn't stay anywhere long. Only now and then he'd sit down, or stand briefly in front of one of the windows, looking out, or by the bed, looking at me. It got so I knew from where he was and the tone of his voice when he started, what he was going to talk about. When he was stumbling around, his voice would be hoarse and his words tumultuous, and then it was always self-condemnation or a blast against Tetley, but with the blasts always ending in blaming himself too, more quietly, as if each time he saw anew the injustice of accusing Tetley. When he was sitting in the chair he would be still for a long time, and then begin, in a low, breaking voice, to remember something about Martin, or Martin's wife and children as he saw them from that letter. The letter was an obsession itself. When he came to stand over me, it was to offer another clear proof, as he saw it now, that the flaw had been in him from the start, that he had never really hoped to save those men or force justice.

Once, when he had subsided into the chair and was silent longer than usual, I could hear that Rose and her husband weren't down in the bar any longer, and after that I listened better.

Even so it was hard talk to hear because there wasn't any answer. It was disordered and fragmentary, but if you admitted the big point, his own guilt, it wasn't illogical, and it was impossible to make him see that nobody else could think him guilty. I tried just once to make him see that, and he turned and stared at me till I was done, which didn't take long, and then laughed hard and suddenly, and stopped laughing suddenly and said, oh, yes, he was trying to play the Christ all right, but it wasn't a part for cowards, and it hadn't needed a Christ anyway; all it had needed was a man. And after that he would end each tirade against himself with another sudden laugh about trying to play the Christ. I had to let him go; if anything would help, that would. We couldn't bridge the gap; he was all inside, I was all outside.

Finally, though, he was played out. He'd talked more than an hour; I wasn't sure, maybe two. From where I was sitting on the bed I could see through the window that it was late-afternoon sun on the eastern hills, and that the snow was almost gone from them already. It was a sad light, but lovely and peaceful, glowing as if it burned within the hills themselves. Then Davies just sat there with his head in his hands, now and then bending it so his fingers ran through his hair, but then lifting his head again, as if each time he decided he wouldn't break, but stand it.

"You better get that sleep now," I said, as quiet as I could.

He looked at me slowly, bringing his mind back. He appeared nearly dead, the hollows of his face so sunken that his skull showed in startling relief. But his eyes were a lot calmer, and though he was shivering, it wasn't with that tightness any longer, but just as if he were exhausted and cold.

"I might as well, hadn't I?" he said.

He got up slowly and came to stand by the foot of the bed again.

"I'm sorry, Art," he said.

"It's all right," I said. "You had to. You can rest now."

He nodded.

I must have forgotten the voices downstairs, which had grown quieter as it got toward supper time, for I didn't even realize that Gil's was one of them now, until I heard somebody running on the boardwalk under the arcade, and coming in below us, slamming the door so the talk stopped. I stood up quickly, still listening, but there was just the one voice, young and excited, some boy, and then exclamations without anger, and a low murmur. I withdrew my hand from the gun belt again. I'd have to get Gil in sight to feel easy.

Davies said, as though it didn't matter now, "I've even thought—" and paused so long I said, "What?"

"I've even thought," he said, "that I wouldn't have needed a gun, that at the very end Tetley knew he was wrong too, and all I'd have had to do was say so."

I shook my head. "No," I said, "you were right in the first place. He was frozen onto that hanging. You'd have had to hit him over the head to bring him out of it."

"I hold to that," he said, like he was really hanging on hard to something. "I hold to that."

And after a moment, "That he couldn't have been moved, that there was for him no realization of sin."

"There wasn't," I said. "You'd have had to kill him."

There was no talk in the bar now, and I could hear somebody coming up the stairs.

"And I couldn't have done that," Davies said slowly. "And though even that might have been better, it is not altogether a weakness that I couldn't."

"Nobody could have done that," I told him. I was glad he'd come back to that idea. It would be a saver for him.

"No," he said wearily, and nodded.

"If I didn't believe that—" he said.

"You couldn't have stopped him any other way," I assured him.

"No," he said.

The door opened, and it was Gil and Canby.

"Hello," Canby said to both of us, and then to me, "How long have you been awake? I just came up to see if you wanted something to eat."

"I'll come down," I told him and, when he asked, said the shoulder was doing fine.

Gil was drunk, all right, in his steady way.

"Sorry," he said, "didn't know you had company," as if he'd found me with a girl.

"It's all right," Davies said, "I was just going."

"Did he wake you up?" Gil asked, belligerently, looking hard at us, to focus.

"I was awake," I said. "Where did you go to get that drunk without my hearing you?"

"I took the horses over to Winder's," he said, "and he wanted to drink. He felt pretty low about the business."

"*He* did?" I said.

"Bill's not a bad guy, when you get to know him," Gil maintained; "only pig-headed.

"Anyway," he said cheerfully, "we won't have to have another hanging. Tetley took care of himself."

It caught me wide open, and I made a bad cover.

"Oh, Gerald, you mean?" I said, after too long a wait. "Yeah, I heard," and tried to signal him off. He didn't get it.

213

"No," he said, "his old man too. After he heard about the kid he locked himself in the library and jumped on a sword. They had to break the door open to get him. Saw him through the window, lying on his face in there on the rug, with that big cavalry sword of his sticking up through his back."

Canby saw me glance at Davies, and I guess I looked as funny as I felt. Canby turned quick to look at him too.

"Who would have thought the old bastard had that much feeling left in him?" Gil said.

Davies just stood there for a moment, staring at Gil. Then he made a little crying noise in his throat, a sort of whimper, like a pup, and I thought he was going to cave. He didn't, though, went out, closing the door behind him. We could hear him on the stairs, whimpering more and more. Once, by the sound, he fell.

"What in hell ails the prophet?" Gil asked.

"Go get him," I told Canby, and when he stood there trying to see what I meant, "you can't leave him alone, I tell you." And then started to go myself. But Canby caught on, and pushed past me, and went out and down the stairs three or four at a time. I went to the window, and saw Davies already out in the street. He was sagging in the knees, but trying to run like he had to get away from something. I saw Canby catch up with him, and Davies try to fight him off, but then give up. They came back together, Davies with his head down and wobbling loose on his neck. Canby was half holding him up.

"What in hell ails him?" Gil asked again, watching over my shoulder.

I heard Canby getting him up the stairs, and went over and closed the door. But we could still hear the shuffle of their feet, and Davies whimpering constantly now, like a woman crazy with grief. We listened while the shuffle and whimper passed the door and went down the hall, and then was shut off by another door closing.

"What's the matter?" Gil asked, scared.

"He had a notion he was to blame," I told him.

"For what?"

"The whole business."

"*He* was?" Gil said. "That's a good one."

"Isn't it?" I said. I didn't want to talk about it. I felt sick for the old man.

We both thought about it for a minute.

"Well," Gil said, "you better eat something. All this time, and losing that blood."

"I'm not hungry," I told him. I wasn't, either.

"You better eat, though," he said. "I gotta eat too," he added. "I can't drink any more till I eat something."

Going down the stairs he said back up at me, "Smith was all for getting up a lynching party for Tetley, till we heard."

"Smith's a great hanger," I said.

"Ain't he," Gil said.

We ate out in the back room, where it was already laid out for us, salt pork, winter rotten potatoes, beans and black coffee. At first it stuck in my throat, but I drank two cups of the coffee, and was hungry again. Canby came in while we were eating, and said Davies would be all right, he'd given him something to make him sleep and sent Sparks up to be with him. There was nobody in the bar, so he stood watching us eat, with his towel in his hand. He said the story was all over town all right, that it took more to pass Smith out than he'd thought. But in one way it was working out good. They were taking up a pot for Martin's wife. There was more than five hundred dollars in it already.

"Even old Bartlett chipped in," Canby said, "but he's not showing his face around much. He sent the money down by Sparks."

"That reminds me," Gil said, as if it hadn't been on his mind, "I put in twenty-five apiece for us."

I squared with him out of my Indian sack.

"She picked a good time for the pot, anyway," Canby said. "Roundup over and none of you guys taken yet.

"It's not a bad price at that," he added, "for a husband that don't know any better than to buy cattle in the spring without a bill of sale."

He went back out to the bar, and we could hear him talking to somebody out there.

After a while, when he wasn't talking any more, we went out, and Gil and Canby had their joke about the "Bitching Hour," and we had a couple of drinks and a

215

smoke. I didn't want any more; what I still wanted was sleep. It seemed as if I hadn't even got started on the sleeping I could do. I've noticed it works that way, when there's something bothering you that you can't do anything about, you always get sleepy. Besides, there were men beginning to come in who hadn't been up there with us. They would look at us, and then stay at the other end of the bar and talk to Canby in low voices, now and then sneaking another look at us. Gil was getting sore about it. He still hadn't had the fight he wanted, and he was drinking like he was just a pipe through the floor. He would stand there, staring at the men, and just waiting for one of them to say something he could start on.

When Rose Mapen came in again, all big smiles and walking like she was at the head of a parade, and the man with the red sideburns right behind her, I was scared. But Gil fooled me. He picked up the bottle and two glasses and said, "Come on, I don't want to fight that guy now. I'd kill him."

Up in the room I stretched out on the bed. Gil put the bottle and glasses on the dresser and went over and looked out of the window into the street. It was about sunset, a clear sky again, and everything still. Gil opened the window, and the cool air came in, full of the smell of the meadows. Way off we could hear the meadow larks. Gil poured himself a drink and lit another cigarette. He blew the smoke hard, and it went out the window in a long, quick stream.

"I gave Winder the ten to give Farnley," he said, like that made up for something.

"That's good," I said.

Downstairs we could hear Rose talking and then laughing and all the men laughing after her, the way they had in the afternoon. She was on show all right.

"If I started a fight with that guy, it would come to shootin'," Gil said.

"We've had enough of that," I told him.

"I know it," he said, "but I don't know how to start a decent fight with that kind of a guy."

And then, like he was giving it a lot of attention, "He's a funny guy. I don't know how you'd start a decent fight with him."

Tink-tink-a-link went the meadow lark. And then another one, even farther off, teenk-teenk-a-leenk.

Then Gil said, "I'll be glad to get out of here," as if he'd let it all go.

"Yeh," I said.

AFTERWORD

IN THE SUMMER OF 1956, the Virginia Players, an imported stock company, were presenting Oscar Wilde's *The Importance of Being Earnest* at the Opera House in Virginia City, Montana. The incongruity between this English farce-comedy and the wild setting and violent history of Virginia City could not have been greater. A wealthy man has done for Virginia City what Mr. Rockefeller did for Williamsburg, restoring the place to a semblance of what it was when it had a reason for existing. The Opera House and the adjoining saloon, the Bale of Hay, are a part of that restoration.

After watching the play as if we were in London, we adjourned to the Bale of Hay to wash the inconsistency of it out of our mouths. The man I came to know as Walter Van Tilburg Clark took a position at the extreme left end of the long bar and held it throughout the evening, which was prolonged into early morning. He drank moderately and talked little, but held his place, seemingly completely

219

absorbed in some world of his own, perhaps investing those bare hills and pine-board houses with the vitality they once possessed.

I suspect it was here that I glimpsed the quality that gives distinction to Clark's novels and short stories. Not content with surface manifestations, he probes for the deeper meaning and the reasons for the westerners' spectacular acts. He is not consciously trying to be either heroic or profound, but rather to see how much he can understand in order that he may make others understand what he sees. His refusal to pander, to join the parade of popular western writers, is something for which he probably deserves little credit. He is bound by his own limitations, one of which seems to be a built-in integrity that forbids him to do what he does not himself respect. Considering his background, one could say that he must have a New England conscience standing guard over his impulses. To such a man fame and fortune come as incidentals, not as a result of a calculated chase.

Walter Van Tilburg Clark has skipped the fortune which he could have had, because, as I shall show later, he can write conventional "horse opery" until the world looks level. I mean he could write it if he were somebody else. Many with less knowledge and skill are living in big houses on high hills. In short, Clark is in one sense a victim of his own standard of excellence.

He was born in East Orland, Maine, on August 3, 1909. When he was eight years of age his father became president of the University of Nevada in Reno. He took two degrees at Nevada, but what is more important, he came to know the people. "Many of our close friends," he says, "were ranching and mining people, and I spent a good deal of time in both these worlds, and a good deal also camping and hiking in the desert hills and the Sierras. . . . Though I was born in Maine . . . I am essentially a westerner, and mostly of the desert breed." Like Hamlin Garland and Eugene Manlove Rhodes, he had to go East before he got started writing about the West. He published *The Ox-Bow Incident* in 1940, *The City of Trembling Leaves* in 1945, and the next year he returned to the West for good. *The Track of the Cat* appeared in 1949 and *The Watchful Gods and Other Stories* was published a year later.

It is not the purpose here to appraise Clark's total

achievements or to guess at his place in American literature. It may seem rash to suggest that any western writer can deserve that honor, especially one who chooses the same characters and situations that have been used so much in pulps and thrillers. The stereotyped story has produced the stereotyped critic who forgets that the western author has no choice but to work with the material *on the ground at the time of the story*. The author or critic may lament with Henry James that there were "no country gentlemen, no palaces, no castles, no manners, nor old country houses nor parsonages, nor thatched cottages, nor ivied ruins" in the West. He who writes about Nevada in 1885 has none of these advantages so dear to the expatriate.

"What is there to do in this town, anyway?" demanded the cowboy who sensed the cultural limitations.

". . . you have five choices," said Canby, "eat, sleep, drink, play poker or fight. Or can you shoot some pool."

As for women, the prospect was even bleaker. After the married women ran Rose Mapen out of town, the only unmarried woman known to Canby was "eighty-two, blind, and a Piute."

On the positive side, what did Clark have to work with in creating high drama in Nevada in 1885? He had scenery —mostly mountainous. He had weather—the wind and the snow. He had men and men only, for the West in those days was a male society. Western writers are notably weak on women. Clark discards them almost completely, refusing to drag them in by the hair. He mentions only two by their full names.

Since there are no unspoiled women, there is no real love affair. Rose Mapen is attractive enough, too attractive, but that problem is solved when she turns up with a husband—"the damned superior son-of-a-bitch" from San Francisco.

Men had two ways of livelihood: either running cattle or mining. *The Ox-Bow Incident* is concerned with cattle, supposedly stolen.

There was a semblance of law, but it was enforced, if at all, almost by common consent. The code required each man to furnish his own protection, and only when the code was violated did the law function. If it failed, or was too slow, the habitually armed men took it into their own hands and considerably shortened the process of justice.

Prior to 1885 wild Indians were a factor in western life, but by the time of the Ox-Bow incident they were irrelevant.

Finally, Clark had Canby's saloon, which was the forum and the club of this male society.

These are the ingredients of western life, and the writer who portrays it can no more ignore them than the English writer can escape the thatched cottages and ivied ruins of Victorian England.

When Clark accepted these limitations and sought to handle his shopworn material in such a way as to create high drama, he set himself a hard task, made more difficult by the hack writers who have cut the psychological ground from under the serious one. He did not deceive himself as to the problem. He says, in a letter dated Mill Valley, California, September 1, 1959:

> Like everyone else who has ever wanted to use western materials, especially from the past (and it seems to me we have to establish contact with the past, literally, before we can handle the present with any depth), I had repeatedly found the stereotypes, both the people and the situations, of the standard "horse oprey" in my way. . . . So, in part, I set about writing *The Ox-Bow Incident* as a kind of deliberate technical exercise. It was an effort to set myself free in that western past by taking all the ingredients of the standard western (which were real enough after all) and seeing if, with a theme that concerned me, and that had more than dated and local implications, and a realistic treatment, I could bring both the people and the situations alive again.

Act One of this five-act tragedy is conventional western, nothing else. Two young men ride over the divide into Bridger's Wells, dismount at Canby's, get a little high, and engage in a poker game which ends in a fight. At that juncture an excited youth arrives to report the rumor that Kinkaid has been killed and maybe fifty head of cattle have been stolen. Lynching is mentioned.

What does Clark do next? Where does he go with his story?

What you expect is that the good guy will lead the

posse and eventually, after much hard riding through the sage and around the boulders, bring the bad guy to bay. And since the good guy has the best horse he will outride his posse and face the bad guy alone, and they will fight it out in a six-shooter duel to the delight of all adolescents from six to sixty. Why, after such a beginning, anybody could finish according to the formula.

But Clark bids farewell to the formula right there. The theme emerges, and the mob forms, finds its leaders, and vacillates because only two of some twenty persons involved really want to participate in the deed of that wild night. The mob is composed mainly of those who lack the physical or the moral courage to oppose it or refuse to be in it. The night riders find three men asleep in a valley where a little mountain stream has designed a course that looks like an oxbow. Only three men vote against the "incident" which takes place at about sunrise. The main body starts back, only to meet Kinkaid, who is very much alive, and to learn that the cattle were bought and not stolen. Tragedy piles on tragedy as the story crashes to its end some twenty-four hours after it began. There is no hero.

The book was immediately acclaimed as something special in western writing. The reviewers were followed by the literary appraisers and the scholars who are now searching all of Clark's work for symbolism, and they are making many guesses. Being leery of symbol hunters, I hit upon the highly original idea of asking Clark what deeper story he was trying to tell. I quote his answer.

The book was written in 1937 and '38, when the whole world was getting increasingly worried about Hitler and the Nazis, and emotionally it stemmed from my part of this worrying. A number of the reviewers commented on the parallel when the book came out in 1940, saw it as something approaching an allegory of the unscrupulous and brutal Nazi methods, and as a warning against the dangers of temporizing and of hoping to oppose such a force with reason, argument, and the democratic approach. They did not see, however, or at least I don't remember that any of them mentioned it (and that *did* scare me), although it was certainly obvious, the whole substance and surface of the story, that it was a kind of American Naziism that I was talking about. I had the parallel in mind, all right, but what I was most afraid of was not the German Nazis, or even the Bund, but that ever-present element in any society which can always be led to act the same way, to use authoritarian methods to oppose authoritarian methods.

What I wanted to say was, "It can happen here. It has happened here, in minor but sufficiently indicative ways, a great many times."

As Clifton Fadiman has said, "Such a book can never be followed by another of the same kind; it stands by itself." It reveals the integrity of the author who has reversed the western formula, preserved the vitality of real life, and proved that western men are pretty much like other men and that literature can be made of their folly.

—WALTER PRESCOTT WEBB